MW00950663

PROJECT

New World

❖

AMANDA BRAUNEIS

CONTENTS

CHAPTER 1

Project New World

*T*he battle raged on around Darius as he began trying to sneak away, but Rafficer saw him. With an angry growl, the old vampire decided to take his youngling down. Rushing from the other side of the room, Rafficer caught Darius just before the 652-year-old vampire could make it through the door to outside. Darius was startled and let out a soft cry while backing away from Rafficer's furious green eyes. He was trapped between Rafficer's arm and the wall that he backed into. Darius watched as the older vampire laughed and felt a chill run down his spine. Rafficer's eyes betrayed his intentions to Darius, and it would be painful. As always, he began with a little taunting.

"Where are you going, Daredevil?" Rafficer asked in a higher-than-thou tone. Darius gave a half-hearted laugh at his nickname and bravely looked at Rafficer's face. His fear was hiding behind his defiant sky-blue eyes. Rafficer's green eyes narrowed. Originally, he thought that Darius had started this battle, but seeing the youngling try and run, he wondered who really did start the battle. Darius knows, Rafficer thought to himself. He wasn't going to let him escape.

"Anywhere but here, Raff!" Darius cried as he tried to feint moving left but actually moved right. Rafficer saw the move coming and caught Darius's throat in his left hand. Even though Darius knew he could survive the attack on his neck, human instincts made him panic and grip onto Rafficer's arm. The 721-year-old vampire *laughed at Darius's useless attempt. Darius shook his head, looking for a weakness in the grip. Rafficer had him, and Darius wouldn't be able to stop anything his sire tried next. Using his vampire strength, Rafficer lifted Darius off the ground and slammed his back into the wall. Darius let out a grunt but made no other noise.*

"I made you, Darius! I taught you everything you know!" Rafficer snapped at Darius. Green eyes glared hard into defiant sky-blue ones as Darius hung from Rafficer's hand. Rafficer could see that this was going to get him nowhere, so he switched tactics. Slowly, Rafficer leaned forward, his black hair melding with Darius's hair, which was dyed black. Darius prepared himself for everything. He wasn't going to let Rafficer get away with whatever he was planning. "Do you regret what I turned you into, Darius?"

"IDONA!" screamed a loud, high-pitched female voice. Idona jumped in the air out of fright, somehow still holding onto the book she was reading, as her wild brownish-green eyes landed on a pair of shiny chocolate-brown eyes. It took a minute for Idona to calm down and recognize the person standing beside her. Idona sighed when she realized that it was her roommate, Minnie. Minnie's face held a rather large and innocent smile as though she had done nothing wrong.

"Why'd ya have ta yell at me, Minnie?" Idona asked, dropping into slang. She really wasn't in the mood to play. Her eyes rolled over Minnie's feminine frame once more.

Idona resigned herself to the fact that she was simply average; her voice was deeper and more robust than most girls' were, her build was almost masculine but her large chest made up for her otherwise manly appearance. Idona was not fat, she weighed only 162 lbs, which was a little overweight for her 5'3" frame, but it suited her. Her dark chocolate-brown hair was short and dangled over her ears and neck. Idona worked out every day, not just to keep her weight in check, but because she liked to exercise. She certainly wasn't the "feminine" type at all. Currently, Idona's clothes didn't really show off anything. She was wearing a band (Santagata) T-shirt, two sizes too large, and a pair of men's shorts that reached her knees.

"Cause you didn't hear me the first five times I called you," Minnie answered with a soft giggle. Minnie's voice matched the slim curvature of her body in a way that showed she was pure female. She had waist-length curly blond hair that was almost always tied in a ponytail with two hair ties, almost like Princess Jasmine from Disney's *Aladdin*, which was Minnie's favorite movie. The girl weighed almost as much as Idona, sometimes she varied five pounds in either direction, but her weight was usually constant. It was just enough for her 5'5" height, something that Minnie loved showing off to Idona and other chubby girls at the school. Today, she wore a tight white sleeveless shirt and a pair of slim fitting shorts that covered very little. Idona thought that the shorts were a second pair of underwear.

"Five times, eh? You still haven't beaten Sue's tolerance of seven?" Idona inquired. Sue was the Resident Advisor (RA) for their floor. Sue was feminine like a model. She had a perfect height of 5'7" and weighed almost nothing. It often worried others because she seemed a little too thin. So like Idona, she used to wear clothes much too big for her size.

"Not yet, but I'm getting closer. So, what'cha reading?" Minnie asked, pulling a wooden chair from under Idona's desk and promptly sitting on it backward. Leaning against the backrest, Minnie waited. Idona rolled her eyes. She knew that Minnie didn't really care. It was just bland conversation. After most of the year had gone by at school, the two had realized that they didn't really have much in common other than their majors. They both were pursuing an English degree. Minnie added Theater to it, and Idona added History so they used to be busy with classes and homework.

"Nothing much really," Idona answered as she began scanning the bed for her bookmark. Minnie rolled her eyes before leaning over to the side and picking the bookmark off the floor. She handed it to Idona and tried again.

"I mean, what is it called?" Idona could tell that Minnie thought that the book was homework related. Surprisingly, even though Minnie was bad at remembering names and dates, she was interested in History.

"*Project New World,*" Idona responded as she took the bookmark and placed it inside the book. Looking over the last line that she remembered reading, Idona committed it to memory. Despite how much she wanted to, she knew that she might not get back to reading that night.

"*Project New World?* Never heard of it," Minnie said as she tried to flip the book and read the back cover for the summary. Idona held the back cover up to make it easier for her. Minnie mouthed a "thanks" and started to read it. Idona rolled her eyes; she didn't want to wait for Minnie to complete reading.

"It's about a group of vampires that don't like humans and are trying to get rid of them. Whether it's by turning the humans into vamps or by simply killing them."

"Doesn't sound very entertaining," Minnie made a face and got off the chair in an attempt to head to her bed. Idona smiled because she knew that Minnie didn't care for vampire novels, but often, she secretly peeked at Idona's novels. Many of those books were sitting on the top shelf of Idona's desk. They ranged from Bram Stoker's *Dracula* to Charlaine Harris's *Sookie Stackhouse* novels.

"But there is a vampire, Darius, on the inside trying to stop the group. Sadly the group's leader is Darius's sire, so it's hard for him to fight back...," Idona explained while thinking of Darius. She felt so bad for him. He had so many things happen to him in the course of his life with Rafficer, but he still couldn't escape. How she just wished she could take him away from Rafficer forever so that he might begin to have an easier life.

"Whoa! You lost me at sire," Minnie replied as she flopped onto her bed. Idona sat up to face Minnie. She forgot a lot that Minnie wasn't into vampires and didn't know about vampire folklore.

"Sire means the vampire that made you. Your sire also is the one who can control you into doing things."

"Oh. Can't he just say no? Or better yet, can't he just kill this sire guy?"

"In most stories, the author has it that if the vampire is strong enough mentally, he can say no. Sometimes, a few vamps have the sire killed off. This author, so far, hasn't done either. I think she's making it that, after a certain amount of years the underling is free from his sire. But I haven't read enough of the series to find out," Idona mentioned as her eyes focused on the two other books she owned of said series. Only three out of the entire series had been released.

"Series? This is a series?" Minnie asked as she sat up fast. Facing Idona in shock, Minnie just stared. "You are kidding, right?"

"No. Actually, this is the third book in the series. The series is called "Project" and each book has a different project. The first book was *Project Old Life,* and the second was *Project New Knowledge.* This one, well, you know what it's called," Idona stated excitedly. Minnie rolled her eyes and leaned back to lie down. She couldn't understand why people would waste so much time reading fiction. But she wasn't going to criticize Idona aloud. "Any more questions?"

"Not right now, I guess. Too much information already," Minnie mumbled before becoming distracted by something on her wall. Idona nodded, pleased that she informed her roommate of the series. She picked up her book again and opened it. Just as she began to read it,

Minnie's eyes flashed over to the clock. A smile came to her face before she looked over to her roommate. "Hey, are you going to your meeting?"

"Meeting?" Idona repeated before looking at her watch. Swearing violently, Idona rushed out of the room. Inside, Minnie was smiling away. Idona was usually late to club meetings. It was so consistent that Minnie began helping Idona try to make it on time. They came upon this agreement when the club threatened to remove Idona. It helped that Minnie would get the room to herself for a little while. Both girls loved solitude. But since Minnie was usually the one running around to classes and practices, whatever amount of time she had to herself was limited. So, she loved to kick Idona out of the room for different reasons. This club meeting was one of them.

Outside, Idona was running down the hallway toward the elevator to go to the ground floor. From there, she flew out the dorm doors and into the evening air. Taking no notice of the charged atmosphere, Idona rushed along until she reached a side building with a note saying *Paranormal Club Meeting*. This club met every night of the week. Apparently, they thought that there was enough going on at the school to warrant it. Biting her lip, Idona sneaked in and even before looking up, she knew the group members were staring at her. This was the third time this week she was late. Most of the members didn't care for her because of her tardiness.

"Welcome, latecomer," growled a senior girl who stood before the large group. Idona nodded a welcome in return and rushed toward a seat in the back. She hated being late, but it was just something that happened. "As I was saying. George has a possible sighting of a ghost in the third floor of the freshmen dorms. Someone needs to help him investigate it."

With that, the meeting went on as normal. After a while, the group began to disband and Idona got up to leave, but a man blocked her path. Idona kept her eyes to the ground. She already guessed who this was. The one man who came to this meeting just to see her. This type of approach would flatter most girls, but Idona found it annoying.

"Hi, Idona!" the man almost shouted in excitement. Idona's lip twitched. She recognized the voice. Slowly looking up, Idona realized her assumption was correct. Marc, the college flirt, was standing there. He was 5'5" like Minnie and slightly muscular. For some reason, the senior had decided that he wanted Idona as his next girlfriend. Idona rejected him every time. It wasn't because Marc was considered one of the "Top Ten Hotties" of the school, which was the kind of person she liked to avoid. She just didn't see anything good in him. Lately, the senior had been giving her the creeps.

"No, Marc," Idona snapped, before she tried to slip around to the exit. He was a little faster and was able to sling an arm around her waist to stop her. Idona rolled her eyes. *Here we go,* Idona thought as she focused on the ground. Some once told her that men got discouraged when their prey, or subject, didn't pay any attention to them. Marc disproved that theory. He only seemed to be more encouraged.

"I haven't even asked anything yet. What if I twist my words around so that you were really saying yes?" Marc asked with an evil glint in his forest-green eyes. He leaned forward so that his short, wavy, dirty blond hair fell slightly over his eyes. A move that never worked on Idona. Girls were beginning to crowd up and sigh. As the girls tried to get closer to Marc, they pushed Idona closer to him. Both Marc and Idona tried their best to ignore the crowd. Idona rolled her eyes and moved back to get out of Marc's arms. He gave her a light smile, and Idona's face turned icy cold.

"What can I do to get you away from me?" Idona growled. Marc's face brightened for half a second before switching to a pondering face. During the half-second pause after Idona's comment, she realized she was going to regret asking the question. During times like this, she thought of asking for help in controlling what she said..

"You can date me, say yes to everything I ask of you, and stop once I get bored and end our relationship," Marc answered in a straight face. A couple of girls gave a displeased sound of protest. Idona made a disgusted face before looking away. It made her sick how "puppy doggish" he got. Every word and advance on her just pushed her further away from him. Not that Marc even seemed to notice. He was used to saying one word to a girl and having her drop straight into his trap, oops, arms.

"Isn't there any other girl out there more suited to your tastes?" Idona questioned. She knew that he had yet to date her roommate. Minnie was available and more than willing to date Marc, if he just asked. Sue told both girls that Marc had this list and it followed it by order of when he first learned the girl's name. Idona regretted every minute after Sue introduced the two girls to him because Idona's name was stated first.

"Yes, but I intend to date every girl in this school. You happen to be next on my list, Sweetie," Marc gingerly stated. Idona jerked at the last word. Her brownish-green eyes narrowed.

"If it isn't for the fact that Sweetie is my last name, I would slug you," Idona barked before backing into a large crowd of girls, all of whom had been staring dreamily at Marc and sometimes even shooting angry glares at Idona. But when she backed into them, they all moved, using it as a chance to get closer to Marc. It took the senior a few moments to realize what was happening. Having realized that he lost his prey, Marc burst into the crowd of girls where he last saw Idona. Joyful at being able to touch Marc's "godlike" skin and body, the girls squealed and pushed ever closer to him, making it much harder for him to get through them.

With the girls working on getting closer to him, they opened a larger path for Idona to escape. She didn't look back to see what was happening as she rushed out of the room. Marc felt suffocated by the crowd and couldn't see Idona. He figured she used their lust for him as an escape and almost wished he wasn't as sexy as he thought he was. After being trapped by the girls for too long, Marc cursed his stupidity just before remembering his escape plan.

"Look, its George!" he cried while pointing to a random spot in the room. Surprisingly it wasn't in the direction that he needed to go. The girls now distracted by the possibility of an even hotter guy, found themselves turning and rushing toward where Marc pointed, but no one was there. While they were distracted, Marc took off, landing himself outside the building. He paused and looked back at the path he had just taken. *Works every time,* he thought to himself with glee. Shacking off his triumph, he began scanning the area for signs of Idona. Marc knew that he hadn't been trapped for too long, so Idona had to be around somewhere. But as he searched the distance, he had a feeling that he had just missed her. Cursing his luck, Marc trudged back to his dorm before the girls from inside noticed that not only was George not there, but he now Marc had also vanished.

Hiding in the shadows by the side of the building, Idona sighed when Marc left. Coming out of the darkness, she slowly made her way back to her own dorm, which thankfully was a different building from Marc's. Thinking back on her past now, Idona realized she had always been good at hiding. She just seemed to vanish into whatever crevice or darkened area was around. It was a talent that made many people think it was why she liked vampires and demons so much. That wasn't true but she wasn't going to correct people who thought otherwise.

Idona rushed and caught sight of her building. The meeting spot for the club wasn't far from her dorm; it just felt that way whenever she had to run to it. Currently, Idona's mind was focused on men. Marc wasn't the first guy who acted like this around her. In high school, many men there tried to date Idona for no good reason. Idona went on a date once, and the kid's mother had joined them. At school, the guy told all his friends that Idona tried to do "things" with him. That was when Idona swore never to date another man.

Why can't more men be like Darius? Sweet, innocent and so...Oh, I don't know, loving. Idona thought. She imaged Darius suddenly standing at the door to her dorm. *His dyed black hair was cut to hang just below the top of his ear. Sky-blue eyes scanned the area. He's looking for someone. His eyes find me, and he smiles before walking down the stairs to meet me.* Idona paused. The imagery in her mind was so lifelike that she wondered if it was real. Squeezing her eyes shut for a moment, she reopened them and looked up the stairs. No one was standing there. She sighed and decided not to think about it anymore. Stuff like this hurt, even if it wasn't real.

Entering the dorm in silence, she showed her ID card to a freshmen sitting behind a large desk. He nodded to her as she headed to the elevator. The floor was empty, so Idona didn't have to put on a happy face. Considering how lonely Idona felt, it was surprising at times how many people were concerned for her feelings. But, they always seemed to show up when she wanted to be left alone. As she tried not to think about Darius, Marc, or anything else, Idona dragged her feet to the room. Upon opening the door to her room, Idona spotted Minnie and didn't believe her eyes when she saw Minnie staring at *Project New World*. It almost looked like she was trying to read it. Normally, Idona would not have cared, but after what had happened, she was in a blur of emotions. In a panic, Idona rushed toward Minnie.

"What are you doing?" Idona screamed. Minnie, in a fright, threw the book across the room. As the book landed, it caused a huge ruckus. The two girls jumped at the sound, but Idona didn't turn to look at her book. As their eyes met, Minnie felt a chill because of Idona's glare. Minnie had never asked to look at the book, and Idona was extremely bothered that Minnie invaded her privacy without a second thought.

"I'm sorry," Minnie cried. Seeing Minnie's scared face, Idona quickly calmed down before going to comfort her. Idona knew that her anger was unnecessary. She sighed and hugged Minnie. Idona had been working hard on controlling her anger, but she took it all out on Minnie. Idona had a quick fuse, and this wasn't the first time she had resorted to anger instead of calmly expressing her feelings.

"No. I'm sorry, Min. I'm not used to people touching my things without my permission. Last year, I didn't have a roommate. Hell, never mind a roommate, I'm an only child," Idona explained. Minnie calmed down. She felt bad for Idona, and as much as one might think she didn't deserve it, Minnie did. Ignoring her own feelings, Minnie leaned over to comfort Idona. Each time that Idona lost her temper, Minnie learned more about her. Although, Minnie was hurt every time Idona lost control of her anger, she understood the reasons. Idona had done this enough to explain all the different reasons for the way she acted. When the girls were moving in, Idona's parents took Minnie aside. They explained that Idona had a bad temper and that she was used to her privacy. She didn't get along well with most people. Idona left high school without a single friend. Remembering all this, Minnie pulled Idona into a hug. Slowly, Idona backed away. "Are you okay?"

"Yes," Minnie replied as she wiped her eyes. Even though Minnie knew that Idona had seen the tears, she didn't remark on it. Idona smiled instead and went to her side of the room. She tended to assume that Minnie was fast at healing from emotional wounds because Minnie never mentioned them again. Minnie just forgave Idona for all the pains when she saw how much it hurt her.

Back on her side of the room, Idona's brownish-green eyes flashed around. Finally, they stopped on an object lying by the end of the bed. There, by the closet Idona saw her book with its bent binding and absence of bookmark. Idona stood still for a moment, clenching her fists to control the anger that began to race through her body once again. Minnie watched and wondered if Idona was going to freak again. Thinking about how she overreacted to Minnie just moments ago was enough to calm the shorter girl. As the anger began ebbing away, Idona started to search for her bookmark.

While searching her mind wandered to Darius again. In her mind, she could see him finding the bookmark and handing it over to her. He'd smile and go to Minnie, whisper something sweet into the girl's ear, and Minnie would laugh allowing the tension that was filling the room to vanish. It was a perfect vision but highly untrue. For now, Idona couldn't find that godforsaken bookmark. Her anger level kept on rising, making the tension heavier and heavier.

"Did you see the bookmark?" Idona asked uncertainly when her search was fruitless. Minnie shook her head no, making Idona frown. She had been hoping that Minnie had it on her side of the room. The bookmark wasn't very important to Idona—she was just bothered because she didn't have another to take its place. "Oh well. At least I remember where I was."

Picking up her book, Idona began to shift through the pages. With a deep sigh, she sat down. Sometimes it was easy to find the page, and other times it was harder. Every now and then, she paused to find her page. It took her a few minutes, but Idona found the spot she remembered. Or so she thought. A few more lines into it, she remembered reading it the previous day. So, she went a little further. Then, she went too far ahead and had to go back. Finally, she found the correct spot and read a full page. A smile appeared on her face before she laid down on her bed.

Meanwhile, Minnie got up and began grabbing clothes. From out of her pile by her closet, she pulled out a pair of Disney pajama bottoms and a Tinker Bell pajama top, both a mismatch, but Minnie didn't seem to care. She headed out. When she returned, she was changed into the pajamas and ready for bed. Of course, with Idona reading, Minnie had to ask to turn off the lights. A rule they came up with when they first began rooming.

"Is it okay if I just go to bed now?" Minnie asked. Idona let out a sigh. Her brownish-green eyes slid over to the window. It was almost pitch black outside. She had forgotten that her club meetings usually ended just before dusk. Then again, she normally forgot the whole meeting anyway. Her eyes wandered over to the clock on her desk. It read 9:45 p.m. Idona sighed.

"Be my guest," Idona answered stiffly, signaling she had still wanted to read. Minnie smiled in relief and turned out the lights, not realizing what Idona's tone had meant. As Minnie climbed into bed, Idona ripped a page from her notebook and shoved it in between the pages of the book. Minnie shifted in her bed to get comfortable and slowly began to drift off. Idona sat up and placed her book lightly on her desk. Minnie was fast asleep in a matter of minutes. Idona looked over quickly and gave the sleeping girl a half-hearted smile.

Almost as if it was waiting for Minnie to slip out of consciousness, tears slowly began falling from Idona's eyes. She felt guilty about having acted so harshly toward Minnie earlier. It took another moment for Idona to realize that guilt wasn't the only feeling that had made her cry. She was upset about her selfishness for wanting to read and bother her roommate even more with a light. Also, she was upset that things in her life kept making it hard for her to survive. There were even feelings of sadness that Idona couldn't seem to find a nice guy to love her. Five minutes passed by with Idona crying softly. Minnie had slid into a deep sleep and missed the whole thing. Half-grateful that Minnie had missed the whole crying, Idona sucked it up and tried to stop.

Looking at Minnie's slim form, Idona noticed the girl was so out of it that she was beginning to snore. Giving a soft smile, Idona tried to lie down on the bed. First she tried to lie on her back, then her side, and finally her stomach. Sadly, no matter how hard she tried, she just couldn't get comfortable. Idona shifted around, but nothing worked. This was a common occurrence. She naturally had a problem with sleeping at night and tended to read until she got tired. Previously, Minnie had somehow found a normal sleeping schedule with letting Idona stay up, but with finals coming up Minnie asked that the rule be changed for more sleep. Idona didn't mind at first, but when nights like this happened, she couldn't help but get annoyed.

Idona shook her head and sat up. She didn't want to keep blaming Minnie for her own problems. It was unfair and Minnie didn't deserve it. She was one of the best things at this school. She kept to herself most of the time, was normally always busy, and was fine with compromising with Idona's needs. This was the reason Idona now found herself sitting there on her bed, the clock ticking to change to 11:50 p.m., and no book in her hand. Idona laid back down and tried to sleep. After shifting to her back for the second time since laying down, Idona saw the clock now read 12:00 a.m.

Finally sighing and giving up on sleep, Idona sat up again. For some reason, she found herself drawn to the window and looked outside. It was still pitch black. No moon or stars were there to light up the night sky. Idona frowned. Lately, she would read with just the light of the moon. But tonight, that wasn't going to happen. As she turned away from the window, something caught her eye. Slowly, she stood and walked closer to the window. Far off in the distance, just over the mountaintop, Idona saw a small star shining its light away. *I shouldn't. Those things never happen,* Idona thought as her vision focused on the star. *But, maybe.*

"God...If there is even a god out there...I wish I could meet someone who held my interests. Someone who could help me along in my life and someone I could help in return. Maybe even have Marc get off my case. Anything is better than what I have now," Idona wished. In her head, she formed an image of Darius. She could see herself falling in love with him. It would be like those special relationships that she had read about in some young adult books. Relationships where the two seemed destined to be with each other. Idona and Darius would help each other grow. With a laugh at the impossibility of her wish coming true or even meeting Darius, Idona looked away from the star as it flared brighter than before.

Sighing deeply, Idona turned away from the window and sat back down on her bed. She shook her head again at her stupid little wish. Some parts of her wished deeply for her to meet Darius. Even if it was for only a minute. Then a sudden feeling of tiredness came over her. Reveling in the fact that she could go to sleep, Idona fell back onto her pillow.

While the two girls slept, Idona's wish was being granted in every way that she thought. *Project New World* began to emit a strange glow. Slowly, the glow got brighter and brighter until the whole room was lit. Minnie moaned and rolled over, covering her face from the light. Once the book was completely smothered in a golden yellow light, the notebook paper shot from the pages and smacked into the wall near the doorway with a ruffle. With the paper gone, the book opened to the page that was marked with the sheet of paper.

Inside the book world, the battle began to pause as the room looked like the sun was appearing as the ceiling. Vampires screamed and began to run from the room. Rafficer looked up to the light and let go of Darius. Before the youngling even touched the floor by Rafficer's feet, he vanished. He landed on the floor and lost his balance. Falling backward into the wall, Darius knocked his head. The golden light was stronger here than it had been before, and Darius slipped out of consciousness. Just as suddenly as the light had appeared, it disappeared, leaving the unconscious vampire with dyed black hair and bruises on his throat laying before the door in Idona and Minnie's college dorm room.

CHAPTER 2

Darius

A rough shake from Minnie awakened Idona. Moaning deeply, Idona pushed the girl away but Minnie would have none of it. Her eyes focused on something by the end of Idona's bed. Idona frowned and tried to go back to sleep. The older girl shook Idona awake again. Through fuzzy vision, Idona noticed that Minnie was saying something, but Idona was so tired that her ears weren't working well. Finally, groaning in defeat, Idona gave in and began to wake up. As her ears started working, Idona heard Minnie.

"He's unconscious from what I can see," Minnie was saying once Idona's ears cleared. Surprised, Idona jerked up. Her eyes fixed onto Minnie. Minnie was switching her attention from something by the door and Idona.

"He?" Idona repeated, wildly. Minnie's eyes were fixated on the "thing." Turning to look at the door, Idona saw him. As she was about to scream, Minnie clamped her hand over Idona's mouth. Idona's eyes focused on Minnie. They were looking at each other. She shook her head and looked back to the man before turning to Idona again.

"Don't," Minnie softly whined. Idona frowned and swallowed the scream. As much as Idona wanted to scream, she trusted Minnie's judgment. It took another moment before Minnie removed her hand. She had decided that Idona really was calm enough. "Let's not wake him."

"You seem rather calm," Idona muttered as she shifted to get more comfortable. Minnie gave her a soft smile. Slowly, she moved toward the end of Idona's bed. It gave the younger girl a clearer vision of the man lying on the floor. The move also placed Minnie just out of the man's line of sight.

"I'm from the slums, you get used to random people crashing at your place. Trust me though, I'm freaking out on the inside," Minnie responded. Idona nodded before looking over to the crasher. He was laying on the floor near the door, blocking it from them. Realizing that there was no escape made Idona worry a little more about who he was.

The man looked like he could stand at 5'9" and he was the perfect weight for that height. His hair was dark black and seemed rather unnatural for his pale skin. It made Idona think that he had dyed hair. With his eyes closed, Idona couldn't tell what color they were but an image of seeing them as sky-blue made Idona gasp. She leaned closer and noticed that he was wearing a black T-shirt that looked like someone had tried to rip. His black jeans also seemed torn because of a struggle. Idona focused on his face again. She had a guess as to who this could be.

"It couldn't be!" she finally squeaked out as she tried to think of another explanation. Minnie frowned now, but before she could ask, Idona rushed over to him. In doing so, she pushed Minnie into the wall. She cried out in shock so softly that Idona didn't even notice. The shorter girl fell to her knees by the man's chest. Her brownish-green eyes focused on his face. "This looks like Darius!"

"Darius?" Minnie responded in confusion. Slowly she made her way over to Idona's side and kneeled down. Idona was squatting as she stared into Darius's unperturbed face. Her face was filled with shock and awe. Minnie couldn't help but hide the new worry that spread over her features. If Idona was so fascinated with Darius, then she could have done something reckless. But what concerned Minnie was that she had heard that name before and didn't like thinking of how she did. All she could focus on was that Darius is from that vampire novel. *That can't be right! Idona must be wrong!* Minnie thought to herself as her eyes glazed over Darius's form.

"Darius, from the book I was reading," Idona whispered as she began to reach out and stroke the vampire's face lightly. When her skin touched his, it sent a chill down her spine. She didn't even register that his skin was as warm as her own was when all vampires should be as cold as ice. Darius stirred from her touch, which made her stop. Once she did, he calmed. Minnie sat there holding her breath while Darius had settled. Slowly she released it as quietly as she could. She looked over to her anxious roommate. She had feared that Idona was going to say that he was a vampire.

"Don't wake it," Minnie called as Idona reached for his face again. Idona turned a brownish-green gaze at Minnie. The once seemingly calm girl was now looking like she was about to freak out. Idona couldn't tell if it was over his history or over his appearance. Either way, Darius didn't need to be called an "it."

"Darius is a guy," Idona snapped. Minnie recoiled in horror. The other girl looked she was going to kill her. Idona had turned angry many times, but Minnie had never seen her this mad. It almost terrified her more than Darius did. She paused a moment, and decided that she needed to explain why Darius was an "it" and not a "he."

"Darius is a character from a book. He can't be here!" Minnie stated. Idona focused on the girl beside her. Realizing she might have said the wrong thing, Minnie changed the subject. Her eyes turned pleading. Idona's narrowed her eyes, expecting Minnie to press the subject. "Please, just don't wake him!"

"I won't," she answered sharply. With her temper still controlling her, Idona focused on Minnie. *I won't try hard, I mean,* Idona thought as her hand again stroked Darius's face. This time when he stirred Idona didn't stop. Minnie bit her lip and watched as the vampire's eyelids began to move. She slowly noticed that Idona wasn't going to stop. Knowing now that Idona was going to wake him, Minnie decided it was for the best not to stop her. Closing her eyes in fear, Minnie tried not to watch. Through blurry sky-blue eyes, Darius noticed he was staring at the faces of two girls. Surprised, Darius jerked backward, using vampire speed, and slammed into the door behind him. The bang that echoed through the room made all three of them tense even more.

"Who are you?" Darius called loudly as his eyes switched back and forth from brownish-green eyes to chocolate-brown eyes. The girls at first said nothing. Idona was still a little shocked that this was Darius. But something inside her mind still wondered if this man before them really was Darius. He had moved quickly, but she had blinked in the same moment that he moved, so it was as if the movement didn't occur at all. One thing she knew was that if this weren't Darius, she wouldn't disclose her name. Minnie, on the other hand, didn't want Darius to know her name. She didn't care if he was real or from the book. She wasn't going to share her name with him. Darius snarled when he realized that neither girl would speak. He focused on Minnie for a second. When his eyes landed back on Idona, he compelled her to answer. She felt the power flow onto her, but she didn't understand what it was and easily fell into it. "Who are you two?"

"My name is Idona, and this is my roommate Minnie," Idona revealed before she even realized she was speaking. Darius nodded tensely. Though he knew their names now, he didn't know how he knew them or even if he should. Minnie and Idona traded looks and mouthed a conversation to each other. Minnie asked why Idona said their names and Idona tried to explain. The vampire's eyes began to wander around the room.

The room had two sets of desks, two beds, two bureaus, two closets that just about reached the ceiling and two mirrors. Everything else was placed against the wall Darius was leaning on. Nothing about this room looked familiar to him. He was used to blacking out after he drank too much, but he didn't remember going out for a drink. The last thing he remembered was staring into his sire's eyes.

"Where am I?" he asked. Minnie stood but froze when Darius turned to watch her. Idona, noticing the tense situation, also stood between them making Darius look at her instead. Feeling like he might be crowded up against the door, Idona backed away. As Idona moved, Minnie followed suit, but he was focused on Idona. As they retreated, Darius became calmer because he realized they weren't setting up a trap.

"This is our dorm room," Idona said once she finished moving away. Darius frowned. He had no idea what a dorm room was. Idona almost smacked her forehead. She had forgotten that the book he was from was written about a time before colleges had dorm rooms. "It's our room at college."

"Why are you so okay with this?" Minnie whispered more to herself than to Darius or Idona. When the two looked at her in confusion, she didn't even notice. She wasn't looking at them anymore. Idona noticed that Minnie was looking for something. *Is she looking for her cell phone?* Idona wondered as she watched.

"What?" Idona asked. Minnie looked at her quickly and realized then that she must have spoken aloud. Her eyes glanced over Darius before looking back to Idona. She really didn't want to speak to the "vampire" before her.

"I mean, we don't know his name, but we don't know how he got here, and he doesn't know anything about us!" Minnie cried. Idona shook her head and decided that Minnie should be left out of the rest of this conversation. The taller girl wasn't taking any of this well. But, Minnie seemed to have other plans. She focused on Darius. "Which speaking of, what the heck is the last thing you remember?"

"Why should I tell you?" Darius countered, feeling rather insulted that Minnie just assumed things. He hated when people had preconceived notions. Minnie frowned. She thought that her last question was helpful and not so personal. Idona shook her head in disgrace. Idona confirmed that he was Darius, so why didn't Minnie believe her. It wasn't Minnie's question that bothered Darius, but the tone in which she has asked it.

"We can help you with the details of what might have happened to you, and maybe get an explanation as to how you appeared in our locked room," Idona cleared up for her roommate. Minnie said nothing. Darius looked back at the shorter girl. She made a good point. With the attention off her, Minnie quickly went back to searching for her cell phone. *If I can find that, I can call the cops!* Minnie thought. *But, if he is a vampire...Cops won't be of much help'*

"The last thing I really, clearly remember is...being choked," Darius told the girls. Idona gasped audibly. She remembered reading that Rafficer was choking him. She walked away from Darius and Minnie and sat on her bed. As she moved, Darius watched her and began to relax visibly. With the vampire relaxing, Minnie found her phone. But she paused. Maybe he was a victim, and if he was, she didn't want to call the cops on him.

"Who was choking you?" Minnie questioned. Darius didn't even look over. He just focused on the ground.

"Rafficer," he responded. Idona winced. She knew he was going to say that. Now she had no doubt in her mind that this was Darius. Idona almost groaned aloud. Somehow, she kept it all in. Minnie almost recognized the name. If she calmed herself down and waited for her mind to catch back up, she might have remembered Idona mentioning the name. But she didn't wait.

"Who is that?" Minnie muttered, not even thinking of the book characters Idona had mentioned. Idona frowned as she looked at her taller roommate. She thought Minnie had read at least some of the book when she came in the night before but she realized now that that assumption might have been wrong. *Heck, I even told her that Darius's sire is Rafficer!* Idona realized.

"My sire," Darius answered in a calmer voice. Idona nodded her head, since she already knew that. Darius saw her nod, and it made him curious. "You act as though you knew."

"Uh," Idona dumbly stated as she stared at Darius in surprise. She had read that he was critically blunt. Rafficer was the same way and so it had rubbed off on Darius. It was a trait that the 652-year-old vampire didn't like but had to deal with. Idona was not good at thinking on her feet. Nor was lying but she had to say something soon. Minnie cleared it all up. She had dropped her phone into a pile of clothes and was now leaning back against her bed.

"So, he really is from that book," Minnie said. It was strangely brave and clear. Darius turned to her, his sky-blue eyes turning dark as he did so. Minnie let out a cry of surprise when she noticed and backed away.

Idona tensed, preparing for anything. She almost expected Darius to attack Minnie. But Darius did not intend to do any damage.

"Where?" he commanded but didn't use his powers. Angered that Darius was talking that way to Minnie, Idona spoke up. Minnie didn't need to be treated badly for not understanding what could be going on. Heck, even Idona barely knew what was happening. Minnie stood up straight. She was going to stand up for her right of not having to answer. But she then noticed Idona getting ready to answer.

"In a book called *Project New World*," Idona snapped as she stood up and went to her desk. Picking up the book, Idona stared at it before turning around and tossing it lightly to Darius. She had paused when she noticed that the new bookmark was missing. Catching the book with practice ease, Darius turned to the back cover and began to read. "It's the third book in a series. The first one, *Project Old Life*, was about your life as a human 652 years ago. *Project New Knowledge* is about you learning how to be a vampire. This one is about you trying to stop Rafficer from killing all the humans."

"Who would write this?" Darius called softly, which made Minnie and Idona exchange guilty looks. As much as this was a shock to all of them, both girls could hardly imagine how Darius felt. He stood there, looking at the book, unsure about how to react. This was a book about him, more than likely it was filled with stories he didn't want others to read. In his thoughts, Darius walked over to Idona's bed and sat down on it. Idona said nothing about him sitting there.

"I'm sorry," she said softly. Placing the book on his lap, Darius looked up to Idona. He was almost at a loss for words. This strange girl shouldn't feel sorry for him. Darius shook his head.

"Why should you be sorry?" he inquired stiffly. At first Idona didn't answer, her brownish-green eyes covered by dark chocolate-brown hair but Darius's sky-blue eyes stared hard. She wasn't sure of her answer. It had just felt like the right thing to say. She almost felt like this whole thing was her fault.

"I'm sorry for what's happening to you right now," Idona mumbled. Sighing, Darius turned away from her.

"Not much you can do now," Darius responded as he began to get up. Idona fixed her eyes on to the floor. Minnie backed away and dropped onto her bed in an attempt to get away from Darius, but when she moved, he faced her. "Did you read this as well?"

"No," Minnie squeaked. Darius nodded and turned his attention back to Idona. He sighed again, walked around her, and dropped the book on the desk. For a moment, he stood there, but then he dropped back down onto the bed. Laying his head on his hands, Darius sat there thinking. Slowly, Idona turned her head to watch him. He looked completely lost. Idona suddenly had a thought.

"What do you last remember again?" Idona asked softly.

"Rafficer's hands around my neck squeezing and him asking me if I regret what he turned me into," Darius answered swiftly. Idona nodded and turned back to the ground. Her thought vanished with his words. She couldn't bring them back. Nor did she really try. The pain in Darius's voice made her not want to ask him anything about it again.

For a while, the three stayed like that. Minnie was watching Darius for any sign of attack, Darius held his head in thought and Idona stared at the ground. Then, almost as if the silence was bothering it, the alarm clock next to Minnie's bed went off. All three jumped at the sudden noise, and Minnie quickly shut it off. With two pairs of eyes on her, Minnie looked over guiltily. She had set the alarm while Idona was in her Paranormal Club Meeting and had forgotten to shut it off when she woke up an hour or so early.

"Sorry. I have to go, my first class," Minnie informed the two before quickly gathering books from her desk. Her mind was so focused on having perfect attendance for her classes that the girl almost forgot about Darius being in the room. Darius watched the girl before he heard Idona swear. His eyes focused on her.

"I have to get going as well," Idona told Darius as she turned to face her desk. "Same class and all."

Darius was shocked. Earlier, the two seemed panicked by his arrival in their room. Now, though, they didn't seem to care that he was there. His mouth was open, like he was about to speak, but no words formed. Minnie snapped to attention. She couldn't have heard Idona right.

"We can't leave him alone!" Minnie cried in surprise, dropping one of her books onto the ground. Two pairs of eyes focused on her again. Her chocolate-brown eyes were staring sharply at Idona. The shorter girl growled to herself in annoyance. Just a second ago, Minnie had seemed fine with the idea of leaving Darius. Darius almost smiled. He had been expecting this reaction.

"Why not?" Darius almost smacked his own head in the idiocy of Idona's question. He just could not believe that these two girls were acting as though his presence was normal. They were unfazed by the fact that he was a vampire that could kill them before they even knew what happened. Not that he wanted to hurt them. He wasn't the type who liked killing. Truthfully, Darius even hated taking the life from someone when he drank from them. In the end, it was better that he just killed them though. Others are not as friendly about leaving "meals" alive.

"This is a girl's room!" Minnie responded as though that explained it all. Idona now made a noise that sounded like a mix of a groan and a snarl. Darius found himself watching the two girls in surprise. Here he was, a 652-year-old vampire, wait, fictional vampire who just appeared in their room and they seemed more worried about people reacting to him being in the room in the first place. Even worse was that they seemed to have forgotten that he was even there. To him it seemed as if school was more important than their own safety or figuring out what happened to him. He wouldn't have minded if one of them mentioned he was dangerous, but both girls seemed focused on their education, which, he could tell didn't happen often.

"That doesn't make any sense, Minnie!"

"I will not allow him to stay!"

"Then skip class."

"And what about my scholarship?"

"So? It's not like you'll lose it by missing one effing class!"

"You bitch!"

"What did you just say?"

"Hello?" Darius meekly called. The two girls were beginning to get rather loud now, and with his vampire hearing he could tell that some other kids were starting to get up. With their added noise, Darius didn't want too many people coming over to see what was making them fight, especially since Minnie seemed so worried that, as a guy, he wasn't allowed to be there.

"I called you a bitch, Idona!"

"Am not!"

"Girls!" Darius said louder.

"I can't skip a class. You do it all the time, why not just do it again?"

"I've skipped too many already! You haven't missed one!" Idona snapped as she crossed the room to stand in front of Minnie. Darius followed before stepping into the middle of the girls. He held out to his to stop either of them if they decided to attack each other.

"Girls!" he tried again, even louder than before. They broke apart and looked at him. His sky-blue eyes were watching them closely. When they calmed down, he said to Minnie, "If I can't stay here, where am I supposed to go? I don't even know where I am."

Minnie opened her mouth to offer a suggestion but couldn't come up with any. The college had recently been enforcing a new rule that every building made you show your school ID to the Public Safety member at the doors. This rule was established when there were too many reports of strangers walking around on campus. Idona sighed and looked back to Minnie. Neither of the girls had any response.

"I won't be back until about six or so," Minnie finally said as she looked at Darius. Idona then turned to the vampire.

"I'll be back at eleven thirty, but will have to leave at one for a couple more classes," she said. Darius nodded, and the girls waited for a moment. After the moment passed, Minnie gave up and began packing her things again. Idona and Darius watched her. As she finished up, Darius realized that she still hadn't said if he could stay or not. He glanced at Idona for a moment before leaving his gaze on Minnie.

"Is it alright if I stay here?" he called softly. Idona turned to him in surprise and Minnie froze. The two didn't answer, and it made Darius look up with his pleading eyes. He didn't want to wander around and risk getting lost. Who knew if he'd be able to find either of the girls again if he left.

"It's alright with me," Idona answered. Her eyes softened at Darius's pleading voice and he sighed in relief. Then he realized that if she was fine with it, he might be left alone. As much as he didn't want to leave, he really didn't want to stay alone. Minnie stood there shifting her weight back and forth. If her parents found out...It wouldn't be good. She could picture the fights in her head now.

"Why the hell not? If you are caught, blame it all on Idona though. If my parents learn that I had a guy in my room, I'd be taken out of school," Minnie informed him. Darius nodded his consent before Minnie gave him a soft smile before mouthing "bye" and heading out. Slowly Darius looked down to the floor and Idona paused. He didn't want to ask her to stay. But just as he finally decided to ask, Idona spoke.

"See you later?" she asked. He faced her. Idona was giving him a sad look. It killed him inside. He couldn't ask her to stay. It would be too much. Slowly, he looked away again.

"Bye," Darius called as he looked up, but Idona had already slipped out the door, her hands empty. She had disappeared down the hall and the door was slowly closing on its own. Slowly, Darius dropped his head back down. He sat there for a while before his eyes turned to look at the book. Frowning, Darius picked it up, stared at the cover with the bent binding, and opened to the last page Idona was reading.

Darius turned to answer Rafficer but as he opened his mouth, a blinding light made Rafficer look away. When he looked back, his hand was holding nothing but air. Darius had vanished. Cursing his luck, Rafficer looked around trying to find one of his generals, but no one was there. Rafficer looked around in a panic. This isn't headquarters! *Rafficer thought desperately. Indeed it wasn't, Rafficer was standing the middle of a great desert. It was the middle of the night, and as far as Rafficer could see, there would be no shade for when the sun began to rise. Panicked, Rafficer set off in a random direction to find some shade.*

Darius shut the book quickly. *No,* he thought before slowly re-opening the book. Turning the page, Darius found his earlier conversation with Minnie and Idona was written down. Swallowing some built up spit in his mouth, Darius found himself turning another page only to find it blank. As he sat there in shock, words began to appear on the top part of the page.

As Idona walked away from her room, she thought how difficult it was for Darius because he was suddenly pulled into her world. Catching up to Minnie in the elevator, the two girls found themselves too worried to talk to each other. Simply giving each other a smile, they went back to their own thoughts. As the elevator reached the lobby and they walked out, Idona spoke.

"Think he'll be okay without us there?" Idona whispered to Minnie. The other girl shrugged her shoulders, and the two continued on to their class.

For the second time, Darius shut the book. *This can't be happening! Not now!* Darius thought as he jumped to his feet and dropped the book on the bed. Spinning to face it, Darius watched as the binding forced it open again. This time it opened to the pages written about Idona and Minnie. Words continued to appear as Darius watched in horror. As the words began to fill the second page, the book somehow turned the page and began filling up the next one. Darius looked away. He couldn't deal with a book that was writing itself. Glancing back to it, Darius became curious. Furious, he started to pace the room. *I will not look!* Darius repeated in his head repeatedly. Finally, curiosity got the better of him. Slowly, heading over to the book, he began to read while leaving it laying on the bed.

Idona sat down into her assigned seat in front of a boy. He had short, wavy, dirty blond hair and forest-green eyes. As Idona began to shift in her seat, the boy leaned forward and tapped her shoulder to get her attention. Spinning around, Idona glared at the boy.

"So, how 'bout we go on a date tonight? We could go to the movies!" the boy asked her. Idona clenched her fists as she glared at him.

"Not if you were the last guy on earth, Marc," Idona snapped as she spun around to face the front of the class. Marc gave off a smile as he leaned back. That can be arranged. *Marc thought sarcastically.*

Darius turned away from the book as he felt a pang of jealousy fill him. He paced the length of the bed before realizing he was being ridiculous. This was something he had to stop. Idona had every right to see this Marc if she wanted to. And Darius couldn't stop Marc from chasing Idona. Growling at the emotion, Darius defiantly turned back to read the newest words.

As the class went on, Idona tried her hardest to ignore Marc's incessant stares. Listening to the professor, Idona didn't notice that the mechanical pencil she had borrowed from Minnie took a life of its own and began to sketch a rough picture of Darius's face on another item borrowed from Minnie. But even as she sketched, Idona couldn't get the vampire out of her mind.

She wondered what he could be doing back at the room. Was he trying to figure out how to work her computer? Or maybe he was reading the books. That would be interesting, *Idona thought with a slight laugh. Slowly, looking down to her notes to see if she was still writing on the lines, Idona found her sketch. Her eyes widened in surprise before she tore the paper from her notebook, shoved it into the back, and furiously began writing.*

Farther back of the room, Minnie took note of her roommate's distress and wrote a note to ask Idona about it later. Returning to paying attention to class, Minnie didn't notice as Idona turned for a split second to look at her. On her own notebook, Idona took a note to talk to Minnie. Both girls had different thoughts pass through their heads about the same subject, Darius.

The rest of the class flew by. Idona couldn't stop thinking about Darius. Whenever her mind relaxed into class, they drifted to the vampire. Minnie was finding that she was also thinking of him. Her thoughts weren't as pleasant as Idona's. She feared that by now he would have been found. Any second the door would burst open and there would be someone calling her name. Her parents would remove her from school and she would be forced to go to a community college near her home. Of course, Minnie's thoughts never happened and all too soon the students were released.

Idona packed her things, faster than she ever had done before, and then rushed over to Minnie. She was just finishing packing her things.

"I need to talk to you," Idona whispered before grabbing Minnie's hand and pulling her roommate down the aisle and out the door. Rushing around to a side hallway, Idona stopped and spun to face Minnie before grabbing her notebook and scanning around for the sketch. Minnie paused to catch a breath and remember her own question. Idona was a little too slow.

"I wanted to talk to you as well. I saw you rip out a paper from your notebook and put it somewhere," Minnie called, making Idona look up from her work. The younger girl nodded. She hadn't thought that Minnie had seen her do such, but it brought it easier to bring the next issue up.

"Yeah, I'm going to need to borrow your notes from the beginning of class later. But the real reason is this," Idona answered as she found the sketch and showed it to Minnie. Her roommate stared at the picture in surprise before taking it and staring at it closer. It looked so much like Darius. As though he was staring at the girl from the page. Even with it just being a pencil sketch, Minnie thought it was a photo.

"Wow, this looks really good. I didn't know you could draw this well!" Minnie excitedly stated as she handed it back to Idona. Idona shook her head.

"That's the point. I can't, and I wasn't paying attention to what I was doing. I was trying to ignore Marc and listen to the professor. When I looked down this was staring back at me!" Idona pleaded. Minnie nodded in confusion but didn't say anything else. "Listen, I need to go see Darius again. I can't get him out of my mind."

"But you have a class!" Minnie scolded. Idona couldn't stop the smile from spreading across her face. Minnie grimaced. She knew what Idona was going to say next. Idona told her the same thing every time the girl skipped a class.

"That's why I'm in most of your classes," Idona answered before turning and rushing off to their dorm. Minnie turned to yell something at her but stopped. Whatever, Minnie thought before turning and heading to her next class.

CHAPTER 3

Book Edits

"This can't be real," Darius muttered. "A book can't rewrite itself."

Slowly, Darius sat back down on Idona's bed. His thoughts focused on Idona. When he first noticed her, he felt drawn to her. It was weird. She seemed to call out to him even though she wasn't speaking. There was something else about her. Something that kept Darius focused on her. He just couldn't stop thinking about the shorter of the two girls. Beside him, the book turned a page. A moment later, he heard a key slide into the door lock and then it opened. Idona stood there and surveyed the room. Everything looked the same except the book being open on her bed beside Darius.

"Darius?" Idona called softly as she entered the room and closed the door. She dropped Minnie's notebooks and pencil onto the floor as Darius looked up, trying to feign surprise, but when her brownish-green eyes narrowed, he knew he had failed. She walked over to her bed and closed the book while it was pausing in its writing. Darius frowned and focused his attention on the book. Idona left her hand on the cover as though to hide it from his sight. "Did you read it?"

"A little," Darius admitted before looking toward the door. Idona sighed. She picked the book up as though the thing offended her.

Turning, she placed it onto her desk. As she let go, Darius focused on the book. Feeling his gaze, she turned and removed her hand before leaning against the desk. The edge of the cover caught on Idona's loose shirt when it tried to open again. She didn't even notice. Darius's frown deepened. Before he read it, the book had never tried to reopen itself. Now, that's all it wanted to do.

"What did you think of it?" she asked. Darius looked over to her, and noticed that she didn't realize what the book was trying to do. Her eyes focused on his face, and she felt a smile emerge. But as he moved, a small beam of sunlight peaked in and landed on his face. Darius barely noticed, but Idona focused on it. Her eyes widened in fear. She knew what it could do to him. "Oh my god!"

Before Darius could react, Idona jumped forward and pushed the vamp out of the sunlight. As he fell backward, Darius's eyes focused onto the light. *I didn't feel that,* Darius thought as he landed on the ground beside the bed. Idona scrambled to her feet before rushing toward the window and shifting the shades to hide the light. Everything happened so quickly that she didn't even see that he wasn't hurt.

"I'm so sorry about that! The light…it was touching your face," Idona cried as she turned to look at Darius. He stood and Idona saw his still pristine face. She froze with her mouth still trying to form a word as Darius walked over to the window, reached around Idona, and pulled the blind up until he was fully bathed in sunlight. Both waited for the vampire to go up in flames or even turn to steam, but nothing happened. "You're not burning."

Darius shook his head. Idona focused on Darius's soft pale skin. Slowly, her right hand lifted and lightly touched his cheek. Sky-blue eyes quickly looked down into brownish-green. Time seemed to stand still. Darius held his breath, as Idona stared into his eyes. Their emotions reflecting conspicuously in their eyes. They didn't know what the emotions meant, but all that mattered was they saw them. Idona filled with warmth as she stroked his face. Darius leaned in to touch her, but she pulled back. Idona pulled away when he got a little too close. The vampire continued to lean in closer, and she felt compelled to move in herself. She pulled back again, and gave him a soft smile. Darius couldn't help the disappointment that flashed through his sky-blue eyes.

"You really aren't burning. How is that possible?" she whispered, not noticing the last feeling he had. Darius shook his head before looking back out the window. It had been so long since he had seen the world covered in normal light. Idona turned to look away but her eyes focused on the book. Again, it was open. "I thought I closed that."

Darius spun to look as Idona walked over to the object. She reached for it and paused. Darius could tell it was filling with words. He could see her stiffen as she read the lines. Remembering his own first reaction to the book, he noticed she seemed rather calm. *Must be because she is still trying to get used to me being here,* Darius thought. Slowly, he moved over to her.

Darius moved to stand behind Idona. The young girl was in shock and didn't even notice. She silently read the book as it filled with words. Her thoughts focused on trying to figure out if what they were saying was true. Darius, having known of the strange magic before, simply stood there watching her read. As she began to grown weary from shock, Idona fell back into Darius's chest. She didn't want to read anymore. When is all this going to end? When is enough, enough? *Idona thought. Her head fell back naturally and fit comfortably into Darius's chest as she relaxed even more. When Darius realized she had stopped reading, he resisted the urge to pull her into a hug in an effort to comfort her. His eyes shifted to read the words as they appeared. It was almost as if he was waiting to see if Idona was going to reject him.*

"Can this day get any weirder? Or am I simply dreaming?" Idona muttered to herself. She moved away from Darius. "Darius isn't standing behind me and my book isn't rewriting itself while I read it."

"I didn't believe it either until you came back to your room. The rest of the pages are blank. It's filling itself back up as we stand here," Darius told her, his eyes reading the words seconds after he spoke them. It seemed strange to him that sometimes their actions appeared before they did them and other times they appeared after. Idona paced over to the other side of the room. Again, the words appeared after she moved. But her speaking began to write before Darius noticed she opened her mouth.

"What did it say?" she asked as her eyes focused on the notebooks. Darius gave her a confused look and didn't answer. He was too focused on the power of the book. Idona asked again, "What did you read?"

"I read about you and your class," Darius answered. Idona looked at Darius before facing the door. "I'm sorry about the drawing. It came up before I looked away."

"I can't actually draw. Stick figures barely look like anything more than squiggly lines. Hell, even my squiggly lines don't look like squiggly lines. But...that drawing...it just...looked so much like you. It was like you were staring back at me from the paper."

"In my experience. Characters from a book are written as perfect beings. They can do everything and even more. If not perfect in whatever way, then the flaws can be fixed by a simple adventure to somewhere," Darius said, not meaning any offense, but Idona turned to look at him in shock. It was as though he had slapped her across the face.

"I am not a story! I'm a living, breathing person who exists in the real world!" Idona snapped, her temper getting the better of her. Almost as soon as she said it, she regretted it. Darius's eyes widened before he looked away. His eyes focused on something outside the window. Idona moaned in disappointment. Why did her temper always make her say stupid things? She focused on Darius and began to wonder. She didn't want to be in the dark, so Idona stepped toward the book and read it.

Darius couldn't help but feel hurt. He recently thought that he was real as well. Then he suddenly appeared in this room and learned his entire life was some sick story that a real person had written. He didn't blame Idona for her temper, nor for saying what she had said. If he didn't have 600 or so years to rein in his own temper, he probably would have reacted the same way as her when he first found out that he was a fictional character.

A silence enveloped the room; Darius's mind drifted to Rafficer. Idona's eyes focused on the name in the book. She had almost forgotten that the other characters might have escaped the book as well. Darius sighed deeply as he tried to figure out what to do next, and Idona was concerned and finally had to ask.

"What about Rafficer?" she asked as her question appeared in the book. Darius turned and saw her focused on the book. *Damn traitorous thing,* he thought before Idona looked up at him.

"I did read a part that said he was in a desert. I didn't believe it then because I was shocked that the book was writing itself. But it said very little before it shifted to you and Minnie," he answered. Idona picked up the book.

"What page?" she questioned before flipping through it. Darius moved closer just as she found it and read. "I don't remember ever reading that there was a desert near where you live."

"I don't even think it's a desert in my world," Darius informed her. Idona almost dropped the book. Darius lunged forward and caught it, their hands briefly touched before the vampire let go. Idona looked into his eyes in surprise. This was the first time that she noticed he wasn't cold. As her mind wrapped around that new information in her head,

Darius focused on the book. The book had flipped to a new page and was beginning a new chapter. A chapter called, *Rafficer*. "Look!"

Rafficer didn't find any shade. Cursing his luck, he began to use vampire speed to make it further. It was almost time for sunrise, and he still hadn't found anything. This can't be happening! *Rafficer thought angrily as he slowed down and finally stopped.* I'm about to die in the middle of a godforsaken desert and no one will know. *Dropping to his knees, Rafficer accepted his fate.*

"Boss?" called a distant voice. Rafficer looked up, surprised. He recognized that voice. It was his First General, Serge. Jumping to his feet, Rafficer looked for the voice and spotted a distant outline on the next dune.

"Serge?" Rafficer screamed back. After a second, the outline used vampire speed to appear before him. Rafficer sighed in relief to the 6'5" monstrosity with unnatural golden eyes and whitish blond hair.

"Daylight is coming up fast, Boss," Serge pointed out. Rafficer nodded.

"There's nothing around to cover us," Rafficer admitted, dejectedly. Serge nodded.

"I kind of figured that when I saw you sitting in the sand. You never give up," Serge pointed out. Rafficer nodded ignoring the fact that Serge didn't end with either "Boss" or "Sir." "So, are we just going to stand here and resign ourselves to death, Sir?"

"I guess so," Rafficer answered, seriously. Serge nodded and turned to look at the sun creeping out of the sand.

"Here it comes, Sir," Serge whispered, making Rafficer turn to face the oncoming sun. For a moment, Rafficer thought about hiding behind Serge. He thought that the youngling might be able to provide enough shade to save him. But not for an entire day. *Rafficer realized, and sighed deeply. It would only prolong his life for a minute or two.*

The two watched as the sun slowly began to rise over the farthest sand dune. Rafficer closed his eyes and Serge faced his sire. Both lifted their arms as though asking for forgiveness before their deaths. Then they waited for the pain of burning underneath the glare of the yellow orb. Serge closed his eyes. Time passed, and the two realized they were sitting there in silence. Slowly, Rafficer opened an eye and stared into the sun. "Uh, Boss?"

"Yes, Serge?" Rafficer asked as he opened his other eye to stare in surprise.

"Are we dying yet, Boss?" Serge questioned, his eyes tightly closed.

"No, Serge," Rafficer said. Slowly, Serge opened his eyes. For a while, the two stood in silence. "Ever see something so beautiful?"

"No, Sir," Serge responded before the two smiled at each other.

Idona looked at Darius and frowned. She almost wished now that she hadn't asked. Maybe if she didn't, this chapter wouldn't have appeared. With a grunt, Idona handed the book over to Darius who willingly accepted it and continued reading.

"Perfect, just perfect! I wonder how many of you guys are out of that book," Idona growled as she sat down on the bed. Darius said nothing. He just stared at the book. For a long while neither said anything. Finally, Darius put the book back on the desk. He looked over to Idona and simply watched her. It was almost as if he was too afraid to speak to her. Minutes passed by before Idona looked back at Darius. "Is there anyone in your world who could have done this?"

"What do you mean?" Darius asked as he sat down near the head of the bed. Idona shifted in her seat to face him.

"I mean connect two worlds? Yours and mine." Darius shook his head. In disbelief, Idona shifted to face forward. Darius didn't even bother to ask about her world. It seemed like there might not be someone in her world who could have done it too. "Now what?"

"I don't know. But, don't you have class?" Darius muttered, trying to change the subject. Idona laughed. She couldn't help it. Having Darius care about her missing class was something she never thought would happen in a million years. But as the thought crossed her mind, she looked at the clock. It was almost eleven.

"I've missed most of it. But even if I didn't, I wouldn't go. Figuring all this out is a little more important, don't you think?" Idona told him. Darius nodded his head. Secretly, he was glad that Idona wanted to stay. He found her presence calming. "How are we going to fix this?"

Darius stiffened. He wasn't sure how to respond. His first reaction was to cry out in anger, and he didn't understand why. He had just meet Idona. It was too soon for feelings of any kind. But Darius knew that he had feelings for her. He couldn't explain it. All his life, he had longed for something, but when he woke up and saw Idona for the first time, his longing vanished. Not that he was ever going to tell Idona that. He respected her now. *Maybe that's why I'm getting so bothered. I respect her, and so I'd like to be respected!* Darius lied to himself.

Idona looked at Darius. She saw his stiff form and felt bad. As she watched him, she realized that he was thinking of something disturbing. When she spoke, she didn't even think of the pretenses that could be taken from her question. As she watched him, she began to think of what he could have differed from her. Slowly, she leaned over to grab the book. Her shifting weight alerted Darius that she was moving, and so he looked at her. As she began pulling the book toward her, Darius's hand dropped onto hers. Brownish-green eyes meet sky-blue ones in confusion.

"My private thoughts should be just that, private. If you respect that, then I will do the same for you," he said to her. Idona looked over to the book. She almost told him that he had read her private situation with the drawing, but when she looked back at Darius all she could do was agree. Time ticked by slowly as they sat there. Every now and then, the book would flip a page.

"If we're not doing anything do you think it's following...You know who?" Idona meekly questioned. She avoided Rafficer's name as though just saying it would bring the older vampire to them. It was something that hadn't concerned her until she realized he was also in her world. Darius looked toward the book with a pondering gaze. He almost didn't want to tell her what he knew but he also figured that if the book were writing about Rafficer, it would be rather gruesome.

"Raff just fed," Darius finally told her. Idona looked at him. He could read the question on her face as if she had stated it to him. "He grows stronger when he feeds and weaker when he hasn't fed in a while. I can sense his power."

"I didn't know that," Idona whispered. Darius couldn't help but smile. It was the first fact he stated that Idona didn't know about. "How can you sense that?"

"When we are young and still weak, we want out sire to be healthy and strong. We can't help it. Some take it to the extent of going and bringing a meal back to their sire to keep up his or her strength," Darius began. Idona nodded. She had read all of that when Darius was going through that stage. Idona had read that Darius was glad he wasn't an extremist who brought food to Rafficer.

"You do that for the first 100 years because during that time, if your sire dies, you do too. But I thought the power left after that age," Idona continued. Darius nodded as he shifted to look out the window again.

"I thought so too. But Kathleen—you know of her, right?" Darius paused, looking back at her. Idona nodded. Kathleen was Rafficer's first bride. She had been changed over the same night by the same sire as Rafficer and he forced them to be wedded even though neither felt any love for the other. Anyway, she told me to feel continuously for when Raff got weak. If there ever came a time when I was stronger than him, I should take my chance to kill him. Thanks to her, I kept that ability in use. Every day, I examined Raff's strength, waiting for the day that I'd be stronger than him. By always using that ability, I never forgot about it and so it didn't fade away. Others who never use it and allow it to fade can't tell when they could have the perfect chance to break free. It's why so few of us break loose of their sires."

"How did Rafficer break free so early? Wasn't he still in his hundred years?" Idona muttered as she thought back. Darius nodded when she focused on him.

"Rafficer was turned at 29 and spent 40 years as a vampire before he broke free. His sire was ill and couldn't get strength from feeding so Rafficer killed him. Raff didn't die because he had killed a weakened sire. Despite, Kathleen having the same sire, she didn't die. Anyway, he then began building an army in fear of his weakness. Every day, he fed for the first 100 years or so after I was turned. I thought he'd never stop that habit, but he began skipping his feeds. I can't remember how many years passed where the days between feedings got longer and longer until suddenly, he was back to feeding almost every day," Darius explained. Idona frowned and looked at the book.

"You tried to attack him too soon. Nini, Rafficer's choice in your girlfriend, told you it was time because he hadn't fed for a month. Kathleen warned you to use your senses but you were so...so..."

"Impatient. I hated him and her so much that I risked everything. It's funny that you can remember that but I couldn't until now. Rafficer had just fed when I came bursting into the room. I attacked without thinking. In the middle of it, I realized that Nini had lied."

"He almost killed you. I remember crying for you. My mom thought I was crazy when I begged for you to survive," Idona laughed lightly as she looked at the door. Darius focused on her. He was surprised that she said that. "Even though I still had a quarter of the book left, I was worried that the author would kill you."

"Raff spared me, but he made sure to never get that weak again. Now he feeds at least every three days. I have to pay attention more than ever now, because I'm closer to his level than ever before. Each feeding I feel closer."

"So, you'll be free of him as your sire, forever?"

"No. Nothing can take that from him. But when I beat him, I'll be my own vampire. I won't have to follow his orders. And if I wanted, I could sire my own vampires," Darius said as he turned dreamily to the window again. Idona faced him and watched for a moment. She never imagined Darius as siring his own vampire. Suddenly, she realized the reason she couldn't was that she didn't want him to.

"Would you?" She asked and Darius faced her again.

"Hmm?"

"Would you sire your own?" Darius paused. The thought hadn't crossed his mind. It was something that nearly all vampires dreamed of doing, but then again, nearly all the vampires that wanted one, liked being one. Darius hated Rafficer for doing this to him. He hated being a vampire. It wasn't his choice to become this, and if he had a choice he wouldn't have become one.

"I don't...I guess it depends."

"On what?" Idona whispered. Darius could hear the fear in her voice now. His eyes meet hers, and they were filled with a horrified curiosity. It was then that Darius realized that Idona had wanted him to say no but the more he thought about it, the more he found he couldn't say it. Shocked by his own discovery, he shook his head and looked away. He realized that with this out in the open, Idona wouldn't look at him the same way.

Idona sat there thinking of what he meant. Slowly she began to real-ize why the situation would depend. So many "ifs" can be inflicted onto a situation. If the person wanted it, if Darius wanted it bad enough, if he was bored, if he was lonely...the list just seemed to go on forever. She closed her eyes. Understanding his reasons didn't make her fear him less, but it did make her more forgiving of him. A minute passed before Darius heard Idona sigh.

"I understand," she finally told him. Darius couldn't help but look at her in surprise. Her eyes were focused on the ground and her hair blocked her expression from his view. But those two words didn't hold any of the fear he had heard or seen before. She even looked calmer.

"What?" he forced himself to say. Shock was making it hard for him to think.

"I understand. Sometimes you might want someone by your side. Or maybe it could be someone you want to control. Or maybe even, a lover?" Idona said. Darius couldn't help but smile. He was glad that she understood. He could tell from her tone that she was asking if she knew whom he wanted to turn. Never before had he truly thought about turning someone. It had always been something he said to the other vampires to get them off his case. Now, as he thought about it more, he realized what he would do. He went to speak again when there was a loud bang on the door.

CHAPTER 4

Sue

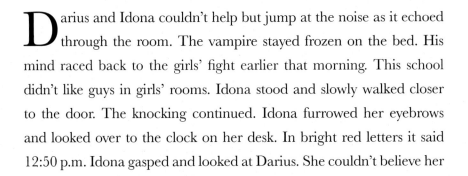

Darius and Idona couldn't help but jump at the noise as it echoed through the room. The vampire stayed frozen on the bed. His mind raced back to the girls' fight earlier that morning. This school didn't like guys in girls' rooms. Idona stood and slowly walked closer to the door. The knocking continued. Idona furrowed her eyebrows and looked over to the clock on her desk. In bright red letters it said 12:50 p.m. Idona gasped and looked at Darius. She couldn't believe her memory lately. Suddenly, Darius knew what was going on. Idona was going to have to leave for her next class. The person at the door must be someone reminding her to go.

"IDONA! COME ANSWER THIS DOOR!" called a loud female voice. Darius looked at Idona in confusion. He didn't know who else Idona knew. But he did know that Idona knew the girl on the other side of the door. The chocolate-brown haired girl swore under her breath. A loud knock came again. "IDONA!"

Idona focused on Darius. He could see the fear in her eyes. Idona was panicking. She knew that outside her room stood Sue, the only other friend she had here. Sue was here to bring her to their one o'clock class. But the main problem was that Sue was a Resident Advisor, meaning, she was the type of person who had to report Idona's unwanted visitor unless she'd get in trouble.

"You have to hide," Idona told him. Just as Darius frowned and tried to protest, Idona argued, "Girls can't have guys alone in their room with the doors closed! I could get expelled!"

"Well, that's very restrictive of them," Darius responded as the knocks continued. Idona rushed over to Darius's side and grabbed his arm. She tried in vain to pull him to his feet.

"Idona? Is someone with you?" Sue asked in almost a whisper through the door. Idona let out a squeak of shock and tugged harder at Darius's arm. Feeling bad for her panic, Darius finally stood as a pounding now replaced the knock. Idona let go of the vampire and looked around for a place to hide him. Her panic was so overwhelming that she almost couldn't think. Under the beds or under the desk risked too much attention, the two bureaus were too small, Minnie's tall closet was so full the door was open and clothes spilled out. Idona's eyes stopped on her closet. When Darius noticed it as the only spot, he stiffened. He really didn't want to hide in there of all places. "IDONA? Answer me!"

"No," Darius muttered. Idona gave him a quick glance and noticed he was also staring at the closet. *I feel really bad, but it's the only place'* Idona thought to herself before turning to face Darius. The vampire focused on the closet. He understood what Idona must have been going through, but it was too humiliating.

"Even you can see that it's the only place," she whined. Darius shook his head. "Please."

"I won't do it," he confirmed again.

"Darius!"

"Don't make me."

"IDONA!" screamed Sue as she pounded on the door again. Idona and Darius looked quickly over to the door. They could tell that Sue was getting impatient. Idona turned back to Darius and he looked at her, his face set in a pleading sad face, but when he saw her panicked eyes, he found he couldn't fight it any longer.

"Of all the indignities!" he finally mumbled before walking around Idona and into the closet. The closet was mostly empty because Idona didn't own many clothes. A laundry basket was on the ground beside Darius's feet. It had very few items in it, but Darius knew that sometimes even a little amount could smell, a lot. He tried not to sniff, but it was a natural reflex and he smelled nothing. At first, he was shocked but he forgot about his shock when Idona closed the door. Just before she closed it, Darius caught sight of her face. After seeing it, he couldn't help but be glad. Helping her calm down helped dissolve some of his humiliation.

While Darius was stuck in the closet with its door closed, Idona centered herself and went over to the main door. Her hand touched the handle lightly just as her eyes spotted the mirror. She looked too awake and aware of herself to try to lie that she had been napping. Shocked, Idona quickly ruffled her hair and patted her cheeks before slouching. Now she looked like she had just woken up. Idona opened the door while a knock was underway.

Outside of the doorway stood a brunette with violet eyes. Her slim figure was dressed in male-like clothing that hid her curves. She stood, mid-knock, staring at Idona for a moment. At her feet was a red reusable Target bag filled with notebooks and schoolbooks. Idona gave the girl a tired smile.

"Hey, Sue," Idona mumbled, trying to sound like she was still sleepy. Violet eyes narrowed before Sue shoved past Idona. Idona stumbled back and watched the other girl in surprise. Sue looked quickly around the room before checking under Idona's bed and desk. She then strode across the room and began checking under Minnie's things. Idona stiffened. Next place Sue would look is her own closet. Slowly, Idona shifted to block it off. "What's up?"

"Where is he?" Sue snapped, looking sharply at Idona. The younger girl couldn't help but flinch at the attitude in the words.

"Who?" Idona responded, feigning innocence. Sue's violet eyes focused on the closed off closet before fluttering quickly back to Idona.

"Let me check your closet," she ordered before stepping forward. Idona hesitated. "That's where he is, isn't it? Last place he could hide."

"Sue, you're talking crazy. Besides, what guy would ever hide himself in my room or even in my closet?" Idona muttered just before Sue rushed toward her. The brunette easily shoved the smaller girl aside and stepped up to the front of the closet. Idona caught her balance and spun to look just as Sue opened the doors.

Having realized that he was about to be caught, Darius prepared himself. Once the door was opened enough for him to slip by, he ran as fast as he could past the two girls. The door out to the hallway was open, so he rushed through it without slowing down. Once he was in the hallway, Darius slipped into the first opening he saw. It was a small lounge area. Thankfully, no one was there. Sighing deeply, Darius relaxed into one of the chairs.

Back in Idona's room, both girls were shocked to see nothing in the closet. Idona slowly moved to stand by Sue's side and looked in the closet. Suddenly it clicked in Idona's mind, vampire speed. Darius ran away and hid elsewhere. After another moment, Idona grabbed the closet door and slammed it closed. "I like to keep my things private."

"But, I heard a male voice," Sue tried to explain. Idona shook her head before looking to her desk. *Project New World* was still open and while she watched, it flipped a page. Idona rushed over, closed it, opened her top drawer, stuffed the book inside, and slammed the drawer closed before the book could reopen. Sue turned and looked at the other girl in confusion. "What was that?"

"Something," Idona responded, knowing that if she said it was "nothing," Sue would press for more information. Sue shook her head and was about to ask about the male voice again when Idona spoke. "So, what are you here for?"

"Hmm? Oh, class," Sue answered, beginning to forget about the male voice she heard. Idona frowned. She had just recently asked Sue to come and get her for this afternoon class. Idona was always either late or skipping. Thankfully, this teacher didn't seem to care about the college's rule of "three absences or more means an automatic fail."

"I think I'm gonna skip," Idona told her. The brunette frowned.

"What?

"Tell the teacher that I'm sick. She'll understand."

"This will be your fourth time this month!" Idona moved to sit on her bed. Sue focused a glare on the shorter girl.

"Mrs. Raymouth loves me. Besides, she knows I get sick a lot."

"Idona, I hate lying to Mrs. Raymouth," Sue said as she shook her head. Idona gave the brunette a soft smile.

"Sue, I can't go."

"Why?" Sue's hands moved to the sides of her hips. Idona's mind almost shut down. Then she thought of it. Standing, Idona spoke.

"I have something else to do."

"Like what? What could be more important than your education?"

"Like..." Idona looked around her room before focusing on her closet. A pathetic excuse occurred to her. "Laundry."

"You can do that after class. Besides, your basket looked mostly empty." Idona frowned. This was why she liked her privacy.

"Homework?"

"Since when do you do homework?" Idona began to panic. She was running out of ideas.

"Clean!"

"Be serious Idona. Outside of Minnie's closet, this room looks immaculate," Idona looked around the room again and found no other plausible excuse. Finally, she sighed. Slowly, she went back to her desk. Once there she began to open her top drawer. She didn't want to show Sue, but this was what it took to be left alone, Idona was willing to do it. Almost as if he could sense something wrong, Darius began to head back to the room. He needed to try to help Idona get rid of Sue.

As the drawer started to open and the book inside got enough room to try opening itself, someone cleared their throat. Idona and Sue turned to the door. There stood Darius. He looked at Idona and willed her to have no reaction to him. Sadly, Idona couldn't help it. She knew that Sue also read the books about Darius. *If Sue is paying attention, she'll recognize him!* Idona thought hysterically. *But how can I tell him?* Darius nodded a hello to the girls.

"Is one of you Idona?" Darius asked, focusing on Sue rather than Idona. Sue nodded and slowly pointed to Idona. Darius faced her. He intended to ask her something ridiculous. Then he sensed someone feeling for him. His eyes darkened. He suddenly looked distant. Like he was listening for something. He came back around just as Sue really began to focus on him. Idona was freaking out. The longer he stayed near Sue, the longer she had to figure out who he was. His eyes were still dark when he spoke again. "Grab a few of your things and come meet me outside, please."

"Is there a problem?" Sue called, frightened, when Darius turned away. Idona froze when she saw his eyes darken. The words barely registered but when they did, Idona realized that might not have been what he wanted to say. Darius didn't look back before speaking.

"I'm not at liberty to say," he told the girls before walking out of sight. Idona released a breath that she had been holding. Sue turned to face Idona. The younger girl could see the fear on her face. It made Idona wonder if Sue would even realize that the man she just saw was Darius. Sue didn't care that she recognized something about Darius. For now, she was too scared to think about it. Even if she wasn't, Sue wasn't sure she'd be able to ask him anything.

"I'll tell Mrs. Raymouth you won't be in," Sue muttered before rushing out of the room. She paused only long enough to pick up her bag. Idona waited a few seconds before opening the drawer the rest of the way and pulling out the book. It opened to a new page.

The terrified brunette met up with the vampire at the elevator. When Darius had hidden from this girl minutes before, he had seen others hit the button with a down arrow painted on it and wait for one of the two doors to open. It hadn't been very long that he waited but many kids had come and gone. He had already hit the arrow and now he wondered what to do next. The kids he had seen before all had friends whom they chatted with or took out a book to read. Since Darius had neither a friend nor a book, he looked around the room. Sue said nothing to Darius while they waited. Even if she had wanted to speak, she had no idea what to say. She wondered why the man needed to see Idona.

Just as she finally began looking Darius over and realizing that she might know someone who looks like him, the elevator on the left dinged and opened. Both entered and waited for the other. It was almost like neither of them wanted to make the first move. Darius stared at the panel filled with buttons. Many had numbers written on them but one caught his attention. It had an "L" written on it. Some more below had words printed on them but Darius didn't focus on them. He was more curious about the ones above those. *What do I hit now? Darius wildly thought.*

"Going to the lobby?" Sue asked, sounding much braver than she felt. Darius frowned. He had never heard that term before. Not knowing what else to do, he nodded yes. The doors closed, and Darius felt a shift in the floor. If not for his vampire reflexes, he would have fallen backward. His eyes flicked to Sue, but she didn't shift at all when the elevator moved.

Darius almost spoke to her then. He wanted to know a little bit about this new contraption, but he realized that she was just used to it being there. If he drew too much attention to himself, Darius feared that someone would learn he didn't belong in their world. Trying to make sure he wouldn't speak to Sue, Darius began to look around. Above the door were more circles, with similar numbers and the one letter. They lit up as they passed the floor, which the vampire noticed between the cracks of the doors. Darius stared at it in fascination. *How can anyone feel that this thing is safe? I could easily rip these doors apart. The vampire thought to himself.*

Relaxing now, Sue watched him, as he stayed focused on the flashing lights. She felt like she had seen him before. He just looked so familiar. But Sue barely left the library and he didn't look like he was from this college. The thought wouldn't leave her mind though. Sue knew this man from somewhere. She opened her mouth, determined to ask Darius about it, but paused.

Finally, the elevator slowed to a stop before the doors opened. Sue calmly walked out with Darius coming slowly behind. She decided against asking, unless she saw him again. The vampire paused in the busy lobby, not sure where to go until he saw an area that looked like the outside. Quickly he headed over and made it in time to see Sue exit out a door. He followed her out that way. When he got outside, Darius froze. It had been so long since he'd seen the outside in daylight. He had seen it from the window in Idona's room, but seeing it like this was, different.

"You okay?" Sue asked. Darius focused on her again. She was watching him closely. He nodded. Seemingly satisfied with his answer, Sue started walking away but stopped short. She focused on him again. Darius tensed. He could see in her violet eyes that she might be recognizing him. She took another minute to stare at him before she shook her head and walked away. Once he was sure that she had left for good, Darius focused his attention on the outside world. It was so beautiful to him...

Idona closed the book and sat down on her bed. Her favorite fictional vampire was now outside in the daylight. *No, that doesn't seem awkward. A vampire out in the daylight.* She sighed before looking around. Even though Darius said to meet her outside, Idona didn't know if she wanted to. It seemed like such a hassle. She could always ignore the request and allow the vampire to explore her world while she forgot about his existence. Then she wouldn't have to worry about trying to fix what happened. It felt like a good idea until she thought more about it. Minnie would know about Darius. It was then that Idona remembered Rafficer. He was roaming free in her world as well, or so Darius said. But if he was, she was the only one in this world who knew.

"Crap," Idona moaned before opening the book. She half hoped for a section on Rafficer just so she could keep her promise to Darius. Sadly, that didn't happen. Idona sighed deeply but continued reading.

I hope Idona gets down here soon. I wonder if she'll come down packed, Darius thought as he leaned against the brick wall, which sat across the road from Idona's dorm. The vampire had sensed for his sire again. Rafficer was just beginning to feed a second time. Darius couldn't tell why the older vampire was feeding so regularly, but he figured it was because of Serge. Even though Serge was Rafficer's First General, the young vampire was only 70 years undead.

"Come on, Idona," Darius moaned, his worry getting the best of him. When he had been sensing for Rafficer, the older vampire paused his feeding. It was almost as if he could sense Darius feeling for him. The older vampire sent out his own senses

and felt where Darius was. It had made the 652-year-old vampire stop when he did feel it. Darius ruffled his dyed black hair before starting to pace again.

His thoughts drifted to a topic that he wanted to avoid at all cost. Rafficer. The older sire was feeding a lot in this world. Darius could only assume it was because whatever Raff was going to do required a large amount of energy. Sire vampires used up a lot of human blood and life energy when they used abilities such as sensing their younglings, calling to them, or using even more normal vampire traits like compulsion, mind reading, shape-shifting, and the like.

The vampire couldn't help but feel horrified that Rafficer was sensing for him. A little unknown fact about Rafficer was he also had the ability to tell when his younglings stayed with a human for any amount of time. It was as if he could either smell or sense the presence of a human on the vampire. Darius hated that ability of Raff's more than any of his other abilities. Many times when Darius fed, he didn't like completely draining the human. It took Darius almost two years to realize that Rafficer would go out, find these humans, and kill them slowly and painfully. When the vampire found that out, he actually didn't feed for almost a month until Rafficer attacked him.

Sky-blue eyes looked at the door but still Idona didn't appear. Darius groaned. She didn't get his warning. He needed to get Idona away from here. Rafficer is going to come to this place whether I leave or not, and if Idona stays here...*Darius couldn't even finish the thought. But the mental images of Rafficer torturing her or even worse, turning her, made Darius feel ill. It was then that he realized Minnie had to leave too. She was around him almost as much as Idona. Darius then turned to look in the direction Sue left in.* She should be safe. She wasn't near me long enough, *Darius thought, the rest of it left unthought-of. He looked back up to the window he thought was Idona's room. His mind focused on her.*

Upstairs Idona began...

CHAPTER 5

Escape

---❮◦❯---

Idona slapped the book closed just as the words wrote themselves down. *Rafficer, after me? No. That can't be true!* she thought. Her mind focused onto the second book in the series. She remembered a small section dealt with an issue where Darius closed down and didn't feed. It took her a moment to realize that it was around that time that Darius learned Rafficer was finishing off all his kills. Idona couldn't help gasping in shock. *Was that the only mention of it? No...*

There was also a human girl, Robyn. After Rafficer had attacked Darius, the young vampire tried to run away and ignore all of his sire's calls for him. Robyn had been there. She stood by him, helping Darius fight the calls. Robyn also went searching for other types of blood for Darius. He didn't accept any of it, but it was nice of her to offer. When Darius felt Rafficer draw near, he left Robyn without telling her. Darius remembered it as the second biggest mistake in his life.

Rafficer compelled the girl to tell him all about her time with Darius and rewarded her by turning her. When someone is turned while under a compulsion, they go insane. Something in their mind just seems to snap and they lose all control. Rafficer called them "inhuman." He loved them like that. Not that he turned many while under a compulsion because the older they got, the harder it was to stop them. One lasted a full year before Rafficer told Darius to kill it. The only reason Darius agreed to do it was that the vampire had eaten another vampire in its search for blood. Darius and readers found out later that other sires wouldn't be so "forgiving" to both human and youngling.

Idona sat on her bed in newfound horror. She couldn't believe the amount of trouble all this was causing. She felt like she was at fault for the whole thing, but she couldn't remember why. Realizing that Minnie had no idea about the new changes in their lives, Idona reached for her phone on her desk. She scanned down to Minnie's name and texted her. Idona's eyes flashed to the clock and realized she was in between classes right now.

"come. min in trouble"

"?" was the response a few seconds later. Idona couldn't help but smile.

"?"s later Idona sent back before dropping her phone on her bed and grabbing her backpack. Her phone rang, alerting her of a new text, just before she dumped the contents of the bag onto her bed. She then grabbed the phone and read the message.

"K." Again, she couldn't help but smile. Normally, Minnie wouldn't skip a class like this for her. The older girl was rather particular about attending all her classes. Sliding her phone into her pocket, Idona then headed over to her closet and opened the doors. On the top shelf, in the closet, was a tan suitcase that she grabbed. It was just big enough to hold two weeks' worth of clothes, which was about all that Idona owned outside of specialty clothes like dresses and fancy outfits. She tossed the suitcase on the bed and opened it.

Idona sighed and looked at all her clothes in the laundry basket. She groaned. There weren't many clothes, but it made her realize that when she left, they'd all have less time on the road. She then began to dig them all out, folding them as she did so, and placing them neatly in the suitcase. Finishing those clothes rather quickly, she started to go through the bureaus for the rest. All of them were folded, so she only had to toss them neatly into the suitcase. When she was just about done, Minnie and Darius showed up.

"Found him outside, which was weird in and of itself, but anyway... Darius said we need to leave?" Minnie asked. Her eyes drifted to the suitcase as Idona closed the lid on her clothes. Minnie couldn't help but make a face as she looked at the dark chocolate-brown haired girl. Idona looked at the two and gave Darius a soft smile. "What's going on?"

"It's hard to explain," Idona began as Darius strode across the room. He grabbed *Project New World*, opened it, and handed it to Minnie. The girl paused before accepting it.

"We don't have to explain," Darius growled as Minnie held the book by its binding and watched it open. All three saw the pages were almost full. Minnie watched in silence as the rest of the page filled with their conversation and then the page turned by itself and resumed writing. With a scream, she dropped the book. Mutely, Idona went over and picked it up before it finished reopening. "Minnie, please just pack. We'll explain everything afterward."

"The book just opened!" Minnie cried as she stared at it in Idona's hand. Idona sighed and looked at Darius. He continued frowning. "WHY ARE YOU TWO NOT FLIPPING OUT?"

"We did earlier. But to be honest, a book rewriting itself is not the biggest issue we have to face. Just pack, Minnie," Idona begged. Brownish-green eyes told the other girl everything she needed to know. Idona was scared of something and that made Minnie worry greatly. Minnie looked at Darius. *How can this be? Why is this happening?* she thought to herself. Slowly, Minnie's eyes meet Idona's before the other girl nodded and walked over to her bed.

She pulled two suitcases out from underneath it and placed on the bed. As she opened them, Darius walked over. In two seconds, half of Minnie's wardrobe was packed neatly into one of the two suitcases. Minnie fell backward on her desk and let out a small cry. If she didn't believe before, she couldn't help but admit it now.

"Oh my god!" she cried as Darius finished packing the rest of her clothes in the other suitcase. Meanwhile, Idona was packing her backpack with her chargers for her phone, iPod, and eReader. Then she packed her iPod, eReader, and headphones. She looked back at her desk. Her laptop was still running. Shutting it down, she started to pack that. "You really are a vampire?"

"You just noticed?" Idona muttered. Minnie looked at her with a sharp glare.

"You knew?"

"He's from my *vampire* book."

"I just thought..."

"You thought wrong. I'm also not the only vampire from there to come here. And trust me, they aren't as nice," Darius finished as he faced Minnie. She stood there for a few more seconds, wondering how things had become so weird in such a short amount of time. Her thoughts focused onto the idea that there might be more vampires out there in her world. Swallowing some built-up saliva, Minnie headed over to her closet. She decided that packing her things might make her forget what Darius told her. On the top shelf was an empty backpack, which she grabbed and began packing full of things similar to what Idona was packing.

"Hey, Min? You got gas?" Idona whispered. She had paused packing and looked out the window. Darius frowned as he watched Minnie also pause and look up at Idona.

"Just filled her up."

"Still have the emergency supplies?"

"Never take them out."

"Good."

"Emergency supplies?" Darius asked, completely lost by the girls' conversation. Idona turned to face Darius as Minnie resumed packing. She was now working on a second bag, which was being filled with makeup, medication, hairbrushes, elastics, toothbrush, toothpaste, and other similar things.

"My car is packed with six blankets, three pillows, two first aid kits, a box of chewy bars, change of clothes for me and three guests, chargers for any electronic device, a GPS, and a cooler filled with chilled water," Minnie explained. Darius's frown deepened. Minnie's mention of a "car" simply confused him even more but he understood that most people didn't pack their cars with half as much as Minnie had in hers. Idona noticed his confused gaze and couldn't help but softly giggle. Darius heard and looked over to her.

"Minnie's gotten lost a few times, stuck in bad weather, and run out of...energy for her car. I'll explain the car thing later, but because of those experiences, Minnie stocked up her car in case something happened. Something like stuck in a snowstorm to an accident, Minnie's pretty much prepared for it all," Idona said to clear up his confusion. Some of it cleared, but Darius still didn't get the concepts of a car, chewy bar, chargers, cooler, and GPS. Darius nodded his head anyway and acted like Idona had helped, but even she knew that it didn't.

It wasn't long after the girls had finished packing everything they needed. Darius grabbed Minnie's two suitcases and Idona's one before marching quickly out the door. Minnie grabbed three of her bags (all of which Idona frowned about) while Idona grabbed her backpack and pillow. The two then headed out the door and met up with Darius near the elevator. His hands were too full, so Minnie hit the down arrow. Darius frowned, remembering his last two experiences with the device, and looked at Idona.

"Is there another way?" he mumbled to her. Idona and Minnie focused on him.

"There are stairs at the end of the hall, but I think this will be faster," Minnie told him as the right elevator door opened. Darius sighed before the three piled on. Idona stood near the panel by the door with Minnie in the middle back and Darius across from Idona. "Don't like the elevator?"

"Never heard of one," Darius informed her as the doors closed. Idona hit the "L" button and they began moving.

"Really?" Minnie whispered.

"Darius's world is really different than ours. It's similar to ours in timeline but it's like the Industrial Revolution hasn't started yet," Idona explained. Minnie gasped as the elevator stopped on the floor two floors down. Darius's eyes narrowed. With all the things they had and their own bodies, it was a tight fit already.

"You poor thing!" Minnie cried as the door opened to a familiar figure.

"Sweetie!"

"Marc?" Idona gulped as she looked into his forest-green eyes. Marc smiled before he noticed Darius's sky-blue eyes glaring at him. Shrugging it off, Marc entered the already crowded elevator. In doing so, he somehow positioned Darius in the far back corner next to Minnie with Marc in front of him and Idona in front of Minnie. Darius growled lightly to himself. "I thought you had class about now?"

"Got canceled. What about you? What's up with all this?" Marc asked. Minnie frowned. Marc's class was the same one as hers and she didn't see or hear that it was canceled. Knowing that Marc lied made Minnie feel better when she answered for Idona.

"Death," Minnie answered. Idona almost laughed at Minnie's white lie. Marc looked at Minnie for only a second. He didn't know that Minnie wasn't a good liar or that Minnie barely ever lied. Darius looked at Minnie and tried to cover his own surprise at the girl's lie.

"Don't look so upset, Sweetie," Marc stated when he saw her holding back a smile.

"My family," Minnie said as she put on a sad look. Marc didn't even bother to see if she looked upset. Darius fought to hold in his anger when he smelt Marc's body chemistry change and filled the small space with the smell of lust. The vampire was ready to rip Marc to pieces when the door opened again. He was about to leave when he noticed Idona's face. She looked so unimpressed by Marc that he almost laughed. The way she was acting, Marc could have been the perfect guy for Idona but she'd still think of him as disgusting.

They were now in the lobby. Marc backed out and waited as the others came out as well. Darius slid around the girls and exited first, placing himself before Marc as though the kid might attack. Minnie came out next, followed closely by Idona. Marc stared at Darius, his green eyes filled with laughter. With Marc's attention on Darius, Minnie and Idona sneaked out behind the vampire and headed for the door. Marc moved quickly around Darius and caught up to the girls. Darius glowered and went to catch up using his speed. Just before he did so, he looked around. It was something that Kathleen told him to do in her best effort to keep vampires a secret from public. He was very upset when he saw too many people around and had to force himself to stop.

"You leaving? It's almost 1:30. Maybe you should wait till tomorrow?" Marc questioned. Idona frowned and looked down at her bag.

"Nope, got to leave tonight."

"Where you goin'?"

"Don't know."

"Can I come?"

"No room," Minnie called as she opened the door. Idona slipped out as Marc frowned and followed. As Darius and Minnie exited, Idona turned and faced Marc. The vampire could see the anger burning through Idona as she glared at the boy.

"Marc, why don't you give it up? I WILL NEVER DATE YOU!" she screamed at him. Marc backed away in mock horror before looking sharply at her. Darius couldn't help but smile. Then again, even if he could stop it, he didn't want to. Minnie suddenly looked horrified at the whole situation. Idona had been telling her that Marc was getting worse, but Minnie didn't believe her.

"I don't believe that," he told her. Darius dropped the suitcases, took two strides before grabbing Marc by his shirt collar, and lifting him to meet his eyes. Forest-green eyes met darkened blue eyes and Marc fell limp in Darius's hands.

"You will leave Idona alone," Darius commanded before dropping the teen. Marc sat on the ground frozen in shock and watched as the three walked to Minnie's dark red Chevrolet HHR. Darius walked backward so he could keep his attention on Marc. He didn't want the boy to break the compulsion too early and attack when the vampire's back was turned. Minnie was shaking like a leaf now. Her fear made

Darius calm down. He didn't want her to fear him; he wanted Marc to. Idona was still in rage. She stormed to the HHR so quickly it felt like she would break the pavement with her footfalls.

As they reached the car, Darius gave Marc a fleeting look of triumph and saw something that shocked him. In the book world, very few humans who could fight a vampire's command and Darius expected the same to happen in this world. But as he stared at Marc, he could see the fight in his eyes. Marc wasn't going to give up. If anything, the guy was now more determined than ever to get Idona to date him.

CHAPTER 6

Where To?

"This is a car," Minnie said to Darius. The vampire stared at the machine as if it was some kind of monster. He was already beginning to forget about Marc and the way he acted. Idona had quickly thrown the suitcases and bags into the back trunk like space of the HHR. Minnie was trying to explain the workings of the machine, which was something the two girls were used too. "The outside is a kind of metal, plastic shell that protects us from the wind, bugs, and weather. Inside are the seats, seat buckles and other things."

"Where are the horses? How long till they are prepared?" Darius muttered, sounding very childlike. Idona groaned before grabbing Minnie's keys, opening the driver's side door and getting inside. Darius circled the car to stand by the window as Idona started the car. Both girls gave Darius credit for his bravery since he didn't even flinch. Instead, Darius became even more curious. "How does it do that?"

"Well, there are gears inside that make other gears turn when connected to strings or something. Uh, there are also these weird cylinders that move up and down with oil and gas," Minnie began explaining. Meanwhile, Idona opened the glove compartment, grabbed the car

Owner's Manual, and got out. Darius watched her as she handed it over to him.

"Read this after you get in. It should make all this much easier," Idona told him, the agitation on her voice was so clear that even Minnie could hear it. Darius accepted the book and began looking at the pages. "We need to get a move on it. The further away from here we get, the better off we'll be."

"You're right," Darius muttered and he quickly read the whole thing, speed reading with vampire senses. He understood most of the book but still had a few questions. Minnie walked over to the other side of the car and opened the door as fast as she could. Idona nodded and sat back down in the driver's seat and closed the door. She buckled and looked up at Darius. He walked to the door behind her and opened it. Pausing, he looked back to the dorm where Marc had last been. The teen was missing. With a frown, Darius slid into his seat at the same time as Minnie. The girl buckled her seat and turned in time to see Darius also do the same.

"Big improvement from not even having heard of a car," Minnie joked. Darius gave her a soft smile and sat back as Idona began to shift the car into reverse and started backing out of the spot. Again, to his credit, Darius stayed quiet. Idona maneuvered the car out of its parking spot and then began to drive it toward the road. "Where we headed?"

"I suggest we empty our bank accounts in case Raff learns what that is and how to track us through that," Idona informed Minnie, forgetting that she still had no idea what was going on. In the big rush to leave, they barely said anything other than "stay, you die."

"Raff? You mean, Darius's sire?" Minnie asked, looking back at Darius. After a second, she looked at Idona in surprise.

"As my sire, Raff has the ability to sense where I am when he tries to feel for me. Earlier today, he did that and learned of my presence here," Darius informed the girl as Idona turned left out of the parking lot. Their minds were distracted by other thoughts and none of them noticed a black Camaro sneaking up behind them.

"So, what does that have to do with us leaving? It just sounds to me like you alone should have left," Minnie said as she twisted in her seat to look at Darius. Idona frowned.

"How fast of a reader are you?" she asked as she took another turn. Minnie shrugged.

"Depends on the book I guess. I read schoolwork rather slowly, but if the book interests me, then I could finish about 100 pages in an hour. Why?" Minnie asked. Darius also looked at Idona.

"At this point, you might as well read the books. Darius, I think my bag is on top," Idona told the vampire as she looked at him through the rear-view mirror. Darius turned to look and picked it up. As he went to face forward, he noticed the Camaro. For a moment, he thought he saw Marc behind the wheel, but then the sun caught the windshield and created a glare. Darius turned forward again and frowned. "The books are in the front pocket."

Nodding, Darius unzipped the bag and lifted the first book, *Project Old Life*. As he looked at it, he couldn't believe that it was sitting there in his hands. Minnie watched Darius as he flipped the book around to read the back cover. He quickly read it and looked up.

"This is about Raff?" he asked. Idona nodded.

"The beginning is all about Raff's fight for freedom and during the middle it switches over to follow your life. It ends when you are turned into vampire. When Minnie's done, you could read it," Idona said. Darius looked back down to the book and scowled. He wasn't interested in reading what he had already lived through. With a disgusted look on his face, Darius handed the book over to Minnie. The girl accepted the book and began to look at it. The cover showed a young man with green eyes and black hair. The sketch had sharp features that displayed that the man would be extremely handsome in real life.

"Is this Rafficer?" Minnie muttered as she stared at the image.

"It looks similar. He's got a huge scar down his right cheek though," Darius told her as he leaned forward and showed where the scar would be. Minnie nodded as Idona slowed the car to a stop. Darius looked up and saw the red light. "What's that?"

"A stop light. Red means to stop, yellow means to slow down, and green means you can go. The light is there to make sure that you don't go speeding through this part of the road and hit another car," Idona told him. Darius nodded. In his world, they were just beginning to introduce the idea of a three colored light that would tell coach drivers if it was safe to go or not. "You might as well get used to the idea of not knowing much of what we have here."

"I figured that. I'm just being nosey," Darius muttered. Idona smiled as the light changed color and she accelerated. Minnie was reading the book now. Darius sat back for a moment before remembering the Camaro. He turned and looked. It was still behind them and there was still a glare. "I think that car is following us."

"This town is almost a one road town, I'd be surprised if someone wasn't following us," Idona said as she turned into a parking lot. Darius spun around and watched as the Camaro drove on. He frowned. Before, he had sworn he had seen Marc. Maybe Idona was right and it was just someone driving in the same direction as them. He faced forward as Idona shut the car off. Minnie lowered the book; she was already ten pages in.

"Where are we?" she asked.

"The bank. Remember I said we should empty our accounts?" Idona said as she unbuckled. Minnie mouthed an "oh" and placed the book down. As she unbuckled, Darius decided to do the same. The three opened their doors and exited in unison. Idona and Minnie slammed their doors closed before walking toward the bank, but Darius paused to look over the HHR and see if he could find the Camaro. He found it sitting, idling in a nearby McDonald's parking lot. Darius growled and narrowed his eyes. Using vampire sight, he tried to see who was inside, but it looked as if the car was empty. "You coming?"

"Yeah," Darius called as he walked after the girls and the three entered the bank. Darius focused his attention on Idona because he didn't want to seem like a fool when he asked what everything was. Minnie quickly walked over to a woman sitting behind a desk and began talking while Idona stood behind some velvet ropes. Darius leaned forward. "When we get back outside and start to leave, can you watch for that car? I really think it's following us."

"I think you might be paranoid," Idona told him as she looked out the big glass windows at the front of the bank. Darius also looked. He again noticed the Camaro. It was still idling in place.

"It's across the road, there," Darius whispered as he pointed to the car. Idona squinted and spotted it through the glare of the sun. She stiffened and all blood rushed from her face. Darius looked at her when his sensitive hearing heard her heart skip a beat. She looked pale, almost like if he had drained nearly all of her blood. It made him hungry for a split second. He noticed the feeling passed quickly but was fearful of the next time. After using his powers so much, he would need to feed soon.

"That looks like Marc's car. But, you compelled him to leave me alone, didn't you?" Idona questioned as she looked into his sky-blue eyes, which had a slight reddish tint to them. Darius shook his head.

"I tried, but Marc seems to be impervious," Darius told her. Idona gulped and looked back across the street. The car was now moving toward the road. She watched as it cut across traffic and pulled into the parking lot for the bank. Again, it parked in such a way that the sun glared the view from inside the car away.

"I'll watch for him," Idona whispered. Darius nodded as he straightened to stare at the Camaro. Marc's imperviousness made him worry that maybe the boy would be a bigger problem than he first thought. The more that Marc hung around, the worse it could be for all of them.

"Can I help you?" called a gentleman, who was sitting behind a second desk. Idona nodded and headed over. Darius moved over toward the windows and watched the Camaro. Narrowing his gaze onto the car, Darius felt better. Even if he couldn't see in, as long as he stayed focus on it, everything would be fine. He waited for a few minutes by himself before Minnie came and stood beside him. She was counting money in her hands. Darius looked over. With the money all fanned out in her hands, he could see the amount of each bill and quickly added it up in his head.

"Two thousand three hundred fifty seven dollars," he mumbled. Minnie stopped counting and looked at him.

"You've got to be kidding me, how did you know that?" she asked. Darius pointed to the money.

"I counted," he informed her. Minnie frowned and looked at the cash still fanned out. With a huff, she closed the fan and dug into her back-left pocket to take out her wallet. Darius sniffed and looked back out to the car. The engine was turned off but no one had come out yet. With the sun still creating a glare, Darius didn't even try to look closer; he just turned and watched Idona. The gentleman behind the desk handed her a large wad of cash. Darius looked closer and noticed that most of it was $100 bills. Doing the math quickly in his head, he assumed that amount could be close to 5 thousand or more. Minnie also turned and looked.

"She comes from a rich family. She's just lucky that her grandparents set up money in funds to get larger. We'll more than likely be stopping other places as well to get the rest," Minnie said, as Idona got closer. Idona quickly shoved the money into a small bag that she had sitting in one of her pockets.

"What rest?" she questioned. Minnie smiled and pointed to her bag of money. "Not any time soon. I'm hoping we can fix the whole thing before I spend all of this."

"Fix the whole thing?" Darius repeated. Idona looked at him. Silence fell over them. Darius focused on her words before his eyes narrowed. It made perfect sense to him now. "Make everything normal, like sending me back into the book. That's what you mean, right?"

"I...I didn't want it to sound like that," Idona muttered as she looked away from Darius. He stiffened and frowned. For some reason, he thought that maybe Idona would want him to stay, but after that, it all seemed very clear to him. Darius nodded and faced the door. He wasn't sure what to say. Finally, he decided to change the subject. Idona watched him in fear. She was afraid of him leaving her for good. It wasn't as if she had meant to make it sound like she didn't want Darius around, it just seemed to come out like that. Minnie stayed silent with every intention of staying out of this little tiff.

"We should just go," Darius stiffly snapped as he walked away from the girls. Idona froze while Minnie watched the two. Her eyes widened as she suddenly saw, in more detail, what happened. Looking back at Idona, Minnie saw Idona's pain written clear on the other girl's face. She decided against bringing it up and walked past Idona. Somehow, her actions made Idona realize that it was over. She had to go now.

Silently, the three headed to the car. Darius quickly got into the seat behind the driver again. Idona paused. She wasn't sure if she should sit in front of him. Minnie looked at her and held out her hand, offering to drive. Idona noticed and gave the girl a soft smile before shaking her head. Slowly she got into the driver's seat. Minnie got into her seat as Idona started the car. She spun out of the parking lot before Minnie had fully buckled and started on the path she would normally take to go home. The Camaro followed, and again none of them noticed.

"So, where should we head to?" Idona said after she had been driving for close to ten minutes. She was well on her way to heading to her house, down Route 2, even though she didn't want to go there. Minnie, who had been reading, put the book down in her lap. She got through a good chunk of the book. Darius, who had been looking out the window, looked at Minnie.

"If we want to try and fix this, I think we should head to someone who might have magical powers. The biggest place of magic that I can think of is either New Orleans or Walt Disney World," Minnie muttered. Idona almost hit her brakes in her surprise. She half hoped that her roommate was joking. "Maybe even Vegas!"

"Seriously? Walt Disney World?" Idona asked, ignoring the Vegas idea. Minnie nodded.

"What is that?" Darius called from the back.

"A theme park," Idona growled. "There wouldn't be anything there."

"No, seriously, think about it, Idona! Everyone says they feel something when they pass by that place. What if it really is magic and we could tap into it?" Minnie cried. Idona frowned and gave Minnie a sidelong glance. After a moment, she shook her head.

"You've been reading way too much Kingdom Keepers. Either way, that's heading south. Get your GPS. I think New Orleans might be our best bet," Idona said. After reviving from the accusation that she read too many young adult novels, Minnie nodded and reached toward a little door sitting in the middle of the dashboard. She opened it to reveal a lot of electrical wire and a small Garmin GPS. Powering the thing up, Minnie looked back at Darius. He focused on the small screen, watching as it turned on.

"Where in New Orleans?" Minnie questioned, her eyes still focused on Darius. Idona shrugged.

"A hotel, I guess," Idona responded. Minnie nodded and looked back at the small device. It powered up but it didn't have a signal. She ignored that and started to set up the directions. Five minutes later, the GPS was ready.

"Continue five miles on Route 2 due East," the GPS called out. Darius raised his eyebrows in surprise, shook his head, and looked out the window again. Minnie laughed. He didn't want to ask about the GPS but even he couldn't stop the curiosity he was feeling. All of this technology was new to him, and even though he was a creature of the night, he was human enough to want to know all about it.

"It looks like it says we'll be there in an hour but I know that it means around a day," Minnie said. Even Idona cracked a smile as she grabbed the GPS. She quickly hit a few buttons and examined the screen.

"Looks like we may have to stop for the night a couple of times. So really, we'll be there in two days or so," Idona informed the others. Darius frowned and remained silent. For them to travel that quickly, Darius assumed the place was close. Minnie frowned. Not only would they have to stop for the night, but they'd also need to refill the tank. Maybe even get food.

"We'll have to stop for gas a few times too. Maybe twice a day. I mean it is fifteen hundred miles or so away," Minnie muttered. Darius jerked forward in response. *It can't be that far away! There isn't anything that can travel that fast!* Darius thought. He looked at the girl, trying to figure out how to bring up his question of speed, but he failed miserably. Meanwhile, Idona bit her bottom lip. She was lost in thought.

"Hmm, I almost feel like we should fly, but then we'll have to rent a car in New Orleans. That's spending too much money too fast," Idona said to herself. She left it unsaid that they could be traveling for a long, long time. Minnie nodded as she looked down at the bag of cash by her feet. After a few moments of silence, Minnie went back to the book.

"In one mile, turn onto route 8A west—then turn right," the GPS called out. Idona nodded and followed the directions. "Continue on route 8A west for nine miles."

Idona again nodded. After a few minutes of silence, Idona reached toward the middle of the dash. There sat a power button, which she pressed, turning on the stereo. Darius flinched when music began blaring through the speakers. The music was Evanescence's "The Only One." Idona smiled before turning down the volume so it didn't hurt any of their eardrums. Minnie paused reading the book.

"Now I can barely hear it," Minnie whined. Idona frowned.

"It's amazing you hear anything when you keep your music that loud," she told the other girl. Minnie laughed before going back to the book. Idona smiled and turned to music up slightly. Darius looked at the two girls who seemed pleased with themselves. He thought back to the dorm and recognizing their differences in the room. It made him laugh when he realized they were complete opposites, and yet they were friends. Sighing, Darius resumed looking outside.

As Idona drove along, she kept trying to maintain constant speed. Minnie would tense up whenever they got too close to another car. Darius was amazed at Idona's driving skills. She was prompt in reacting to the changes in the road, sometimes even before other cars got in her way. Although Minnie tried to distract herself with the book, she kept looking over to make sure that Idona wasn't driving her car too rashly.

Idona rolled her eyes at Minnie's controlling attitude. She had driven a lot, and had only one accident on her record. The accident was the fault of the other driver who was trying to overtake her during a stop signal. The accident damaged her car but it was nothing she could control. During the drive, Darius sometimes focused on the license plates of other cars and sometimes read the road signs. He easily got bored from both of these tasks and started looking inside the other cars. Most of the people ignored him but little kids seemed to enjoy making faces at him. Not sure what else to do, Darius made faces back. He worked hard to make sure the faces wouldn't scare the kids. He just made them laugh.

Time passed by slowly. Idona followed the GPS through a few more turns until the GPS finally said there were 51 more miles remaining. Outside of the music playing through the speakers, it was quiet in the car. Darius kept playing with kids who passed by while Minnie read. After about an hour, Idona pulled a blue cord out of the center console area and an iPod. She plugged one end of the blue cord into the iPod and the other into the dashboard before messing with the iPod. New music began to pour out the speakers. Darius was shocked when a song jumped to a new one before completion. Every other song or so, Idona would play around with the iPod. Finally, one of the girls' stomach began to growl in hunger. The two traded a look.

"It is five," Minnie mentioned, after looking at the clock. Idona nodded and looked at the GPS. The next turn was coming up soon. She memorized what the turn was and handed the device over to Minnie. "What do you want me to look up?"

"A familiar name," Idona told her. Minnie smiled and began flipping through things on the GPS. A moment later, she found a familiar name.

"There's a Panera Bread coming up. I'm not sure how far off course it is," Minnie stated. Idona looked down at the dashboard and noticed they were at a quarter of a tank. She grimaced.

"We're low on gas so let's just take an hour to eat and fill up," she responded. Her brownish-green eyes flickered on the rear-view mirror and looked at Darius. "You okay with that?"

"I guess. I'm not the one who knows about cars or even has to eat actual food," Darius sarcastically stated. Idona frowned and focused on his image. She noticed that he looked upset by the events of the day; she sighed and decided to deal with it when they eat. Minnie added the new stop into the GPS and it called out the new route. Both girls were pleasantly surprised that it wasn't that far away. Ten minutes later, Idona was pulling off the exit and onto the road that Panera was on. Minnie finished the book and turned around to hand it over to Darius.

"Can I have the next one?" she asked. Darius nodded and reached into the bag and handed her *Project New Knowledge* before putting the other book away. Before he fully zipped up the bag, his eyes caught sight of *Project New World*. Very slowly, he reached for it.

"Hey look, a gas station! And it's so close," Idona called as she pointed it out. Minnie looked over at the sign and frowned. In the back, Darius opened the book and began reading the last few minutes of the journey.

"Fishkill Mobil Mart. Hmm, I wouldn't trust it. I thought I saw a Mobil station on the sign just before the exit," Minnie stated. Idona looked at the girl. Darius stiffened in shock.

"I thought you were reading?"

"I was, but I just happened to look up the moment before it passed. I also saw Cracker Barrel on the sign if we don't want to stop at Panera," Minnie said. Idona smiled and faced forward again. It amazed her that Minnie could divide her attention while reading something as riveting the Project books. Idona herself missed a few conversations when she was reading it. Shaking the thoughts from her mind, she took the turn down the road for both Panera and Cracker Barrel. Minnie put her book down in her lap and watched the road. A moment later, they pulled into Cracker Barrel's parking lot. Minnie and Idona unbuckled and began to get out before they realized that Darius hadn't. They both looked at him and saw him reading the third book. He felt their gazes and looked up.

"Marc has been following us," he muttered just before headlights shined into the car. The girls looked forward and saw the black Camaro as the headlights turned off. Marc sat there in the driver's seat. His forest-green eyes were narrowed and glaring at Idona. He shut off his engine and got out. Minnie panicked and locked the doors. Marc laughed when he heard the click as it automatically engaged for every door. Darius dropped the book down on the ground. He straightened, preparing for a fight.

"I'm not here to hurt you guys. Just wanted to see what you were up to," he loudly told them. Idona grunted. She didn't believe him in the least.

"That's why you followed us almost one hundred miles," she cried. Marc smiled and moved toward the driver's side of the HHR.

"I'm determined," he mumbled, turning an angry glare at Darius. The vampire prickled with his own anger. Minnie and Idona looked at Darius in surprise. Idona then focused on Marc. She tried to fight back a chill, but failed. Marc was really beginning to scare her. The worst part about it was that Idona knew she should fear Darius more, but his presence was comforting.

"I'm going to say no to you, Marc. I will never go on a date with you. Why can't you just leave me alone?" Idona questioned. Fear was beginning to get the better of her. A few other girls who has dated Marc had told her that he was slightly obsessive and that she should just give in. Idona called them insane, but she was the only girl who had resisted Marc. Marc smiled before focusing on Idona. He wasn't going to let her get away.

"I just want one date. After that, I'll leave you alone," Marc calmly said. Idona frowned and looked over at Minnie. She focused on the other girl before sighing deeply. As much as it pained her to admit it, Idona was going to have to give in. She didn't want to. It almost hurt too even think about.

"Marc, just take no as the answer. Deal with it, cause that's all you're gonna get from me," Idona told him. Her eyes shifted down and to the left. A telltale sign of a lie. Marc noticed. He gave a sly smile and looked at Darius. The vampire furrowed his brows before focusing on Idona. He saw that she had already given up. This part of the fight was just a pretense. Darius stiffened. Not once did it cross Idona's mind to wonder what Darius would think.

"I never get a no forever. And I think you're beginning to understand that," Marc threatened. Idona turned back to look at Marc, pulled the handle to unlock, and opened the door. Minnie quickly unlocked the other doors and opened her door. Darius nearly shot out of the car so fast that he almost hit Idona. When he noticed she got out, he paused.

Minnie leaned against the top of the HHR, watching the others from a distance. Marc focused on Idona.

"Promise, only one date and then it is over," Idona told him, defeat clearly dripping off every word. Marc nodded as his eyes glided over to Darius.

"Agreed," he said before holding his hand out to Idona. She grimaced and accepted her fate, allowing herself to be dragged into the restaurant. Minnie waited by the car for a minute before looking to the doors and then to Darius. The vampire was frozen in the spot. He was paler than Minnie had ever seen and his sky-blue eyes were now vibrant red. She hadn't noticed them changing. The reason was that Darius used up all the rest of his strength to try to compel Marc to leave them before Idona agreed to the date. Again, sensing her gaze, Darius turned to look at Minnie. She swallowed in fear.

"Go inside and watch them, I'll meet you guys later," Darius growled out. As he spoke, Minnie noticed that his fangs had finally appeared. She felt all the blood drain from her face, and Darius twitched. Very slowly, she began moving to the restaurant. She made sure that with each step, she watched Darius closely. Once she made it through the doorway, Darius suddenly vanished.

CHAPTER 7

Marc's Date

"Where's your date? I thought it'd be nice to go on a double date," Marc purred when he noticed Minnie rushing toward him and Idona. She had been fearful that she wouldn't be able to find them if they had been seated, so she was glad to see them waiting. Minnie felt a chill run down her spine when she heard Marc's tone, but she focused on Idona rather quickly. "My Sweetie might relax and enjoy it more."

"Darius had other plans. He'll meet up with us later," Minnie stated. Idona moaned. She couldn't believe it. *Why didn't I think about him?* Idona thought.

"Did he say where he was going?" Marc asked. Minnie shook her head. Marc shrugged his shoulders as a server came over. She saw the three of them standing there and picked up three menu cards without asking. Minnie saw that and stopped her.

"No! Just the two of them!" she cried. Idona looked surprised and then horrified. Marc frowned.

"Come on, it's fine," Marc told her.

"But I don't want to be a third wheel, so I'll sit elsewhere if you two don't mind?" Her eyes hinting to Idona that if Marc changed this "date" in any way then he might not consider it a date. Idona got the hint but couldn't help the frown as it appeared on her face. Marc noticed it and looked at Minnie.

"I think we'll take your third wheel company. Wouldn't want you to eat alone after driving this far," Marc cooed. Minnie felt another chill. Idona fought off a chill as well and pulled slightly away from the boy beside her. Forest green eyes snapped into focus on her. "Where you goin'?"

"To the restroom. Long drive and all that. Really have to go," Idona lied before she could even think about what she was saying. Marc smiled as Idona gave Minnie a sidelong glance. Minnie caught the look and nodded.

"I should go too, you know. Girl things," she told Marc. His snarled at her, and then nodded his head. With his permission, both the girls snuck toward the back of the store area and headed into the women's bathroom. Meanwhile, the server led Marc to a table. Once the door closed, Idona swung on Minnie.

"What really happened?" she asked, guilt was flowing through her. Somehow, she knew that Darius was doing this because of her and Marc. Minnie shrugged her shoulders, not wanting to admit the full truth to Idona.

"When you left, I looked over at him, and he changed. He was pale and his eyes had turned red probably with anger. But I could tell that it wasn't really anger. It was more...I don't know, something primal I guess," Minnie tried to describe. Idona gasped. How could she have forgotten that detail? He even mentioned the idea of not eating real food. Idona felt even worse now. Not only did she not think about how he'd react to Marc, but she also thought about his need to feed at some point.

"He's going to feed!" Idona cried. Then she smacked her own head and walked over to one of the sinks. "I can't believe I forgot! He's been using his powers all day to sense Raff, make sure we're safe, and compel Marc. Of course he would need blood by now!"

"Well, where is he going to get it from?" Minnie wondered. Idona looked at the other girl. She almost couldn't believe that Minnie had just said that. It was almost like forgetting that cats' have claws or dogs' have teeth. Not giving time for Minnie to realize her mistake, Idona said, "Where do you think?"

Minnie gasped and held a hand to her mouth. Idona gave her a look that seemed to state "yeah." The taller girl groaned and felt silly.

"Oh my god! And I just stood there! There must have been a big huge sign on me that said gullible idiot, ripe for the picking!'" Minnie cried. Idona tried not to laugh at the girl but it was too tempting. Minnie was a ditz. It felt good to laugh at the older girl, even though Idona had gone through a similar mind track earlier. Minnie began pacing the bathroom as Idona watched her. At almost the same time, a thought crossed their minds and Minnie stopped pacing. "But he didn't touch me."

"Darius isn't that type. Even if he did attack you, he may not have drained you completely," Idona mentioned, having already thought about it. Minnie balked at the idea and Idona laughed. Shaking her head to get the image out of it, Minnie held up her hands. She didn't want to think about Darius's vampire senses anymore.

"Okay, change of subject. What are we going to do about this date with Marc?" Minnie began pacing again. She was still focused on Darius and his hunger. Idona, meanwhile, sighed deeply. Idona wanted to avoid thinking about the date. The simple idea of being on a date with this creep was too scary for Idona to imagine.

"I don't know. I have this bad feeling that this won't be the last date he tries to get me on." Again, Idona thought back to the warning she had been given. She almost wished that she had listened. But at the same time, wished that Marc would actually give up.

"I think the same thing. That's why I kept trying to get you to say you didn't want me there. Now, he can easily call this an outing between...'friends.' Ugh, like I'd ever be friends with him," Minnie cried. She gave a shake as if there were spiders crawling up her back. Idona smiled. As much as Minnie had cared for Marc at the school, the teen seemed different now. Minnie appeared to be as uncomfortable by his presence as Idona was.

"There isn't much we can do about it now," Idona said. Minnie nodded. "Let's just hope that he doesn't become too big of a pain."

They stood there for a few more seconds in silence. Neither one wanted to try to start a new topic. Both were afraid it would lead back to Darius or Marc again. Minnie sighed and headed to the door just as Idona looked in the mirror. She never did re-brush her hair from when she messed it up when Sue came over earlier that day. Even though she didn't like Marc, Idona still wanted to look decent. With a sigh, she began to fix it. Minnie smiled and came over to offer her own help. After a minute or two, Idona looked better. Not good enough for an outing with any other than Marc, but better.

"Guess we should head out."

"Guess so," Minnie agreed before the two headed out.

Meanwhile, Darius sulked around the restaurant. He hadn't feed yet. For some odd reason, he just didn't want to. He knew that he should, but he just couldn't find a human he wanted. Every time he thought that he found a human he'd be willing to go for, his thoughts went back to Idona and her asking him if he would turn someone. But it wasn't just that thought. He kept thinking of the first time he saw her, of the first time she smiled at him, and of how she was concerned of him burning in the sunlight.

Idona was something different. Darius could tell that when he began to really focus on her. She was nearly perfect for him. *Nearly? No, she is. Idona is the perfect girl. My parents would have been proud of her. Her parents should be proud.* Darius thought. Suddenly he realized what he was doing. While thinking about her, he had started walking toward the entrance.

He stopped on the roof of the restaurant. Shaking his head to clear the thoughts of Idona, he found they then floated to Robyn, the human that Rafficer turned. She was similar to Idona in everything but looks. Where Idona was manly in shape, Robyn was thin and fragile. Idona also had a significantly larger chest than Robyn. Darius sighed. Robyn was such a sweet girl. He almost could have said that he fell in love with her. Then Rafficer got his twisted hands on her. He turned her into a vampire while she was still under a compulsion. Even a newly turned vampire could tell that doing that was going to be bad on the mind of the human. Robyn went insane until she turned so bloodthirsty that Rafficer ordered Darius to kill her.

"And that was him being more 'forgiving' than other sires. Ha, like I'll believe that," Darius muttered to himself. Below, he could tell that Marc, Idona, and Minnie were ordering food. He snarled. Marc was different. Darius didn't know how he could tell, but he just could. Most vampires, like Darius and Rafficer, could sense other vampires. It was almost like a homing beacon. They stood out in a crowd, not that they looked any different. Seemed more like a feeling that Darius had. But, either way, Darius knew that Marc wasn't one. But, it was weird. Marc simply didn't feel human.

Darius didn't realize, but Marc wasn't the only one who felt different. Minnie and Idona had also begun to feel different. It didn't feel as pronounced as Marc, but the difference was there. Something about them was also changing. Being around them, the vampire couldn't feel the change. It moved too slowly.

Darius's eyes focused on the HHR. A thought made him wonder if the book had any answers. But he had left the book inside the locked car. With a snort, he jumped down off the roof and slowly walked over to it. He stared in through the back window and saw the book lying clearly on the ground. It was still filling with words. He looked at the driver's side door and realized that it was locked. Darius couldn't clearly remember when it was locked, he just knew that it was locked and he wouldn't be able to get in. *Perfect. Just perfect.*

Suddenly, he sensed something close by. He snarled before turning to the back of the parking lot. It was another vampire. He could tell it was back there. His red eyes scanned the parking lot until Darius finally saw it. Hiding in the shadows, was a figure. Darius could tell it was a female. Although she was wearing heels, she was shorter than he was. He watched her step forward. Darius gasped in shock. It was Rafficer's first bride, Kathleen. She had dark reddish colored hair and deep blue eyes, and she looked sickly thin. She wore a halter-top, tight denim-shorts, and heels.

"Kath...Kathleen?" he whispered. She nodded and strutted toward him. Darius stayed put. If one wanted to compare what Kathleen was to the younger vamp, it would be as if she were his Queen and Rafficer his King. Darius dropped his eyes as she got closer. When she was within arm's reach, she touched his chin and lifted his face higher.

"You know how I feel about that," she whispered to him. Darius nodded. As much as it irritated Rafficer off, Kathleen wanted all his younglings to think of her as their equal. "You look hungry, young one."

"I'll be fine," Darius muttered a half lie. One thing about Rafficer and Kathleen that not many knew was that their younglings had to speak mostly truths to them. It was impossible to lie even if one became stronger than either one of them. Rafficer's five other wives didn't possess this strength because they didn't have the death connection that Kathleen and Rafficer had. Also, this connection stopped the two elder vampires from killing each other. Kathleen gave Darius a small smile.

"What are you doing out here? So far away from your sire?" Kathleen asked. Darius frowned and watched as she began to walk in a circle around him. As she moved, Darius stepped closer to the HHR.

"I could ask the same of you," he said. She laughed, giving the younger vamp a chill. With her path cut off, she changed her direction.

"Oh, I love these games you play, Darius. All these half-truths and misdirections," she murmured, placing a hand on his chest and smoothly sliding it around in a sexual manner. Darius gave her a sarcastic smile. He had to force himself to not attack her hand and throw it off him. "I'm out here because while in the middle of that battle that you underlings started there was a flash of light. And I appeared here. I didn't sense you around until a little while ago. So where were you, and how did you get here in the sunlight?"

"This world isn't like ours. We can walk in the sun like any normal human," Darius answered. Kathleen snarled, thinking he had somehow gotten around the lying trait of all younglings. Darius stiffened, knowing that her temper was just as harsh as Rafficer's. "It's the truth. I've walked in the sun. Even Rafficer has."

"You sound as if you know where he is," Kathleen purred as she tilted her head. She continued to walk around Darius; her nails were scrapping the paint of the car next to the HHR. Darius shifted his weight. He didn't fear her. The younger vampire knew that he'd be able to hold Kathleen in a fight, but he did fear answering her questions because he couldn't lie even if he wanted to.

"Last I know, he was in a desert with Serge," Darius honestly told her, hoping that she'd drop the subject. Kathleen laughed. *Now she won't.* Darius thought almost angrily.

"You couldn't know that," she muttered. Darius paused. His still red eyes looking into the back of the HHR at the book. It filled with his answer before he even thought of anything to say. He felt compelled to read them. It didn't feel like a vampire compulsion, he had been under one of those. This one was different.

"I do. This world has changed the rules. Everything is different, Kathleen. We can walk in sunlight, blood will last longer, and...I may have new powers," Darius said without hesitation. He noted that everything the book made him say was true except the last part. There was no new power. Kathleen paused in her walking, she could tell that Darius had lied but she had no idea how he did. *Maybe the rules are different here. That might be why Marc wasn't compelled!* Darius thought as a small smile spread on his lips.

"How?" Kathleen tried again. Darius paused. He was unsure if he wanted to try it again. Slowly, he sighed and opened his mouth to say he had received a new power and it didn't work. *Or maybe, it's true because I was reading it.* His eyes stole a glance of the book again.

"I may have gotten a new power," he lied yet again. With his attention elsewhere, Kathleen quickly snatched her hand out and caught Darius's throat tightly. Darius was so shocked that he was able to lie so easily while reading that it took him a moment to react. But like before, Darius grabbed her arm as though he needed to rip it off so he could breathe.

"How did you just lie to me!" she snarled. Darius kept his mouth shut. He didn't trust himself to try to do it again without looking at the book. Kathleen shook the vampire. "Answer me!"

"I think this world may have changed some of the rules!" Darius croaked out, not really a lie. It was an opinion or a guess. Kathleen snarled again but she seemed pleased with this answer, so she let go of him. Her darkened blue eyes were now turning red. Darius paused as he stared at them. It took him a few seconds before he realized why her eyes were changing.

"Were you compelling me?" he asked, shocked that she had the gall to try to compel another vampire. Kathleen scoffed and tossed her red hair. Darius noticed it and frowned. "I can't believe you would do that."

"I can do whatever I want, youngling. Now, excuse me. I'm going to find some food in there," Kathleen told him as she pointed to the restaurant. Darius froze when he noticed the finger pointed to the doors he had seen Minnie run through earlier.

"No," he whispered so softly he thought that he didn't say it aloud. But as Kathleen spun onto him yet again, Darius realized he was wrong. She slammed his body against the HHR. Her fangs were out and her face had darkened. Darius confidently stared into her pitch-dark red eyes.

"What did you just say?"

"No," Darius brazenly told her.

"How dare you tell me no. What gives you that right?"

"Nothing, but I will not take it back," Darius bravely stated. Kathleen growled and lifted him off the car by his throat again. *What is with vampires and going for the throats of each other?* Darius randomly thought as Kathleen lifted him. He felt the muscles in her arm tighten, preparing to throw him across the lot. It made him tense his own muscles in preparation for the landing. Suddenly, headlights lit up the lot.

Kathleen dropped Darius and ducked behind the door of the neighboring car. Darius remained standing as the car approached and then drove past to a nearby open spot. He watched as the car shut off, an elderly couple got out of the car, locked the doors before closing them, and headed in. Darius nodded a hello to them when they spotted him and the gentleman waved but the woman tucked in closer to his arms. The second they were inside, Kathleen stood back up.

"We are not through. But for now, I must feed. Do you wish to join me?" she questioned. Darius focused on her. He could tell her anger was gone but he still didn't want to risk staying around. Shaking his head, Darius turned.

"Have a good night, Kathleen," he muttered, trying to act as if he didn't care, before walking toward the back of the parking lot. He heard her scoff before she also spun and walked in the opposite direction. When he was sure the shadows covered him, Darius turned in time to see Kathleen enter the doors and slip into the restaurant. "Idona."

Inside, Idona, Minnie, and Marc were "enjoying" their food. Marc was the one doing most of the talking. He told the two girls all about his childhood, his friends, his many fabulous pets, and other random topics. Idona wished she could have joined in on the conversation a few times, but her thoughts kept drifting to Darius. She wondered if he had finished feeding already or even worse, if Rafficer had called the young vampire to him. Quietly eating, Idona barely noticed that Minnie was talking to Marc, distracting him from the silent Idona.

"So Idona, enjoying your pancakes?" Marc asked, rather loudly. Idona snapped and looked over to the boy. A panicked thought entered Idona's mind. *How many times did he ask?* She knew that if it were too many, he'd know Darius distracted her. And she didn't want to think about the repercussions on doing that.

"Yes. Are you enjoying your..." Idona paused. She had forgotten what Marc had ordered. Minnie swallowed a bite of her biscuit and looked over.

"His Southern fried chicken?" Minnie supplied. Idona nodded and gave Minnie a relieved look. Marc barely noticed.

"Yes, that?" Idona finished. Marc smiled and looked down at his plate. It was completely empty. Idona couldn't help but make a sickened face. People eating food too fast always made her feel ill. It had been like that ever since she saw her cousin do it one Thanksgiving and then threw it all up on the dessert table.

"I loved it. This meal has been perfect. Does anyone want dessert?" Marc calmly questioned. Idona put her fork and knife down in disgust while Minnie shook her head.

"I'm good," Idona muttered before looking toward the entrance to the store. At that exact moment, the waiter came over to take the plates away. Minnie told him that Idona was done with her food because she was too frozen to speak. Blood drained from Idona's face until she looked almost as pale as Darius had looked earlier. Minnie noticed and also looked down the aisle and saw a woman standing there, waiting for something. Red eyes focused on the table before she smiled. Marc, noticing the girls were focused on something other than him, also looked.

The woman was about Minnie's height without the heels. To the girls, she looked sickly thin, but Marc thought that she was like a supermodel. Her reddish color hair glinted in the lights of the restaurant and made her red eyes even brighter. Every man in the establishment would find her sexy, and to make it more obvious to them she wore a form-fitting halter top and tight denim shorts. Mostly to the females, she looked like a red-haired hooker with fake contacts. But Idona knew better.

"Wow, is she hot or what?" Marc mumbled more to himself than to the girls. "Wonder who she is?"

"Kathleen," Idona whispered. Minnie now froze. She thought that she had recognized the woman from somewhere. Now, she realized that she had read her description in *Project Old Life*. Kathleen stalked toward the group. She reached the table without a single server bothering to ask if she knew where she was going. Idona and Minnie stood still. Both girls wanted to get up and run for it, but something trapped them. It could have been curiosity, fear or maybe the small bit of compulsion that Kathleen had placed onto the table. Idona only noticed the compulsion when she saw the vampiress's eyes deepen in color. Kathleen stopped at the end of their table and looked straight at Marc, ignoring the girls.

"Is this seat open?"

CHAPTER 8

Dangerous Kathleen

"**N**o! Go ahead, take the seat," Marc said before Idona or Minnie could deny her. Kathleen smiled, showing off perfectly normal teeth. Idona frowned, with the vampiress's red eyes, she should have been showing her fangs already. Kathleen sat in the seat beside Marc, which put her across from Minnie. The blonde couldn't help but shake in fear. Red eyes focused on her. "My name is Marc. What's yours?"

"Kathleen," the vamp said as she looked over to Marc. Forest green eyes flickered over to Idona for a mere second before looking back at Kathleen. Marc was stuck. His mind briefly flashed to his list of girls. Kathleen was last on the list of over 100 girls or so. And Idona wasn't going to make that list move. For a second, Marc wondered if he should actually count this as Idona's date and break up with her. The second wasn't long enough. "How 'bout your friends? What are their names?"

"Idona and Minnie," Marc stated as if the girls couldn't speak for themselves, which they couldn't. Kathleen focused on Idona. The vampiress could sense something was different about her. Something that caught the older woman with such interest that Kathleen couldn't stop her fangs from showing slightly. Minnie gasped lightly, which made

Kathleen realize what happened. She drew them back and looked straight into Minnie's chocolate-brown eyes. Idona could almost feel the compulsion before Kathleen spoke.

"Relax, hun, it's not like I'm going to eat you," she compelled. Minnie and Marc quickly relaxed and even laughed at Kathleen's statement. Idona stayed silent, which made Kathleen focus the compulsion on her. The teen stiffened but didn't feel a change. Red eyes narrowed before the vampiress stopped compelling Idona. Once she stopped, she traded a look between Marc and Minnie. Kathleen made a mental note to try again when Idona wasn't paying so much attention to her. What Kathleen didn't count on was that Idona wasn't going to get distracted. "So, how has your night been? It looks like I may have destroyed a gathering of friends?"

"This is supposed to be Idona's and Marc's date, but I think because I'm here Marc won't consider it a date. So he'll stalk us down to New Orleans until Idona agrees to do this again with just the two of them, alone," Minnie calmly stated in such a way that Idona looked at her so quickly there was almost an audible pop. Marc laughed as he placed his hand down on the table beside Idona's hand. Kathleen nodded. Her gaze shifted slowly to Idona. It wasn't that she was jealous or anything, it was just tiresome how this girl seemed to be in the way.

"This is just us meeting and getting to know each other before we really date," Marc informed Kathleen, foregoing his list for the first time in his life. The vampiress smiled and looked at Marc once again. "I'm still free for someone else, if they are interested."

"Oh my," Kathleen said and waved her hand before her face as if she were getting hot. Marc smiled and moved his hand toward Kathleen's. Kathleen smirked at him and shifted her gaze to Minnie. Knowing that Marc was clearly hers, the vampiress began working on

Minnie. She almost wanted to see if this girl was the key to getting Idona under her compulsion as well.

"Why are you going to New Orleans?" she asked.

"We have to fix something that went terribly wrong," Minnie began. Idona focused on her roommate. When Minnie went to speak again, she kicked her, hard, under the table. "Want to know a secret... OW! What the hell!"

"Foot slipped," Idona lied. Kathleen again focused on Idona and snarled; if Idona hadn't interrupted then Minnie would have spilled the beans. Idona's desperation to keep her secret increased Kathleen's curiosity.

"What kind of secret, Minnie?" Kathleen questioned. Minnie smiled. Idona was panicking. She worried about the vampire and Marc learning about their secret mission. She was willing to put herself in more danger to keep their secret intact.

"There are fictional characters in our world. Dangerous characters," Minnie said. Again, Idona kicked her. "OW! What the hell Idona! Let me tell her."

"I think we should go to the restroom. You've got something on your cheek," Idona lied as she pointed to Minnie's right cheek. Minnie gasped and grabbed at the offensive cheek. She nodded and the two stood up. Kathleen watched, her red eyes growing ever darker by the second. "We'll be back."

"See you in a moment," Kathleen commanded. Idona felt the compulsion and noticed Minnie nod before she grabbed Minnie's hand and dragged her away. She knew that Minnie would want to return to the table quickly. But for Idona, the command made her want to stay away even longer. Trying to keep her pace as normal as possible, Idona stood up, pulled Minnie along, and walked back into the departmental store attached to the restaurant. They felt Kathleen's eyes on them. When they entered the bathroom, Minnie rushed to the first sink and looked in the mirror. Meanwhile, Idona turned around to lock the door behind her. She didn't care if anyone else needed to go. This conversation was supposed to be between just the two of them.

"I don't see anything on my cheek," Minnie stated after examining herself fully. She turned around and looked at Idona as the other girl walked toward the second sink and began to run the cold water. "Were you lying to get away? Oh my god! Are you jealous of Kathleen?"

Idona didn't respond but she did bristle at the statement. To any normal person, this might seem like jealousy, but Idona knew the compulsion was making Minnie think that. Minnie continued to speak behind her. Rolling her eyes, Idona tried to ignore it.

"You are! I can't believe it! I thought you didn't even like Marc! Heck, maybe that's why you've been stringing him along. Were you trying to make him want something he couldn't get? All just so, you could hold on to him longer! Oh, that sounds so romantic!" Minnie gushed. Idona grimaced. If Minnie said anything else, Idona would have walked away. Focusing on the water, she waited. When she believed it was cold enough, Idona cupped her hands into the stream. Minnie stepped forward, as though looking forward to see what Idona was going to do. Just as the liquid began to overfill her cupped hand, Idona tossed it all into Minnie's face. Minnie gasped in shock as the water hit her and began to spit out the droplets that got into her mouth.

"What the hell was that about?" Minnie sputtered as she reached for paper towels to dry her wet face. Idona focused on her roommate. She had to be sure that Minnie was out of the compulsion. Idona intuitively felt that she was out of it. Minnie just seemed to feel right, not that she had been wrong earlier. It was just a feeling of the true Minnie.

"Kathleen compelled you to relax. By doing that, you thought of her as a normal human or even a friend and began telling her almost everything!" Idona snapped. Minnie stopped drying herself off in surprise. She looked over the towel to stare at Idona's reflection in the mirror.

"I didn't," Minnie begged. Idona frowned.

"You did. You even just accused me of being jealous of her a few seconds ago," Idona informed her roommate. Minnie groaned and went back to drying her face.

"I can't believe that! I'm so sorry, Idona," Minnie mumbled through the towel. Idona nodded as she moved to sit on the countertop. "It was such a strange feeling. Almost like I had known Kathleen my whole life." Minnie stopped drying and threw the towel out before facing Idona. "How come you weren't affected?"

"I don't know. But Marc was. Which is weird. Darius had tried to compel him earlier and it didn't seem to work. Marc was able to get out of it. Kathleen's is different. Weird or potent, almost. I could feel the amount of power she was releasing to try to get me to follow her wishes. But I didn't change or fall into it. I just sat there watching her. She knows about me though. I wouldn't be surprised if she knocks..." Idona began to say as someone knocked loudly on the door. Minnie and Idona looked at the locked door. "I locked it."

"Idona? Minnie? You two still in there?" Kathleen called through the door. Idona stiffened as Minnie looked into the mirror, fear plainly written on her face.

"I can't go out there right now," Minnie whispered. Idona frowned.

"Yes, Kathleen. We'll be out in another minute. My stomach doesn't feel right," Idona lied. Kathleen scoffed lightly behind the door.

"Okay, but be quick. Markey wants to show me his cool car outside," Kathleen proudly stated. Idona froze. She knew that Kathleen was baiting her, which meant that Kathleen figured Idona knew what she was. Minnie and Idona traded glances before Idona jumped off the countertop.

"Marc," Idona moaned. She didn't want Kathleen to do anything to him, even though she didn't care for him. Minnie could see the concern on the other girl's face. Groaning inwardly, Minnie looked at the door.

"Just a second. We'll come too," Minnie cried mimicking the voice she had when she was under compulsion. Idona stared at her friend in shock. She hadn't felt Kathleen using any power but when Minnie winked, Idona realized the blonde was faking it. Idona gave Minnie a relieved glance. It took them a moment before they realized that they actually should get going. "Off we go?"

Nodding in agreement, the two headed over to the door and unlocked it. Kathleen stood there. Her eyes were now a more pinkish blue color. Idona couldn't help but feel the horror. Kathleen had consumed someone's blood. Not a lot, but it was enough to give her more power. There was only one person whom she could have fed from without causing panic...

"Where's Marc?" Idona asked, fearing the response. Kathleen smiled, showing a small bit of fang, which made Minnie stiffen. The vampiress's smile vanished. She could see that Minnie's compulsion was gone. A fact that surprised her. Minnie hadn't seemed strong enough to break it on her own, which meant that Idona had helped her. Kathleen was now even more curious about Idona. Something was going on and Kathleen was determined to find out what.

"Waiting by the door for me. Let's go," she said before spinning on her heel and sauntering off. Idona and Minnie again traded a glance before following after her. A sudden sense that all of this might have been a trap left Idona wondered what to do. Fighting back the urge to run away screaming, Idona focused on where Darius might be. She felt that if he had been here and knew about Kathleen, he'd protect them all. But she also knew that he might not be able to fight for them. Kathleen was his Queen, not just a simple vampire or even a human. She was more important to Darius than anyone outside of Rafficer.

It didn't take long to meet up with Marc at the door. By the looks of him, Idona could tell that he wasn't in much more danger than Minnie and herself. Marc held out his arm, when he noticed Kathleen, and waited for the vampiress to hook into it, which she did. Again, Idona bristled, fearing what Kathleen could do to the poor boy. All four headed outside and walked straight to Marc's Camaro. Minnie slipped past and headed over to her HHR, unlocking the doors as she went. Idona followed and stood beside Minnie, near the driver's side door.

"Where was Darius supposed to meet us?" Idona whispered. Minnie shrugged. Both girls noticed Kathleen pause at the name but she continued her walk to the Camaro. Marc walked with her, describing as much about the car as he knew. Sometimes, she threw in a question or two but for a vampiress who came from a world without cars, she seemed to know what one was. That made Idona even more nervous.

"Would you like to go for a spin?" Marc asked. Kathleen smiled so big her fangs peeked out a little too much and Idona was surprised Marc didn't freak out. Minnie looked down toward the ground. As her eyes drifted, she caught sight a small line of blood on Marc's finger. The finger was on the hand that had been closest to Kathleen when they were sitting in Cracker Barrel. Surprised, Minnie tapped Idona's sighed and signaled her head to it. When Idona stiffened again, Minnie knew she had seen it. *She cut him! Marc's dead if we don't get him away soon!* Idona thought.

"Would I! That would be wonderful, Marc. You are such a sweetie," she told him before putting both her hands on his face and pulling him in for a quick kiss on his left cheek. When she let him go, Marc was blushing softly. Idona scoffed and looked at the other side of the car. Minnie groaned and wondered when this night would end. So much had happened to them, it was getting to be a bit much.

On the other side of the parking lot, Idona noticed something. From the shadows, Darius appeared. His eyes were still red, which meant that he was yet to eat. Kathleen didn't sense him coming over yet. Idona bit her lip to stop herself from crying out to him. The longer it took Kathleen to notice he was there, the better off they would be.

"Kathleen," Darius called when he got closer. Idona almost began crying then. She had hoped that he would have waited a little longer. All attention turned to him. Kathleen gave him a large smile. Darius's eyes narrowed when he noticed her eye color was closer to returning to normal. She stepped toward Idona and Minnie, dragging poor Marc along with her. Darius then looked Idona over quickly. Kathleen's smile dipped.

Minnie stood back, wondering if Kathleen or Darius would chase after her if she were to run. She dismissed the thought when she realized that there might be other vampires walking around. That was when she decided that being with Darius and Idona might be safer. Meanwhile, Marc remained compelled by Kathleen's power and couldn't tell what was going on.

"Hello, young one," she answered. Marc glowered before stepping in front of Kathleen as though she needed his protection. Darius stopped a car length away. The parking lot was mostly empty. Kathleen placed both her hands on Marc's shoulders. "What do you think? Promising?"

"No. Too weak," Darius muttered. Kathleen noticed his eyes were still on Idona. She stepped toward the girl and watched as both of them tensed. Her smile grew larger.

"So, have you enjoyed your night, yet?" she questioned, slyly looking at Darius. Idona shivered as Minnie latched onto her arm. Kathleen's smile grew dark and dangerous. Darius focused on Kathleen. He needed to get her away from the girls...and Marc.

"Not yet. Still waiting for the correct...timing," Darius explained. Red eyes glanced over to the girls. He didn't want to reveal that the girls knew about them, so he pretended not to know the girls in front of Kathleen. Kathleen straightened, grabbed Marc's injured hand, and pulled it toward her mouth. She pushed two fingers on the cut to make some more blood to appear and gave the younger vamp a smile. She licked it all off lightly which made the teen groan. Darius tensed and moved to step closer while both girls recoiled.

"I'm enjoying mine," she stated before latching herself onto Marc's cut finger and sucking the blood out. Marc moaned as his eyes rolled back in pleasure. Darius moved forward. He wasn't the only one. Idona also moved closer to Kathleen and Marc. She almost felt like if Darius tried to get into a fight with Kathleen, she'd have to grab Marc. Minnie moved further away, as though she was hiding herself.

"Stop this," he ordered. Kathleen dropped Marc's hand. Darius could tell she was pissed. Her eyes, which had turned to the usual blue, were beginning to turn black in anger. The humor that she had gotten from goading him was now gone. But he had barely noticed; Darius was more distracted by the fact that he had just compelled Kathleen into stopping.

"You can't tell me to stop," she growled, pretending to have stopped on her own. Marc felt a chill up his spine that turned into a shiver, but no one could tell if it was from fear or pleasure. Minnie quickly moved to stand by the back door of the car. For the first time, she realized that maybe being in the car would be the safest. Idona also shifted so she could make a quick escape into the driver's seat. Holding out her right hand behind her back, Idona made an offer for the car keys. Minnie nodded and handed them over. Once the keys were in her hands, Idona prepared herself. She would need to be quick in grabbing Marc and getting into the car. Of course, that was only if Darius starts a big fight with Kathleen. "If I want to drink from this boy, I will."

"You can drink from me all night," Marc slurred, still under her compulsion. Idona groaned as Darius stiffened. She couldn't believe that Marc had just said that. Darius forced himself to remove his focus from Idona.

Kathleen noticed something and glanced in Idona's direction. When she shifted toward the driver's door, Idona actually placed herself within reach. Kathleen smiled and grabbed Idona's throat. Her movements were quick that even Darius failed to notice. She pulled the girl closer, but made sure her grip was not too tight. Idona gripped Kathleen's arm as though she could pull her off.

Marc was about to collapse beside the vampiress. He could barely stand on his own, so Kathleen lightly held onto him. Darius moved another step closer. Now only the front end of the HHR and the Camaro separated them. Minnie also moved forward but backed off as soon as she realized that she didn't want to approach Kathleen.

"You should drink as well, Darius," Kathleen told the young vampire before tossing Idona into his chest. Minnie gasped in shock. *Would he really do it?* Minnie wondered. Darius quickly caught the girl and pulled her close to protect her and Idona settled close against him. As Idona settled deeper into Darius's chest, her mind was focused on Marc. He looked almost drunk. She half wondered if Marc even knew what was going on.

Meanwhile, Darius concentrated on what to do next. If he did bite Idona, it would harm his relationship with Idona and Minnie. On the other hand, if he didn't, Kathleen would make everything harder. Idona would be in danger, just like other humans who had helped him in the past. Kathleen's eyes widened in horror when she noticed Idona relaxing against Darius. She had assumed that the girl knew what was going on, but this was different. Thinking that maybe Idona wasn't as smart as she seemed, Kathleen focused on Darius. Darius was staring at Idona. That was when she snarled.

"Again, Darius? When will you learn?" Kathleen asked. Darius said nothing as he looked up to face Kathleen. Minnie and Idona looked to him in surprise before Idona gasped lightly. *How could I have done this? I should be as terrified of Darius as I am of Kathleen! I'm so stupid! Now Kathleen knows* Idona was blaming herself, even though the fault was shared with Darius, who forced himself to look away. Her eyes burned with anger. When Idona noticed it, she then realized the truth of what was going on. *Darius cares for me?*

"Robyn," Idona whispered softly, and Darius hoped that Kathleen hadn't heard her. When Kathleen raised her head but kept her eyes glued on Idona, he realized she did hear. Kathleen snarled again.

"How do you know about her, human?" Kathleen commanded. Idona felt it again and closed her eyes, hoping that she wouldn't be affected. Minnie, surprisingly, even felt it. She stiffened but failed to fight the compulsion.

"She read it in a book," Minnie automatically stated. Kathleen looked at her sharply and Darius hissed.

"Minnie," he snapped, using his own command to knock her out of Kathleen's. Minnie shook in fright when she felt the compulsion slide off her. Her eyes turned to look straight at Kathleen, whose eyes were turning red yet again. Almost wishing that she had indeed run away, Minnie sulked behind the HHR.

"Read of Robyn in a book?" Kathleen asked. Minnie shook as she felt Kathleen try to compel her again. Darius was quick to respond with his own silent one. But even Minnie could tell it was getting weaker. Darius really needed to feed if he wanted to fight Kathleen. The older vampiress focused on the younger one. Idona was still tucked inside his arms. "Do you care for these humans, Darius?"

"What does that matter to you if I do?" Darius snarled. Kathleen couldn't hold back her laughter. Darius shook out of his anger for a moment before glaring at Kathleen. He knew that since she had fed from Marc, she was definitely stronger than he was now. His eyes flashed around. They were still alone in the lot.

Minnie then realized what was coming and covered her mouth with her hand before she said something she'd regret. Kathleen then took that moment to stop laughing and focus harshly on Darius. The young vampire stiffened when he felt her strong compulsion falling over him. He knew that the next words that came out of her mouth would be something he was forced to follow.

"Darius, you will feed off the girl in your arms, the girl whom you seem so fond of," Kathleen ordered. Idona stiffened when she realized the strength behind the command. Darius wasn't going to be able to fight it. Following the command, Darius pushed her slightly away from him, enough distance away to be able to lean down onto her throat. Surprised that the vampire felt tense, Idona spun to look at him. Brownish-green eyes stared up into compelled hungry red eyes.

Idona felt prepared for what was next. She knew that Darius was compelled and was ready for him to feed off her—even drain her dry. She knew from the moment that he had appeared that the vampire would drink from her. She had prepared herself from the moment she laid eyes on Darius.Darius, meanwhile, focused on anything other than Idona. He didn't want to bite her. Outside of Robyn, Idona was the first human who was not afraid of him. But Darius knew that all of that would change with a single bite. He didn't want it to change. The thought of Idona fearing him was as bad as the memories of Robyn as a compelled vampire. Idona looked up to Darius and saw he wasn't looking at her.

"Darius?" Idona softly called to the vampire. Tears were beginning to form in her eyes. She knew that nothing would stop Darius now. She couldn't tell if she was tearing up because he wasn't in control of his bite or because he wasn't ready for it. Darius opened his eyes to look at her. She saw his heart in them. His fangs snapped into place as he leaned closer. Idona felt him pull her into them. She closed her eyes and opened her neck, knowing that fighting him would just make it worse for both of them.

Darius shut down his mind and heart, knowing that if he kept thinking of the consequences, he'd bring Idona pain. He wanted to feel nothing, almost as if that would make it all go away. Even though he had seen that Idona was ready for this, he wasn't. His breath was warm on her skin and only touched her for a second before there was a sharp pain of the fangs sinking in, then nothing.

Suddenly, it was like the world burst into focus. Neither one of them had felt anything like it. It felt somewhat like a heavy orgasm, but better than that. Idona could feel Darius draining the blood from her neck, but she could also feel the power he was pulling from her. Darius could feel through Idona's blood that he was hurting her and so he calmed himself. She relaxed into him, making it even easier on him. The radiance of the bite spread through them even more.

I'm so sorry, Idona, Darius thought as his lock down on his heart and mind burst. Idona was flooded with his being; emotions, thoughts, everything. It felt warm, kind, and comforting. But she also felt his fear and pain. She felt that he didn't want things to change.

There is nothing to be sorry for, Darius, Idona thought. She sent out her own feelings to the vampire. He almost let go in the shock of feeling them. Not once before had he ever had such a connection to someone he was biting. Her feelings of comfort and caring seemed to calm him.

Both of them fell into each other and moaned in utter joy as they pulled each other in. The connection grew deeper. In that moment, all of their dark secrets were revealed to each other. As each drop of blood slipped past Darius's lips, they drew into each other. Idona began to grow weaker.

As she dropped more of her weight into Darius's arms, it struck him. The compulsion was gone. He could let go of Idona. *Don't.* Idona moaned in her thoughts. She could tell that he wanted to pull away. But the connection was growing deeper. Idona needed to feel what Darius felt when they first met. Darius heard her thoughts and was shocked. He had to let go. Out of concern for her safety, he quickly removed his fangs and backed away, but held her in his arms in case she fell.

Idona dropped slightly before she caught herself. He hadn't drunk much from her but...the experience left her shaking and weakened from something other than fear. Darius stood there, his eyes completely normal. Idona moved to lean in closer to Darius. It was all a surprise to her, but it felt so good. She was almost upset that it had ended so quickly.

Darius was feeling the same way. He had never gained so much strength from such a small feed. He could tell now that he was stronger than Kathleen was, which was another shock. Normally, the only one he could sense their strength from was Rafficer. Now, he could sense Kathleen. He could tell she still needed to feed a little more to get to her full strength. But even her full strength was less than the power Darius now had. Thinking about it even more, Darius noticed he wasn't even truly at his full strength.

CHAPTER 9

What Happened?

"How did you do that?" Kathleen growled. She could tell that he was stronger than she had ever been, even though he barely fed from Idona. The vampiress stepped forward, shoving Marc onto the hood of his car. Minnie huddled down behind her HHR while Idona moved closer into Darius's chest. He engulfed Idona in a hug. Kathleen got closer, and Darius could smell the fear off her. His eyes widened in surprise before he could mask the feeling. "What did you do?"

"I followed your order," Darius snarled, trying not to betray his own thoughts of awe and shock. Kathleen's eyes were bright red again. Darius's eyes flickered over to Marc. The boy wasn't drained enough to be unable to move. But he was smart enough to know that he shouldn't draw attention to himself. Kathleen snarled at the young vamp. Darius turned to face her.

"I know. But how did you get so powerful?"

"I'm just as clueless as you," Darius stated as he pulled Idona closer. Idona settled comfortably inside his larger frame and relaxed. She could tell that Darius was in control now. Kathleen's power was nothing compared to Darius's new power. But her question made Idona wonder about the answer, until the thought crossed her mind. Idona's brownish-green eyes, which now looked more sea-green, focused onto Minnie through the windows of the HHR. Minnie straightened up when she noticed the gaze. Idona mouthed "the book" a few times before Minnie understood. Nodding, she shifted so she could open her door. Darius's eyes flicked over to the other girl so fast that Kathleen didn't even notice.

"You had to have felt something," Kathleen growled as Minnie opened her door. Darius focused on Kathleen. He went to shake his head and found he couldn't. It would have been a lie and he couldn't lie to Kathleen. Swallowing a bit of blood that had stayed in his mouth, Darius felt the connection for a fleeting second. Kathleen's eyes widened when she noticed Darius's eyes changing from his normal sky-blue to Idona's brownish-green eyes. She looked down at Idona but couldn't notice a change outside of her eyes now looking more sea-greenish than brownish-green. Kathleen snarled again before looking into Darius's eyes again. "I order you to drink from her again!"

"You have no more power left to order me around, Kathleen," Darius pointed out when nothing happened. Kathleen snarled. She wondered if maybe Marc could give her enough power to become stronger than Darius. Not wasting a second more, she turned toward the teen. He was still cowering on his Camaro. Her red eyes glared at the boy before she stepped over to him. Marc froze. She grabbed him by both arms and pulled him off the car. As she lifted him to her, she opened her mouth and released her fangs. Noticing what she was about to do, Darius paused. He almost wanted to let Kathleen drain Marc dry, but he knew it would hurt Idona. So he let go of Idona for a moment and held out his right hand. Using all of his power, he commanded Kathleen with one word. "STOP!"

The vampiress froze out of sheer surprise. Her mouth was wide open and her fangs were just scrapping Marc's throat. The boy was shaking with fear. He was just beginning to realize the danger he was in. Very slowly, Kathleen pushed Marc away from her. Darius watched as her eyes darkened even more. She was getting pissed off. Finally, she broke the command and tossed Marc into his car. He hit with a loud bang and dented the hood. Marc barely whimpered. His fearful forest-green eyes focused on Idona's. She gave him a comforting glance, but she could tell it didn't work. Kathleen stepped toward Darius and Idona. She emanated with her remaining power. Idona shivered and Darius quickly held her tight again.

"You will regret that," Kathleen snarled so darkly that even Darius was frightened. Then, she vanished. Darius's sky-blue eyes followed her fast pace path out of the parking lot. He had half expected her to stop at the tree line and wait for him to leave. But his senses told him that she actually had left.

With Kathleen's disappearance, everyone else began to relax. Darius was the only one who didn't, even though he knew she had left. Marc shifted uncomfortably on his car. Idona and Minnie focused on him, wondering if he'd remember everything that happened under the compulsion. Marc indeed had remembered, mostly because he had slightly broken out of it when he got outside. Admittedly, he had never needed a compulsion to stay by Kathleen. Her looks kept him around. When she began biting him, he had wanted to run, but fear kept him still.

Idona fell back into Darius's chest in an effort to relax. When the vampire felt her, he forgot to feel for Kathleen for a moment and looked down at her. She seemed so calm. Almost like none of the events from before had even happened. He was glad. While Idona relaxed into him, she felt her human fear beginning to appear. She had figured it might happen, but she couldn't tell why she felt this way. It wasn't that she was afraid, but something was just off.

Minnie stood, realizing that it was finally safe for her to come out from behind the car. While Idona and Darius focused on each other, Marc was getting pissed off. His forest-green eyes were beginning to grow darker in anger. Minnie couldn't tell if it was because he was remembering what Kathleen had done to him or the scene before him. Finally, a minute passed and Marc sat up on his car. He looked at Idona.

"What the hell was that?" he snapped. Idona stiffened. She had no idea what to tell him. Darius relaxed even more and walked over to him. Sky-blue eyes meet forest-green ones. Idona and Minnie felt Darius's power as Marc began to tense. Darius strengthened his compulsion and watched as Marc slowly fell into it. *Hmm, only girls can easily compel him, I guess,* Darius thought as he stared at the senior student.

"You will forget what you saw here. When you wake up inside your car, you will be driving toward your school. You will remember following Idona to this Cracker Barrel, but you will not care to follow her anymore," Darius commanded. In the back of his mind, Darius almost wondered if this was the right choice to make. *Should the teen forget everything?* Marc shifted his weight when Darius told him not to care that he was following Idona. Darius frowned and repeated it, just to make sure it stuck in the boy's head. "You will go back to your school and tell all of Minnie's and Idona's teachers that they are busy attending a funeral and will not return for some time. Do you understand?"

"Yes," Marc answered. Darius nodded and released his hold on the teen. Marc quickly turned around, got back into his car, and turned it on. Idona rushed to Darius's side.

"He may need gas," she stated. Darius nodded and looked back at Marc.

"Don't forget to get some gas before leaving," he quickly commanded. Marc nodded absently before shifting gears and pulling from the spot. Idona, Minnie and Darius watched in silence as he drove out of the lot and down the street. Suddenly, Idona got a chill. Darius looked at her.

"I feel like I'm going to see him again but...he won't be the Marc I know," she muttered before looking at Darius. He frowned and looked after the trailing taillights. Staying silent was the only thing Darius felt he could do for Idona because once Marc had passed the edge of the parking lot, he had felt the same way. He sighed before turning to look at Minnie. She still stood by the open car door. Darius could see that she was shaking with fear and almost felt bad. Idona was also shaking beside him. Closing his sky-blue eyes, Darius finally looked down at Idona.

"Get in the car. I'll drive," he said. The girls nodded mutely, forgetting that Darius didn't know how to drive. Even Darius didn't think about what he had just stated. Idona quickly handed the keys over and headed for the passenger seat. Minnie entered the back seat and shut the door. Darius paused for a moment outside the car before looking around. When he still didn't sense or see anything out of the ordinary, he entered the driver's seat, turned on the car, and began to drive away.

The girls curled up into their seats, each not speaking while Darius drove a little way down the road to a Mobil station. He was tempted to ask both of them how they felt after what had just happened. But he knew that it was too soon to ask. As he parked the HHR at the pump beside Marc's Camaro, Darius looked at Idona. She was shaking. He gave her a sympathetic look. Very few humans that he had fed from reacted the way she did. They behaved as if their system had gone into shock. In the back, Minnie was fine.

Darius slowly exited the car and shut his door. Marc was standing there silently, already filling his tank. He tried to act like he didn't see Darius. Knowing otherwise, Darius nodded to the boy but Marc didn't do anything in response. With a sigh, Darius moved to the pump. He didn't intend to bother Marc, and he hoped that his compulsion would stick this time.

Distracted by trying to figure out how to fill the HHR, Darius stared at the machine, not sure what to do. His eyes drifted over the pump, trying to get some sort of clue. Not really focusing on the details of the machine, he almost missed the directions that were printed on it. He quickly read the directions. Some of the numbers confused him for only a moment. He had never heard of a credit card before. But just like his new driving skill, he suddenly had the thoughts fill his mind. Slowly, Darius turned and looked at Marc.

"Can I borrow your credit card?" Darius asked of the teen, not using compulsion. The vampire did not intend to bother Idona or Minnie for the plastic item and Marc was the only one here he knew. Marc tensed at Darius's voice before turning to look. The boy gulped in shock. Darius then knew that his compulsion might not fully stick. He could only hope that Marc would think of it all as a nightmare.

Marc got over his shock quickly before digging into a pocket and pulling out a little plastic card. Darius looked at it for only a moment. He noted that it was printed full of numbers and had Marc's full name there. The card was a VISA, a type that this station accepted. Nodding, the vampire slid it into the machine and waited. The card cleared. Pleased that he had figured it all out, Darius handed the VISA back to Marc. Marc forced himself to nod as he finished filling up the tank of his own car. He started to undo the pump and get his car ready to drive off. Darius, meanwhile, prepared the HHR for its own fuel. Somehow, it all felt like second nature to the vampire. Neither Darius nor Marc noticed that it shouldn't be like that. Before Marc got into the Camaro, Darius looked at him again.

"Thanks," he told the teen. Marc again stiffened. The door to his car was open and he had just about been ready to get inside. Marc was on the verge of panicking. He had hoped that once Darius had compelled him earlier, he would never have to see him again. But it looked like that might not be so. *I wish I really could forget this whole thing,* Marc thought to himself. Forest green eyes looked toward Darius. The senior student nodded his head.

"No prob," Marc muttered. As he closed the door to his Camaro, Darius realized suddenly that his compulsion might not have stuck on Marc. Darius heard the engine start and looked toward the car. Before he could stop the boy, Marc had already shifted the car into gear and driven off. Darius could feel the regret burning inside him as he stood there filling the HHR. Red taillights grew dimmer as Marc drove away. Darius frowned. Allowing Marc to leave was an even bigger mistake than allowing Rafficer into his house those some odd 600 years ago.

It took Darius about five more minutes to fill up the car. His mind focused on other things now, and he barely realized what he was doing. He quickly undid the pump, closed off the tank, and got the receipt. Realization suddenly hit him. Kathleen might have returned in the time it took to fill the tank. He paused before looking around. And like before, nothing seemed out of the ordinary. Frowning, Darius stepped inside the car and started it up.

As he drove away, he reached for the GPS. Idona had left it out in the open when they stopped at Cracker Barrel. He felt for the power button and pressed it, turning the GPS back on. For a moment, he feared that it wouldn't remember the destination that Minnie had chosen, but when it told him what exit to get on, he calmed down. A few seconds later, they were on their way down to New Orleans again.

While he drove, Darius suddenly realized he hadn't seen what the girls were doing. Idona wasn't shaking anymore, which was good. But

Darius almost feared that something might have happened to Idona during her shock. Looking in the rear-view mirror, sky-blue eyes focused on Minnie. She was curled up in her seat. For a moment, Darius wondered if she was buckled in. Then he noticed it was sitting at an odd angle against her side. *How can she sleep like that?* Darius wondered briefly before shaking it off. Turning back toward the road, Darius drove on, and seemed to focus on driving so much that he couldn't think of anything else.

After they had been driving for thirty minutes or so, Minnie was awake. Through her blurry sight, she noted that Idona was in the passenger seat. Almost pleased that Idona wasn't driving again, Minnie turned to go back to sleep. It was then that she wondered that if Idona was in the passenger seat, and she herself was in the back seat, who was driving? She sat up and noted the dyed black hair that shifted into her line of sight. Minnie then leaned forward. Her eyes were wide. Idona, who had also seemingly woken from either sleep or her own thoughts, turned to face her. Her now sea-green eyes were filled with raw emotions, many of which Minnie and Darius couldn't figure out. Darius drove calmly, knowing that Minnie's chocolate-brown eyes were focused on him.

"Since when do you know how to drive?" she asked. Idona frowned and then looked over at Darius. Her eyes widened and her bottom jaw dropped as she stared at the vampire. Darius almost smiled until he realized that Minnie presented a good point. He shouldn't know how to drive. Idona was horrified. How could the two of them allow Darius to drive? *He knows nothing about cars and now he's here, driving rather well.* Minnie sat in the back, now simply curious. She didn't want to give into fear unless it was truly deserved. There were hundreds of people on the road who didn't know how to drive. Why not a vampire?

"She's right. How do you?" Idona muttered. Darius stared at his own hands. With both girls focused on him, he knew that he'd have to answer them, but he didn't know how to. He didn't think about driving. It came naturally to him. Orders went to his hands and feet from somewhere other than his brain. Then, Idona looked forward again. A thought had struck her. Now, she just needed to form it. Darius looked at her quickly before focusing again on the road. "Could it have been... my blood?"

"But I read that vampires don't learn anything from a person when they drink," Minnie mentioned. Darius nodded.

"That is true. We don't. I don't know how I know how to drive. It was just, sort of, instinct. Almost like, I know what to do before I can think it," Darius told the two. He looked toward Idona and said nothing. She was staring out the windshield. Almost as though she had shut down, which was what Idona had done. She didn't want to think about any of this anymore. For the first time, Idona was beginning to regret asking for something new in her life even though she still couldn't remember what she had asked for. Minnie sighed as Darius turned to face the road again.

"Well, as long as you're driving, we might as well drive all night," Minnie stated. It was a valid idea. Since Darius was a vampire, he could stay up for all hours doing things like driving. But he wasn't concerned about speed. He'd rather this trip go smoothly. The girls' health came first. Darius shook his head before looking at Minnie through the rear-view mirror.

"I'd rather us stop. You two need actual rest and I should try to see what Rafficer is up to. More than likely Kathleen will be looking for him to tell him of my...disgrace. She'll want to keep up appearances," he said. Minnie mutely nodded. Slowly, she sat back in her seat. Idona turned and looked out her window. Darius sighed before looking back at the GPS. They still had many miles to go. He put the unit down in the cup holders by his side.

As the girls began to drift off into their own worlds, Darius focused on different things on the road. For a while, he read the plates on the cars. Then he switched to bumper stickers. Finally he read the road signs. As those finally got boring, Darius looked at the dashboard. Earlier that day, Idona had turned music on. He didn't remember how she started the music so he started hitting the buttons slowly. Most of them did nothing. One made a round silver disc appear just above the clock. Darius tried to put it back by pushing it in and the car made a hissing sound to him.

"Do you want music?" Minnie softly asked when she heard the hiss. Darius was almost embarrassed to say yes. Somehow, the girl knew that that was what he wanted. She leaned against her seat belt and pushed a few buttons before a CD came on. It was Disney music from the theme parks. Darius didn't know that. He was just glad for the distraction.

"Thanks," he whispered to her. She nodded and went back to reading one of the books. Darius had lost track as to which one she was on. He drove mile after mile listening to that CD at least three or four times. Not that he minded that in the least. He was fascinated by the music, by the CD itself and by the technology behind it working.

Since stopping off at Cracker Barrel, Darius had been driving for two hours. He looked at the girls and noticed that Minnie had fallen asleep and Idona was just beginning to drift off for the third time. *They're exhausted,* Darius thought to himself before almost cursing. If he had been paying attention to them, he would have stopped off somewhere earlier in the evening.

Sighing, he moved lanes on the road. He ended up in the slow speed lane. Watching for the exit signs, he tried to recognize a familiar name for a place to stay for the night. As he read each sign for the next two exits, Darius realized that he didn't know even one. Holding back a groan, Darius looked at Idona. She was still drifting off. Licking his lips, Darius placed a hand on her shoulder before facing the road again. She stirred.

"We there yet?" she moaned. Darius couldn't help but smile. She was being cute. It almost made him want to pull her into a hug. Idona stirred even more when they hit a small bump in the road. In the back, Minnie groaned when her head hit the window, but she didn't wake. Darius again couldn't help but think of how cute Idona was. This time though, there was an added thought of being with Idona for all eternity. He almost flushed when he noticed that he thought that. Just as he was about to shake the thought from his head, Idona shifted to sit up in her seat. He looked at her.

"We aren't there yet. I'd like to stop for the night, and I don't know where we could," Darius admitted to her. Idona nodded and held her hand out for something. Her mind was still focusing on her dream and so she barely knew what she was doing. Darius frowned. He had no idea what she wanted. They sat like that for half a song before Idona came to understand what she was doing.

"The GPS? I can look up hotels in the area," Idona told him, her thoughts were clearing now. Darius mouthed "oh" before looking around. He put it down a while ago and now couldn't remember where he did. Idona took a minute to notice that he was looking around. "Well?"

"I put it down around two hours ago or so," Darius muttered. Idona laughed, making Darius face her. She shook her head in humor when she saw him watching her.

"This is such a big change for you. You're suddenly acting like all this technology has been around you your whole life," Idona mentioned. Darius paused before giving her a soft smile. He didn't realize how true that was until she mentioned it. With it out in the open, he had to admit that she was right. Idona's face suddenly sobered. She remembered reading a vampire book once before where the vampire took on parts of the memories and personalities of the human they drank, but the effect wore off after a few hours or so. If that was going to be the case for Darius, she really didn't want him driving when it wore off. "Do you think it will last?"

"I don't know," Darius answered after a long pause to think about it. Idona gave him a soft smile and looked down to the cup holders. She then saw the GPS. Letting out a cry of triumph, Idona held the unit up. Darius nodded congratulations and looked back out the windshield. Idona then began hitting different parts of the screen, moving through different menus to find what she wanted. The vampire almost wanted to watch, but he found himself forced to watch the road when an exit got a little crowded in front of him. After a minute or two, Idona sighed.

"Looks like we've got a Holiday Inn Express Hotel and Suites right near an exit."

"What's a Holiday Inn?"

"Forget it, we'll just go there. You'll have to trust me," Idona stated as the GPS called out the remaining miles until the new turn. Darius sighed deeply in relief. Over the past few miles, he was sick and tired of driving. Along with getting bored of games he played with the license plates, bumper stickers, and road signs, Darius had seen flashing red and blue lights, heard car horns and other drivers screaming at him. It was getting on his nerves. So much so, that Darius had begun to slow down to the same speed as other drivers.

But, when he saw the flashing red and blue lights, it became a game to see how quickly he could lose them. *Rather easy when you are a vampire. Just turn off your headlights and swerve around traffic*, he thought. Without those lights, the HHR turned into a shadow car. Especially, if Darius never touched the brakes. Not knowing of Darius's games, Idona settled back down into her seat. It took Darius two miles before he realized that she had fallen asleep again.

"Hmph," Darius mumbled to himself. He had been thinking of asking Idona about the biting incident just seconds before. Now that she was asleep, he couldn't be sure there would ever be a time when they could talk about it. Darius drove in silence, both in voice and in thoughts. Disney Theme Park music still played softly in the background, but Darius didn't try to listen. He was beginning to close up.

It took around fifteen minutes more before the vampire pulled the HHR into the parking lot of the Holiday Inn. He parked the car near the front entrance. Shutting off the engine, he wondered what to do. For a moment, Darius sat there and watched the doors. Another car pulled up. In the dark, Darius couldn't tell what it was at first. Once it got into the light near the door of the hotel, he saw it wasn't the Camaro. It was just another car.

When it parked in the entryway, there was a long minute of nothing happening. Darius used his vampire sight to look inside. There were four people sitting in the vehicle. The two in the front seemed to be arguing with the two in the back. Finally, there seemed to be some sort of agreement and two people got out of the car. They were both from the right side of the car. Slowly, almost methodically, they headed inside. Darius noticed the driver wasn't one of the two. Ten minutes passed by slowly before the two people came back out and got into the car. A few more minutes of discussion passed inside the car. Then it started backing up and drove to a spot further away from the door. Parked in a spot for the night the four people ended up getting out. They grabbed bags and suitcases before turning and walking into the building.

CHAPTER 10

The Hotel: Night One

Darius cleared his throat. After he watched the group of five people enter the hotel, the vampire had been trying in vain to wake one of the two girls. He had tried everything from tapping them to blasting the music to speaking to them. Minnie stirred when he cleared his throat, he could only assume it was some ingrained history. This was his fifth attempt to wake her. She stirred even more but calmed. Darius focused on her even more. His throat was starting to hurt from the number of times he had been forced to clear it. "Ahem, Minnie?"

This time, her eyes fluttered before she settled. Darius groaned. He wasn't sure he could do it again. Placing a hand on her knee, he went to speak. For some reason though, this time the touch woke her. Chocolate-brown eyes peeled open and she focused in Darius's direction.

"Hmm?" she groaned as she tried to clear her vision. The vampire knew when she had fully woken, because she suddenly stiffened beneath his hand. He kept it still in case she wanted to attack it. Minnie's eyes focused on it before she narrowed a glare at Darius. He quickly removed the hand. With the pressure gone, Minnie finally took her chance to look around. She didn't remember anything. "Where are we?"

"At a hotel that Idona chose. I don't know what to do," Darius answered. Minnie moaned and then nodded her head. She then reached a hand to her forehead. It was red from hitting the glass repeatedly when Darius ran over bumps in the road. Slowly, almost as if it pained her, Minnie unbuckled her seat belt. Now free, she began to stretch across the back of the HHR. Darius smiled at her softly, but she didn't notice. He then looked at the still sleeping Idona. *How am I going to wake her now?* He thought to himself as Minnie opened her door and got out. She faced Darius and Idona before shutting the door.

"I'll get us a room. You wake her," Minnie ordered before closing the door. He watched her go with the soft smile still on his face. When Minnie turned and saw it, she shivered. Guilt filled Darius when he noticed the movement. As she spun back around, Darius sadly noted that Minnie had sped up to a half jog, half run to the entrance. Once she vanished inside, Darius faced Idona and tried to forget what he saw Minnie do.

Darius contorted his face into weird angles and shapes as he thought of how he could go about waking Idona. In the end, he placed a hand on her knee. Nothing. He shook the knee. Again, nothing. Rolling his eyes, Darius sat back and stared. The conversation didn't wake her so he knew not to speak to her. Shaking and gripping her didn't seem to bother her sleep. *Maybe a light touch,* Darius thought. He reached up and began to rub her face lightly. She stirred and began moaning. Seconds later, she swatted his hand but opened her eyes.

"Wha…What?" Idona snarled when she realized she was being awakened. Darius didn't answer. He just continued to rub her face. They took a few minutes to realize that this was how Idona had woken him just that morning. As she became more aware of what was going on, Darius had to give her credit for not tensing or even moving away.

She just sat there. It took another minute before her sea-green eyes focused on him. "Are you done?"

"Hmm?" Darius asked before realizing that she was referring to the rubbing. He took his hand away. Idona found herself laughing very lightly at the vamp. Darius even started to smile but when Idona saw his teeth, she looked away from him. The smile vanished as he tried to fight the hurt that ached through his heart. Idona sighed and looked back at him, but he was now facing the windshield. She frowned and looked toward the dashboard. *I know he's a vampire. I know that he drinks blood so he can survive. So why does it bother me so much? Hell, it didn't bother me then.* Idona thought. No matter how much she had thought she was ready to be bitten, it almost seemed life changing afterward. She just couldn't look at Darius the same way.

They stayed in silence. Idona and Darius both had unbuckled in preparation for Minnie to come back. The tension in the air was so thick that one could cut it with a knife until Minnie came back out five minutes later. She looked distracted when she came over. Idona stepped out of the car, quickly, as though she had been looking for an excuse. Darius came out much slower.

"So?" Idona asked. Minnie faced her.

"Our room is 712," Minnie answered. Darius looked at Idona and saw her brows furrow in confusion. He had also noticed that Minnie only stated one room number. It was hard to believe that a place like this was brimming with guests.

"And Darius?"

"Um, 712," Minnie whispered. Darius looked surprised. Idona looked so pissed that Minnie was ready to run away. It took the shorter girl a minute to calm. She had been debating what best to say. Just as she opened her mouth to speak, Minnie began trying to explain.

"Apparently this is a really popular spot! There are a few weddings and some type of convention! Nearly all the rooms are full. We're lucky to even get this one!"

"Is it at least a double?" Idona muttered. Minnie shrank back. Idona closed her eyes and waited, trying to calm her rage and even fear. Idona's fear bothered Darius. He had liked that she wasn't afraid, even though it was smarter for her to fear him. Minnie didn't speak. She didn't want the other girl to snap. After a moment, Idona opened her eyes and walked to the back of the car. With it unlocked, she easily opened the back hatch and started to grab her things. Minnie slowly headed back to join her. "Bring only what you need for the night."

"Of course!" Minnie called, almost insulted that Idona would accuse that she would do anything else. Idona nodded and backed away holding her pillow, her only bag, and her suitcase. Darius fought the urge to say that she was bringing all of her stuff. He figured that if he did mention that, then Idona wouldn't speak to him. The younger girl grabbed her stuff and headed to the front of the car to wait. Just as she made it there, Minnie put her stuff on the ground behind her. She had grabbed two bags and one suitcase. She backed away and closed the hatch. Slowly, she then walked over to Darius and held out her hand. "Keys."

"Oh, yeah," Darius mumbled before handing them over. Minnie locked the doors. When she nodded, Darius snatched up the two suitcases. Idona stiffened but said nothing. Minnie shouldered her two bags before walking off toward the hotel. Darius and Idona traded a look before she took off after her roommate. Sighing, the vampire followed them.

When they got inside the hotel, Darius was shocked to find it mostly empty. He paused in the lobby as Idona and Minnie continued walking. Sensing there were humans around, Darius sighed. He had a feeling that maybe Minnie had lied or the person giving them the room had lied. For a packed place, he didn't sense the presence of many people. He was so focused on that detail that he almost missed that Minnie and Idona had vanished into a nearby hallway. Darius slowly headed after them and then noticed Minnie leading them to an elevator. Without speaking, Idona pressed the up arrow just as the vampire realized where they were.

"Really?" he asked. Minnie's eyes narrowed. She was too tired to care about his or Idona's feelings. They were only moments away from being able to go to bed and resting for a night. This behavior is common, when humans get close to the end of something they get closer to freaking out at little things. Darius, on the other hand, didn't care if they were close to an end of the day; he didn't want to get on another elevator.

"Hey, you just drove a car here. I think you can get used to an elevator." Minnie told him harshly. Idona held back a harsh laugh as the elevator door opened. Even though the older girl's attitude was harsh, Idona thought the comment was funny. Her humor showed that she was really tired. Darius didn't agree with either girl. The girls got inside the machine and turned to face the vampire. Minnie stood in the back while Idona went to the button panel. She held the door open for Darius. He lightly glared at Minnie. She gave Darius a look that told him no matter what he thought she wasn't going to back down. Darius frowned before entering the elevator in defeat.

"The car had a manual that I could read. The elevator doesn't," Darius responded. Minnie groaned as the door closed. Idona pressed for level seven and they headed up.

"Fine, I'll go onto my computer, pull up a manual for the elevator, and you can read it," Minnie snapped. Darius frowned but didn't press anymore. He was now curious as to what a computer was. But with the girls were so tired that he didn't want to ask. The rest of the ride was silent. Darius couldn't help but feel that it was his fault. Just as he went to say something, the doors opened on seven. The vampire rushed out and was shocked when he noticed he was standing in a hallway. He could go either right or left. Idona came out next and she turned to wait for Minnie. When the other girl exited the elevator, the doors closed again. Darius was still standing there wondering where to go. Minnie noticed two signs and read one of them before turning right. It took Idona and Darius a minute to notice.

Minnie arrived at the room just as they started to follow her. She quickly took out the little package that the hotel's desk clerk handed her and pulled out of the plastic key cards. Sliding it into the electronic lock, Minnie waited for the red light to turn green. It did and she took the key back before opening the door and slipping in. Idona and Darius just made it to the door before it closed. Groaning, Idona opened the door for Darius. He went in and headed toward the back of the room. Sighing now, Idona walked into the room and froze in the entryway.

The room did look nice. In the entryway was a small closet and a door to the bathroom on the left-hand side. On the right wall, just past the entrance, was a large HD TV sitting on a nice wooden set of drawers. One full-size bed sat almost against the bathroom wall on the left side of the room. Minnie was already unpacking some of her things onto it. There was a second full-size bed just past the first and a small night table.

"I thought this wasn't a double," Idona stated, after surveying the room. Walking toward the second bed, she began dropping off her things. Minnie looked back at Idona; most of her stuff was tossed across the first bed. Darius stood off to the side. His back was to the porch door and the desk was to his left.

"I never said it wasn't," Minnie said in a playful tone. Idona closed her hands into fists for a second before relaxing them. She decided it would be best if she didn't answer her roommate. Calmly, she grabbed her pillow again and brought it to the head of the bed she was now claiming. She placed it down lightly as though it was a fragile artifact. Once it was in place, Idona went back to her bag. She pulled a wire out of the top pocket and plugged it into the wall near the couch.

The girls weren't paying much attention to Darius, who looked down at his hands. He still held onto the suitcases. He sighed and headed over toward the beds. Darius separated the two suitcases just before Idona came over toward him. Slowly he backed off and headed back toward his area.

On his way, he glanced to the TV and wondered what it was. For some reason, he thought pictures could appear on it and sound came out of the back part. Shaking the thought from his head, he spun around and moved the shades on the door. Finding the lock, he unlocked the door, slid it open, and walked outside. Idona took that moment to spin around to go back to the bed when she noticed Minnie's mess.

The girl's things were everywhere. She had wires, electronics, papers, hair products, and other assortments of things placed all over that side of the room. Even with all those things out, Minnie was still searching for something. Idona winced and walked over. For a moment, Idona thought it looked like Minnie was trying to make piles. She wasn't. Frowning, Idona began to clean up after her roommate.

Together, the two had everything on the bed placed into piles. There was a pile for wires, a pile for electronics, a pile for hair elastics and gels, a pile for shower things, a pile of unnecessary paperwork, and a pile of small knick-knacks that could be helpful later on. With the things organized, Minnie grabbed the pile of shower things and looked at Idona.

"Do you have to go to the bathroom for anything? I'm thinking of taking a shower," Minnie told her. Idona waved to the bathroom. The younger girl knew that if she needed it, she'd get the restroom after Minnie was done. With a nod of relief, Minnie rushed off. Idona sighed and headed back to her bed. She still needed to take some things out. Darius heard the bathroom door close and lock before he looked toward Idona. She was busy unpacking her own things and even repacking most of it. He sighed. In one swift movement, he entered the room, slid the door closed and locked it into place. Idona shivered but continued to unpack and repack. Darius walked toward the couch and sat down. He watched her.

After a few minutes, she put the bag at the foot of her bed. She had four stuffed cats sitting around the pillow at the head of the bed. Her phone was plugged into the wall beside the couch. They were the only things left unpacked. Darius glanced at the bag and noticed that it didn't seem to be as big as it was moments before. Idona picked up her suitcase next and opened it on her bed. Very carefully, she began looking through the piles. She took out a pair of jeans shorts, a white pair of underwear, and a dark blue, sleeveless tank. Keeping them folded, she placed the pile of clothes on top of her bag.

She then walked over to the closet; she opened the doors and pulled out a plastic bag, which she brought back to her suitcase. Again, she carefully dug into the bottom of her suitcase. Slowly she pulled out clothes that Darius had seen in her laundry bin. Each bit went inside the plastic bag. When she finished that, she closed her suitcase, placed it next to her bag, and then put the plastic bag on the ground beside the suitcase.

"Idona, we need to talk," Darius finally said, as there was a loud crash from the bathroom. Idona and Darius focused their gazes onto the bathroom wall.

"OW! Crap!" Minnie cried. There was a slight pause. Darius wasn't sure if he should say anything. Idona bobbed her head as though she was mentally doing a countdown. She mouthed "zero" just as Minnie called out again. "I'm okay!"

"Idona," Darius sighed when the shorter girl went and sat down on her bed. She was now facing the TV, but she made no move to grab the remote from the nightstand beside her. There was a moment's pause before Idona turned to the vampire. At first, she had no idea what to say but then she sighed and turned away again. Darius went to speak.

"I'm sorry," Idona whispered. Darius froze. He had never expected her to apologize. Idona sighed when Darius didn't respond. She closed her eyes and leaned back against her pillow and the headrest. "I'm sorry for acting differently, I mean. I know what you are and still, when you do what you do naturally, I just…can't seem to believe that you did it. I guess…no, I thought that I might be different. Special. The one you would never bite."

"But, you are——" Darius began. Idona held up her hand. Sea-green eyes faced him. A fleeting thought passed through Darius's head. He wondered if Idona even knew that her eyes had changed colors. It took him this long to even notice it, and he certainly didn't want to bring it up just yet.

"Let me speak," she told him. He nodded and she looked at the ground. *Where do I start?* Idona thought before sighing so deeply it sounded like a groan. "I've read about vampires since I could first read. Most of my school projects have been based on them, and I know almost everything about them. While I had never actually met one, many called me an expert on the subject. But this world is full of so many stories that sometimes the information contradicts each other.

"Many stories have vampires as evil villains who only get close to humans long enough to drain them. These are normally allergic to garlic, hate Holy Water, can't go near a cross or Holy grounds and die from a simple stake to the heart. They also die from a beheading, or the sun, or even fire but most authors are fascinated with the stake. In those stories, vampires are nothing more than animals. They can sometimes barely speak or even understand the verbal word. In other tales, the vamps are more human and they spend a little more time with humans.

"More modern day vampires are like us, just trying to survive. They love, they die, they hurt, they feel some emotions, but they still need to drink from humans or blood at least. It's here that they become a little more confusing. Modern day vampires have lovely little twists added to them," Idona stated. Darius's brows furrowed. *No wonder why she wasn't afraid of me.* He thought. Idona shook her head and leaned forward. She was more relaxed now, almost as if Darius never bit her and changed their relationship. Darius smiled. He didn't want her to be tense around him. It was very uncomfortable. "Vegetarians, ha."

"Vegetarians?" Darius repeated before he could stop himself. Idona didn't tense. She simply nodded and shifted to face him better.

"They drink animal blood rather than human blood."

"Hmm. Never thought of trying it."

"Don't. Some stories it works like human blood. Others it works but not as strongly. Some lead to the vampire getting sick and weak. And few, but just enough have them die." Darius couldn't help but swallow some saliva in fear. If he risked the chance of dying, he more than likely wouldn't try it. This time, he was the one who looked away.

"It would have been interesting to try," Darius admitted. Idona nodded. She had always hoped that he would say that. She also hoped that one day, he would take the risk and try, only he'd survive and it'd be like human blood. But there was still the chance that he wouldn't.

"In this day and age, vampires have been romanticized. An eternity of love and devotion; what person wouldn't want that? Somehow that doesn't happen. Sometimes the person who is turned into a vampire is different in both a physical, mental and even spiritual way. They change at the core."

"The excuses and inhibitions change so quickly that one copes without really thinking about it. Once it's time to think, it's too late. Death is on their hands," Darius provided. Idona nodded again. She already knew that that might have been the case.

As she thought about it, Idona realized that Darius was speaking from experience. The author of the "Project" series didn't delve deep into the thoughts and feelings of her characters and so many don't know the inner workings of why each character does what they do. Darius closed his eyes as images of his victims flashed through his mind. He remembered nearly 90 percent of them as images. Few of them had names that matched the images. Seeing Darius thinking of something painful, Idona decided to move on.

"With these romanticized vampires around, authors began changing many of the old rules. Holy ground, Holy Water, garlic, the stake, and even powers began to change. Even sunlight started to affect them differently. Vampires became impervious, even more deadly, some might say human and a few even turned...dare I say it...sparkly..." At that, Idona shuddered. She hated the idea of a sparkly vampire. These creatures of the night were fearful. They shouldn't shine like gods.

"Sparkly?"

"The sunlight doesn't burn them. It makes them look as though their skin is infused with thousands of little diamonds," Idona explained.

Darius couldn't help but burst into laughter. Idona jumped at the noise. After a few seconds, even she began to laugh. The laughter dispelled the remaining tension. For some reason, the thought kept them laughing. It took them a few minutes to calm down.

"Oh my, that is priceless. Do they really sparkle?" Darius asked. Idona nodded. She shifted even more, moving to the other side of the bed. Her legs now dangled off the side near to Darius and she fully faced him.

"Remind me to show you later," Idona told him. Darius nodded as another laugh caught in his throat. He really hoped that she wasn't being serious about that, but it was funny. Idona's smile dropped away, as did her eyes. "Vampires aren't as evil as they used to be in the past. Back then, it was black and white, good and evil. They attacked humans, killed them, God shunned them, and it was a man's job to deal with them. The man had to hunt and kill the vamp before all the humans died. Now vampires can be just like any other human, the potential to be good or evil. Still, humans would fear and try to kill all vampires. Unless there was a girl in the story.

"Now-a-day vampires can change from evil creatures to good all because of a pretty little girl they had seen. She's always attractive, smart, brave, and defiant, and normally has some crazed man in love with her. Sometimes, she's in love with the man first but then changes. Anyway, she meets the vampire and suddenly their lives change. The vampire can't get the girl out of his mind and she can't seem to get him out of hers. They fall in love and must battle with the idea of being hunted for all time or leaving and trying to find peace somewhere together. A perfect love story. Danger, death, fights, magic, and love.

"But now…ever since…since Kathleen compelled you to bite me, I've been trying to figure out what I thought. When I first started reading the books, the vampires had been romanticized. You held a passion that I expected. I began to feel like I could be the girl who changed you. The one who helped you be good and not follow Ra…him. Kathleen… she…shattered that image in an instant. You became a vampire to fear, one of the old-school, kick-ass ones. I didn't know what to say or do to stop that. Even now…I'm still…" Idona tried to explain. Before she could finish, Darius used his speed to place a finger on her mouth to silence her. Both of them froze from the touch. Uncertainty made neither of them move for a minute. The sound of Minnie's shower cutting off spurred Darius into speaking.

"Don't finish that. I can't handle hearing you say it. I knew things were going to change. You were going to realize the true danger. I had just hoped it wouldn't happen so quickly. For some reason, Idona, you mean so much to me. I want your approval. Not your fear," Darius explained before he removed the finger. Idona nodded. She wanted so much to give him that approval.

Very slowly, they leaned closer. Inch by inch, until their breath began to mingle. Idona titled her head just slightly and leaned over closer. Their lips grazed each other before Idona's mind flashed back to the bite. She backed away so sharply that she flipped over the edge of the bed to the other side. Her cry made Darius rush over to see if she was all right. He made it halfway before it hit him that she had backed away. He stood there; sky-blue eyes expressing a swirl of emotion, while Idona lay there realizing what she had just done.

Tears welled up into Idona's sea-green eyes before she righted herself on the floor. It wasn't that the bite was painful or anything. The bite was almost like a pure bliss that Darius sent her into, but she was afraid of it nonetheless. As she sat upright on the ground, crying, Minnie opened the bathroom door. She rounded the corner in her PJs and stopped at the sight. It took her maybe five seconds to misunderstand the situation and rush to Idona's side.

"What happened?" Minnie cried as she reached for Idona and pulled the shorter girl into a hug. When Idona took longer than two seconds to respond, Minnie shot a darkened glare at Darius. "What the hell did you do?"

"Wha—?" Darius called, shocked. Idona shook her head as her crying began to ebb away. His sky-blue eyes still showed the pain of Idona rejecting him even as he stood there, stiff from shock. Sea-green eyes couldn't focus on the vampire.

"Not him! Me," Idona gasped out between sobs. Minnie's glare vanished and she focused on the girl in her arms. "I couldn't...couldn't..."

"Oh, hun," Minnie whispered as Idona burst into fresh tears. Darius frowned and walked away. Even with Idona blaming herself, he couldn't stop thinking that it was his fault. Darius slipped over to the locked porch door slowly because he didn't want to bother Minnie and Idona. In another swift move, he unlocked and opened the door. He shot Idona a last glance before slipping outside and closing the door.

Inside, Minnie continued to hold Idona. The shorter girl was still crying hard. Minnie whispered calming words to her. Idona heard her voice but couldn't tell exactly what those words were. When the older girl noticed that her words weren't having the fully desired effect, she started rocking back and forth. It took five minutes more of Minnie rocking Idona for her to calm. Once she was sure that it was over, Idona looked at Minnie.

"I think I'm okay," Idona muttered. Minnie backed away. Her chocolate-brown eyes showed that she wasn't going to press Idona for information. Minnie thought Idona hadn't completely stabilized and could burst into tears before the end of the night again. The two stood up in unison. Idona began looking around for Darius as soon as she was up. She needed to apologize yet again. Minnie looked toward her things. She sighed before grabbing one of her bags and started to repack everything as neatly as she could. Halfway through, Idona finally looked at Minnie. "My turn to shower. I'll be out soon."

"Okay. I'm heading to bed. Been a rough day...for all of us," Minnie stated as if Idona didn't already know that. Idona gave her roommate a soft smile. She knew what the other girl meant. So much had happened to all of them. It all seemed to be jammed packed into this one day. The events could have spanned longer but they didn't.

Idona sighed before heading to the bathroom. In her haste to grab everything from her dorm, Idona never packed up her shower things. She had some bathroom items, but her shampoo, conditioner, and razor were still at the college. It almost made her laugh. Normally, Idona was just as prepared for things as Minnie. Thinking back, Idona remembered that even if she had tried to pack all of that, she had no room. She would have needed an extra bag.

Once they were inside the bathroom, she locked the door and looked into the mirror. For the first time, she noticed the change in her eye color. She gasped in disbelief. Her eyes were sea-green. Thinking back, Idona wondered exactly when her eyes changed. *Could it have been when Darius?* Idona thought. She couldn't finish it all. All she knew was that fact wasn't written in any book she had ever read.

For a long while, Idona stared at her eyes. She did some small tests to make sure she was looking at her eyes. Deciding that they had indeed changed color, Idona turned from the mirror. She didn't want to look in it again. Then, something spurred her to check her neck. Pulling her hair aside, she saw...nothing. There wasn't a single mark. It was what she had expected. Vampires can heal the bites so that no one would know. Many don't; they like it to be sort of a claim on the human. Thinking back to her eyes, Idona had a thought pass by as a smile spread across her face. *Maybe, I am special.* Sighing in an attempt to brush the idea away, she turned and started up the shower.

CHAPTER 11

Darius Alone

Outside, Darius focused his thoughts on feeling for Rafficer. He didn't want to think of Idona or Minnie. In his mind, his love story had concluded prior to beginning. Minnie had feared him ever since she found out that he was a vampire. Now, Idona feared him because of Kathleen. He shook his head to clear out his thoughts and focused on his sire. He closed his eyes, as though it would help him. He could tell that Rafficer and Serge had made it out of the desert. Raff felt weaker than earlier that day. *Almost like he…*

"No," Darius muttered, his eyes snapping open. Rafficer had turned a poor soul from this world into a vampire, draining his energy and strength. Darius pulled his power back. He had no idea what to think or say. With Rafficer using his sire advantage to get information from this new youngling, Darius knew that Idona and Minnie were in even more trouble than before. The 652-year-old stood still staring out into the night. He stayed there for about ten minutes trying to steer his attention away from Rafficer. Just as Darius decided to go back inside to find the book, the door opened behind him. Idona stepped out. "Hey."

"Hey. Minnie's out," Idona said. She sounded tired and still upset. Darius nodded. He figured that Minnie would pass out quickly, since she had been tired. Darius spun around to lean against the railing. The view was rather boring at night. Idona sat down in one of the two chairs. She stared at the night sky. It was clear with many stars and the small sliver of a moon, Idona almost mistook it for another star.

"Was your shower good?"

"Warm. A little unusual for me. At school, I'm always getting cold showers," Idona muttered. "It's not like the school has a set amount of heated water or anything. It's just always cold. Never seemed to matter the time of day."

"Why aren't you heading to bed?"

"I was wondering what you'll be doing all night. Do you even sleep?"

"Not really. I can lie down and rest my body, but I'll be aware the whole time. The only time vampires can get close to sleep is when we get knocked out or drink so much alcohol that we keel over, unconscious." Idona frowned and remembered first seeing Darius. He had looked like he was asleep. But unconsciousness and sleeping did tend to look the same. It was something she learned at college. She also learned the names of almost every type of alcoholic drink, not that she even wanted to know them.

"So what were you planning on doing? While we sleep, I mean."

"Hadn't really crossed my mind."

"I think, maybe, you should watch out for…Raff. Pay attention to what he's doing." Darius frowned. He didn't want to pay attention. It used too much of his power and it risked Rafficer sensing Darius watching him. Darius suddenly remembered the book. Now that the girls were going to sleep, the book should focus on his sire. Darius looked at Idona. He didn't remember her grabbing the book.

"Where is *Project New World?*" he asked Idona. She jerked in surprise. Her sea-green eyes focusing on Darius's face.

"Should be in my bag. If not then, it's still in the car," she answered just before a huge yawn caught her off guard. Darius almost laughed as her mouth extended, but he held it back with a smile instead. He thought that it was cute that Idona was trying to hide her sleepiness from him. But she did need sleep. As her yawn dissipated, Idona focused on Darius. "Okay, I'm heading to bed. If you leave the room, be sure to bring your room key."

"Room key?" Darius repeated as Idona stood. She nodded and rocked back and forth on her feet. Darius moved closer in case she were to collapse. She didn't. It was almost as if she was using all her force to move. Once moving, she slowly made her way over to the door and opened it.

"I'll show you," she responded before heading inside. Darius followed after and closed the door while Idona went toward Minnie's nightstand. The small packet with a key card lay on the stand. Idona snatched that off the little table and pulled out one of the two remaining key cards. She then put it back before spinning around and handing the card to Darius. He took it and stared.

"This isn't a key. It's a credit card," Darius said, confused. Idona laughed softly.

"Keys at hotels look like credit cards, but they are keys. That black strip holds the information to unlock the door. Wait, when did you see a credit card?" Idona realized. Darius shrugged.

"Had to get gas somewhere," he said. Idona frowned and lowered her head. Her gaze stayed focused on him though. She didn't remember him getting gas. Then she remembered that the HHR needed some after Cracker Barrel. Just as she went to ask how he knew what to do, Darius spoke. "There were directions on the pump that told me what to do. I borrowed Marc's card because you and Minnie were too out of it.

Speaking of, I'm not sure how long my compulsion will stick. He looked like he might be fighting it."

"Great. Next time, we might as well let him come with us. It'll be easier to not have to worry about him," Idona muttered, heading for her bed. Darius sighed deeply. He really didn't want Marc to join them. And he could tell that Idona didn't want him there either. Minnie moaned in her sleep as Idona sat on her bed.

"I know it'd be easier, but I'd rather send him away again. He gets on my nerves just a little too much. I'm almost afraid of losing my temper and doing something I'll regret," Darius admitted. He hadn't wanted to say it because of Idona's fear of him. But after she admitted that she was fearful because of her own reactions, he'd figured he was safe. Idona didn't tense in fear or even look slightly scared. She just let out a sigh and lay back on her bed.

She had seen that Darius barely reigned it in the last few times that he had seen Marc. But with Rafficer on the loose and knowing that he kills humans that had been near Darius, Idona couldn't stop thinking about Marc and even Sue. They would be collateral damage. Darius could see that Idona understood his point, but he realized that she wasn't telling him everything. He looked away and then headed toward the couch. As he sat down, Idona rolled onto her side and watched the vampire.

"I'm worried about Sue. What if Rafficer finds her? She had no idea who you were," Idona whispered. Darius thought back to that girl. When they were in the elevator, it had looked like she could vaguely recognize him. The vampire decided not to mention that, but he also worried about Sue. Though he hadn't been with her for a long while, Rafficer still might sense just enough of him on her.

"Rafficer turned someone while we were driving. I don't know who it was or what Raff knows of this world. I'm guessing that he's learning faster than I am because he can just relax away and learn. Whereas, I have to learn on the run," Darius offhandedly mentioned. Idona tensed. This really wasn't good news. It scared her that Rafficer had already turned a person. *What would happen now? Could they fix all this if too many people died or even changed? Maybe Raff can keep the turning to a min. Oh wait, this is Rafficer that I'm thinking about!* Idona thought with a deep sigh. Darius almost immediately regretted telling Idona about Rafficer. He hadn't meant to state it so bluntly, but he just couldn't seem to stop.

"Wonderful. Now nothing can stop him from appearing at my school before we reach New Orleans. Hell, he could be waiting there for us right now!" Idona cried as she turned onto her back. Darius shook his head.

"Raff wouldn't be that fast. He'd wait to see how long it would take me to go back to his side. If I return before he really goes looking for me, then he won't go after me. He won't attack all the humans I've met. That is...if I can beat Kathleen. But even so, if Raff finds out about you, then he will go after everyone until he finds you," Darius told her. Idona already knew this. That was why she didn't fight with Darius before, to make him leave her and Minnie alone. "I should have left before it got to this."

"I would have followed you," Idona weakly called. Darius paused. He almost wondered if he had heard her right. *She couldn't have said that. No...why would she? She didn't even know me outside of the book.* Darius thought. It took him a little while to build up the courage to look at her directly. He almost wondered if he had heard her correctly. But as he thought about it, he again remembered the book. Darius stood up and headed over to Idona's bag sitting at the end of her bed. He opened the first pocket, expecting to find nothing but was shocked to see the book there. *Minnie must have put it back when I drove here.* Darius thought as he took the book and stood.

As he straightened, he looked back at Idona. She had fallen asleep over the covers of her bed. His eyes glanced over Minnie, who was tucked under her sheets. Sighing, Darius headed toward the closet in the entryway. He opened the door and took out an extra blanket and pillow. Leaving the pillow, he brought the blanket to Idona and draped it across her body. She snuggled into it as though she had been cold.

Slowly, Darius went over to the couch and sat down. Considering what he told Idona, Darius really didn't want to read the book and follow Rafficer. His eyes focused on the book. *Never thought that Minnie would have had the foresight to pack this back into Idona's bag,* he thought. He was grateful that it was there. Minnie had never shown another way back out to the car outside of the elevator. For a moment, Darius fought the idea of lying back and faking sleep. Then he decided that Idona was right. He should watch for Rafficer. He looked at the book, frowned, and picked it up. Slowly, he opened it. He had been right before. The book was focused on Rafficer.

Rafficer stood before his newest youngling. He was a middle-aged man with dyed blonde hair and contact lenses that turned his natural brown eyes into a bright blue. Serge met him at a club in the town where they were staying. Normally, Rafficer hated turning anyone over a certain age. But Serge explained to Rafficer that this man knew things that could help them. The man had said his name, but Rafficer had already forgotten it. He did recall the youngling telling him that they were in a "state" called "New Mexico" or something.

The man claimed to be skilled at a contraption called, "the Internet." He offered to help Serge find out where Darius was and where the other younglings where. When Serge brought the man to Rafficer, the older vampire saw the importance of this man's service. So he turned him before the man had properly introduced himself. Unlike other vampires, Rafficer didn't have to wait a night for the man to rise, meaning die and then come back to life as a vampire. He could make him rise early. It was dangerous; not many survived it. But Rafficer was certain that almost anyone could help him find the younglings that might not return at his "calling."

"New one!" Rafficer cried. The youngling stepped forward. When Rafficer tried to call him "boy" earlier that evening, the man had protested. Rafficer didn't like the idea of the protest but figured the youngling didn't know any better yet. He'll learn quickly. Rafficer thought to himself with an evil smile.

"Sam," the man reminded his sire for the tenth time since his rising. Rafficer snarled. He didn't care for the name of the man. All he cared about was that "Sam" was supposed to be a genius of technology. Rafficer liked that idea, not that he understood it, but mostly wanted Sam to teach him as much about this new world as he possibly could. The old vampire was disappointed that Sam couldn't explain why the others could live through the daylight. In his haste for knowledge, Rafficer almost killed him then. But Serge reminded him the real reason for Sam's presence.

"Where is that information I asked for?" Rafficer ordered. Just minutes ago, he asked Sam to pinpoint where the vampire had felt Darius. Without more than a few simple feelings and guesses, Sam was fumbling along, staring at a map.

"Without more details," Sam began. Rafficer snatched the man's throat with his hand. He didn't like to be angered. He pulled the new one close.

"Then show me a map," he snarled. Sam nodded as Rafficer let him go. The man rushed to his computer and brought it to his sire. The map was focused on the United States. Rafficer pointed to the New England area without knowing its name. "There."

"Let me zoom in some more," Sam muttered. Once the page reloaded, Rafficer narrowed it down to Massachusetts. Again, Sam zoomed in. This continued repeatedly until it was narrowed in close enough for satellite images. Finally, Rafficer pointed to a tall building on a college campus. The vampire smiled.

"I'd like to visit there soon," he said. Serge stepped forward. As much as he knew not to defy Rafficer's orders, Serge hated that his sire picked on Darius. It's a wonder that the 652-year-old hadn't killed Rafficer yet. *Serge thought to himself.*

"*Darius may have already moved on, Sir,*" *Serge stated. Rafficer narrowed an angry glare onto his First General. The 721–year-old felt that Serge really didn't know anything about him.*

"*Of course he has! But, I'd like to see what brought him there, so far away from me,*" *Rafficer growled out. Serge nodded. While Serge was an expert on following Rafficer's orders, Sam still had a lot to learn.*

"*What good will it do to visit if he is already gone?*" *Sam asked. Rafficer snapped. He hit Sam so hard that the youngling flew into the wall and almost went through. Sam stayed down. The other two knew that it hadn't killed him; he was just in shock.*

"*I will find out why he is staying away.*" *Rafficer growled. Darius was his oldest vampire. If he were already fighting the impulse to follow Rafficer, then who knows how much longer the older vampire would last. Rafficer didn't want his time to end but he knew that Darius wanted his freedom. Could Darius already be stronger than him? Strong enough to kill him? During the battle that sent them here, Rafficer had every intention of killing Darius. It made the vamp wonder if Darius knew. It would explain why he was away.* Wonder where he is, *Rafficer thought before thinking of sensing for his youngling.* "*That reminds me. Where is my meal?*"

Serge stepped away. The First General clapped his hands and two vampires holding onto a young girl walked in. Her brunette hair hid her eyes while she fought against the creatures holding her. Rafficer smiled. He had been so pleased to find many of his younglings in this strange town. In fact, only a handful had been in a different state than him. Earlier, he had sensed for them all and "called" to most of them individually. Kathleen, Darius, and three others were along the eastern coast of the U.S. Sam chose that moment to sit up. His eyes widened.

"*Vanessa!*" *he called, surprised. Vanessa looked at the newly turned vampire. Her hair covered her eyes still, but she could see the man.*

"Dad?" she whimpered just before the two vampires holding her forced her to look at their sire. Rafficer let his fangs drop as he stood up to prepare. Vanessa froze; her bright brown eyes were focused on the pointed teeth. As much as Rafficer didn't like knowing his meal's name, he was happy that Sam knew this girl. Heck, it made him feel great that Vanessa might be Sam's daughter, even though he knew that personal connections to feeds made the new vampires violent. This case was no exception. Sam jerked forward as though he was going to stop his sire. Serge rushed from his spot and stopped Sam. He wasn't going to let this new one interrupt Rafficer's feeding.

Rafficer bit into Vanessa's neck and ripped a large chunk of skin away. Blood spurted from the wound as he spit the skin to the ground. He licked the stream of red fluid as it drained down her shoulder. It took Rafficer a moment to realize that she didn't scream. He paused to see why and saw that he had torn away so much of her throat near the voice box that it couldn't work. His smile looked more evil because of the blood that stained his face. Vanessa died a second before Rafficer actually began to drink from her.

Darius snapped the book closed. No matter how many times he had seen his sire feed, it still made him sick. Sky-blue eyes closed as he tried to erase the images of Rafficer feeding from his mind. As the images began to vanish, Darius half wondered what Minnie saw when he fed from Idona. He tried to imagine it, but he didn't like the violent image that appeared. If that was really what Minnie saw, it was no wonder why she feared him. Still slightly sickened by the images, Darius placed the book onto the couch.

As he looked at Minnie, it suddenly hit him. A feeling of hunger so strong, he almost doubled over. He knew that he needed more blood than what Idona had given him earlier. He hadn't thought about it at all while he drove. Gasping, he jumped to his feet. The feeling made him think that he might be getting into the beginning of a bloodlust. Vampires can easily fall into one when they are desperate for blood and stop after they've had a sufficient amount. Either way he needed to get away from the girls.

Quickly, he ran to the bathroom. Though he knew it wouldn't stop him if he really were having a bloodlust, he closed the door. With it closed, he focused his eyes onto the bathroom mirror. Once before he had gone through a lust like this. He had gotten over it without feeding by staring at his reflection in a small lake. But when he noticed his reflection this time, he paused. His eyes were still sky-blue. Leaning forward, he wondered if it was somehow a trick of the light. It wasn't.

"What the—?" Darius muttered to himself. He checked his eyes by moving into different angles and opening his eyes wider. Not a single speck of red was in his eyes. Vampire eyes turn red when they are hungry as a final warning to others. Sometimes if a vampire has red eyes for too long, they attack their own kind just to get their fix of blood. If his eyes weren't red, then why was he so hungry?

Feeling as though the girls were safe, he slowly walked back out the bathroom. Maybe the book would have an answer. He crossed the room but stopped at Idona's bed. Sky-blue eyes focused onto her sleeping figure. *No, she ate already. Didn't she?* Darius thought to himself. He thought back to Cracker Barrel. When he bit her, he had gotten a memory of her moving her food around on her plate and not really eating. Darius shook the idea from his head.

"I'm sure she ate," Darius mumbled to himself. Idona rolled over onto her stomach. She didn't look hungry. For all Darius knew, Idona could have eaten five meals in Cracker Barrel. But in reality, the memory that flashed in his mind was correct. Being with Marc had made her lose her appetite. Now, almost three hours later, her stomach was trying to get her to eat. The connection that Darius and Idona had felt when he was drinking from her was still there. Neither of them could feel it, but their bodies knew and communicated it with both of them in an attempt to get it solved. Darius walked back to his seat on the couch. He kept thinking about how her hunger was bothering him.

On the other end of the couch was the book. It had opened and was working on flipping a page. Darius sat down and stared at it for a moment. He didn't want to read it yet. For some reason, he thought that the book was narrating Rafficer's story. And if it was, Darius feared that it was still focusing on him feeding. When Rafficer got too violent, he always had to have a second meal right after.

Hunger pains still bothered Darius. He felt that it wasn't his hunger that was bothering him, and he wondered if he should go outside to the HHR. There he could lock himself in the car and not worry about hurting people. Slowly, sky-blue eyes watched Idona. Each time the pain that he felt became almost unbearable, she would roll over or shift. The vampire was half-surprised she didn't wake up. Especially when the pain made him groan a few times. Both girls slept through his vocal sounds as though he was silent.

After what seemed to be a half hour of him fighting the hunger pains, the book started a new chapter. Darius looked at what it said. When he read the title, a smile crossed his face, and he picked it back up. Rafficer really wasn't the only one it could follow.

CHAPTER 12

Kathleen

*K*athleen was furious. That youngling had compelled her to stop. Her irritation increased when she found that she couldn't break the compulsion easily. Even though Darius had felt like Kathleen had left, she had stayed and watched. One of the vampiress's secret powers was the ability to block other vampire's senses. That was why Darius failed to sense her.

She watched as the younger vampire tried to compel the human that she had bitten. Kathleen smiled. After she had first taken blood from him, she gave him a constant compulsion that made it so he'd only follow her or Rafficer. As much as she wanted Marc all to herself, as the first bride of Rafficer, Kathleen couldn't stop him from overpowering all of her compulsions. It luckily worked both ways though, which was something Kathleen enjoyed.

When Marc drove from the Cracker Barrel lot, Kathleen stalked him. She followed him to the gas station. For a while, she just watched him. She almost wondered if Marc would wonder what she was or if Darius's compulsion had stuck a little. Just as she decided to go see Marc again, Darius pulled up beside the human. Kathleen watched as they exchanged words but she couldn't hear what was being said. It took a few minutes more before Marc entered his Camaro and then drove off. Again, Kathleen followed.

She thought she would lose him when he sped away, but luck saved her. Marc had to pull onto the exit to return to school. When he went to enter the exit, he slowed down just enough. She noticed the change in speed and knew that he'd have to speed back up soon, so she had to time it right. Kathleen ran to the side of the car, opened the door, and jumped in all in a smooth moment. She was half-surprised that she could easily get in. Humans were as dumb as they looked. Marc looked at her once she closed the door and he screamed.

"What the hell! Jesus, Kathleen!" he screamed as he lost control of the car for a moment. He regained control just as they reached the top of the ramp. Kathleen gave him a soft smile. Forest-green eyes were focused on the road. Angered that he wasn't watching her, she leaned close to him.

"You left without giving me that ride you promised," she purred. Marc shuddered. His memory flashed back to what happened. Suddenly, he didn't want Kathleen near him. Her ordering Darius to feed off Idona made him so terrified of both vampires that he was half debating following Darius's command, even though it didn't stick. Now more than ever do I wish that it had, *Marc thought again.*

"Had to go. Missing classes and all that. Maybe I can give you that lift another time?" Marc asked as he looked to make sure he could move over a lane safely. Kathleen held back a snarl. She didn't like that answer. Is he fighting my compulsion? Or did **Darius's** really stick?

"I'd like it now."

"Oh. But I'm going home."

"I could join you back home, okay?"

"Well, I'm not really going home."

Kathleen paused. She swore that he had just stated that he was going home. Was he now lying to her? Pouting, she leaned even closer. Marc tensed. She decided to press him about it later.

"Even better."

"Um…how did you even get in my car? I'm going like 70," Marc asked. *Kathleen smiled. She had a good answer for that, or so she thought.*

"I ran," *she told him. Marc's eyes showed his disbelief. The vampiress almost cursed.* I ran? *she asked herself, incredulously. She knew that there was a better excuse than that. But as she thought about it, she couldn't come up with even one.* Of all the questions to ask, why does it have to be one of the harder one to answer? *Kathleen opened her mouth to speak but stopped. The thought left her head as quickly as it came. Shaking his head, Marc went to speak. But he was interrupted by music blaring from something in the car.*

"Shit," *Marc cursed before digging into his right front pocket of his jeans. Kathleen watched as he took out a small device. The vampiress could tell that it was the item making the noise. Marc touched a part of the device and put it to his ear.* "Hello?"

"Hey, Marc," *called a female voice. Kathleen frowned. She couldn't see another woman there. Nor did she notice a wire to allow sound to travel to the small device. The whole idea was making her uncomfortable. Noting that Marc wasn't shocked about this whole thing, Kathleen kept her fears silent. If she acted too odd in this moment, nothing would be able to take it back. Kathleen would lose all she had worked for. Keeping the vampire secret was important and she wasn't going to lose such a wonderful meal.*

"Sue? Since when do you have my cell number?" *Marc asked. Sue sighed through the phone. Kathleen sat back. The cell was so loud that she could easily hear the other girl.*

"You gave it to me when we used to date. Actually, you gave it to me two hours before we broke up. When you first noticed Chelsea." *Marc nodded as he remembered that he broke up with Sue to get with Chelsea.*

"Yeah, I remember. What's with the call now?"

"I wouldn't call if it wasn't really important." *Marc's eyes narrowed. He didn't like when Sue sounded like this. The main reason why he hadn't gotten bored of her.*

"What's up?"

"Are you with Minnie or Idona?"

"No."

"God damn it..."

Marc moved the phone from his ear for a moment as Sue screamed even more frustrated words. Once he was certain that Sue was calm, he brought it back. Kathleen had a confused look on her face. Why does this girl care about if he was hanging out with one or two other girls?

"Whoa! What's wrong? You never speak dirty..."

"They've vanished. Neither one will answer their phone, nor will they answer their door. I had to get Paul, their RA, to open their door."

"So?"

"Their stuff was gone. Almost like they left with no intention of coming back!" Marc bit his bottom lip. How could he tell her that they did without letting her know that he had been with them? Kathleen leaned against her door. She couldn't help but wonder how Marc was going to deal with this situation.

"Maybe they did. Don't see why you're so worried."

"Marc! Earlier, some strange guy told Idona to leave with him. The front desk never sent him up to her room in the first place! He went with Minnie, after I had already seen him with Idona. Plus, I swear he looked familiar!"

"Did he say his name was Darius?" Marc questioned without really thinking. Of course, he didn't know that Darius was from a book. Nor did he know that the vampire was from a book that Sue had read.

"What? No! Wait. OMG! That's how I know him! This guy looked like the exact description of Darius, a vampire from this book series that Idona and I read," Sue quickly explained to Marc. If it weren't for the fact that Kathleen ripped the phone from Marc's hand, he would have dropped the phone. This was the first *mention he had heard of Darius being fictional. Kathleen brought the phone to her ear.* If Darius is from a book, could I be from the same thing? *she wondered.*

"Hey," Marc cried when he noticed that the vampiress had grabbed it.

"Was there another character called Rafficer? Or even a Kathleen?" the vampiress asked. Sue hesitated. She didn't know this voice. Nor did she know if Marc knew the voice. He didn't seem friendly when he cried out. Finally, she decided to answer.

"Yeah, they're both in the series. Why?" Sue responded just before Kathleen dropped the phone. A book series? I'm a character in a book?

"What the hell, Kath?" Marc screamed. Thankfully, the phone had landed in her lap, so he easily picked it back up. "Did you say they are?"

"Yeah, why? Who is that with you?" Marc slowly looked at Kathleen. Her eyes weren't focused on him. Fear raced through him. He knew about that series. When Idona told him she was reading those books, he tried to read them. He had never liked vampire stories, so he didn't get past the back cover. "Marc?"

"Kathleen is with me," Marc called before looking forward. What he saw next terrified him. He hadn't been watching the road. It was just enough time for traffic in front of him to be backed up to a standstill. Marc was still going 70.

Darius tossed the book away. He didn't want to read the rest. As much as he disliked the senior student, the vampire never wished that on him. Slowly, Darius stood up. He wanted to find Idona's or Minnie's phone. Although he wasn't sure what phones looked like, Darius searched. Thankfully, Idona's was sitting, powered up, on the nightstand by her head. Darius rushed over and grabbed it. He began pressing buttons and going through the phone as though he had owned one all his life. Idona had indeed missed almost 30 called from Sue and 10 messages. Darius dialed Sue's number. After one ring, the girl picked up.

"OMG! Thank you! Idona, where the hell are you?" Sue's voice loudly demanded through the phone's speaker. Darius winced at the volume and looked at the girls. Neither stirred even though it was close to them waking up soon. The clock read 7:10 a.m.

"This isn't Idona," Darius muttered. Sue gasped. She recognized that voice as the man from outside Idona's room. The one that looked like...Darius.

"Who are you? Did you kidnap her?" Sue growled into the phone. Darius smiled. At least she was concerned for Idona's safety.

"Not really. Idona and Minnie came willingly. It was for their safety that we all left," Darius responded, not realizing how much it sounded like he had kidnapped them. Sue sounded angrier when she came back on.

"Who are you?"

"My name is Darius." There was a long pause.

"What?"

"Darius Remount Visl-"

"Vislaw Murrow. Nineteen years old, almost 20, but really a 633-year-old vampire?" Sue cried before Darius could even finish his name. Darius smiled. The book really was useful for people in this world. They knew everything. Of course, that's only if they read from it. Suddenly it made Darius wonder if Idona's book was the only one that was rewriting itself. He'd have to remember to ask Sue about it later.

"652 if you add my human age." There was another long pause. Sue was holding her breath so Darius couldn't tell if she was even still on. Frowning, the vampire realized he didn't care for cell phones. One couldn't gauge the reaction of the other person. Darius was surprised that Sue hadn't fainted yet. His smile vanished. *Or maybe she had!*

"Sue?"

"Still here," she squeaked. Darius smiled again as Minnie began to stir. Then it happened. Sue seemed to snap. "Oh my god! Oh my god! Oh my god, oh my god, oh my god ..."

Darius held the phone away as Sue continued to scream those three words repeatedly. Her loud voice quickly woke both girls. They snapped to attention. Once aware that Sue wasn't there, Minnie grabbed her ears as if in pain. Idona focused on the phone. She waved her hand to signal that she wanted it. Darius quickly handed it over with no objection. The girl was still going at it.

"Sue. Sue? SUE!" Idona cried into the phone, matching Sue's volume by the end of it. Somehow that snapped the Sue out of it. Idona switched the phone over to speaker, even though she was sure they didn't need it. Darius sat back down onto the couch. He was grabbing his head like he had a headache, which in fact, he did, thanks to Sue.

"Idona?"

"Yes, Sue?"

"Oh good! I was having a weird dream that I was talking to Darius. You know that vampire from the *Project* series?" Darius smiled. He sat up straight. This was the second time that someone thought he wasn't there. It was beginning to get insulting.

"You weren't dreaming," Darius called from his seat.

"Oh. Are you playing a cruel trick on me?"

"No offense to Darius, but I wish we were," Minnie said as she moved to sit on the edge of the bed closest to Idona. The conversation went silent. Minutes passed.

"I wish you would have just lied to me. Maybe then I wouldn't have spoken to...Marc..." Sue trailed off, as Darius looked away. He felt bad that she had been on the phone with the human boy when—*No! I will not finish that thought!* Darius said to himself as though finishing it would make it true.

"What's wrong with Marc?" Minnie asked. Sue gasped. Darius closed his eyes, wishing that Sue wouldn't tell them. There was a moment's pause.

"I think...I think he got into a...car accident! Kathleen, the vampiress, was with him!" Idona dropped the phone. Sea-green eyes focused on Darius. Chocolate-brown eyes focused on the book, laying on the floor near the foot of her bed. "Idona, tell me I'm wrong! Please, God, tell me this is a dream!"

"I'm sorry," Darius whispered. There was a clatter of Sue's phone falling on the floor, followed by the sounds of sobs. Idona looked back to her phone. Tears were streaming down eyes. Even Minnie was crying.

"Sue, did you call 911?" the youngest girl asked.

"Yes," Sue sobbed. Her voice was distant, meaning she still hadn't picked up her phone. "But, they can't help unless they know where he is!"

"I'm sure someone called it in," Minnie tried to reassure everyone. It didn't help.

"Kathleen was with him," Darius reminded them. Idona looked at him in horror.

"She wouldn't!"

"She seemed rather attached to him. I mean, she did follow him."

"No...Not Marc! Anyone but Marc!" Idona moaned before tears freely fell from her eyes. Sobs racked her body before she dropped her face into her hands. Even Minnie seemed shocked by this news.

"You can't mean that! Marc would never want to be turned!" Minnie almost screamed. Darius shook his head. No vampire relied on a choice of the human. They tended to turn the person and expect them to be happy about the change.

"Minnie, think of it this way. If you were going to die a painful death in a matter of minutes or be turned and live forever, what would you do?" Sue called, her voice sounded closer to the phone. Idona and Darius looked at Minnie, waiting for her to respond. Tears still fell from her eyes, but Idona seemed a lot calmer. Minnie was freaking out. She started shaking her head, as though removing a thought from her mind.

"I'd die," Minnie answered confidently, but Idona knew she was lying. Idona shook her head in disbelief. Minnie's chocolate-brown eyes focused on her. "I would!"

"I'm sorry. I just don't believe you. I mean, I know I wouldn't choose that," Idona muttered. The end was so soft that everyone else almost missed it. Minnie frowned.

"Neither do I. Personally, I'd be turned in that moment. I know now, when I can think about it rationally that I would choose to die. But in the heat of the moment, I wouldn't care. Even if I turned into a senseless killer," Sue added. Two sets of eyes focused on Darius. The vampire simply sighed. He assumed she might have forgotten his presence again. Before anyone could remind Sue of his presence, she cried out. "Oh! Not that I would be, I mean...oh God, I'm sorry, Darius!"

"I know what you meant," Darius mumbled before standing up. His eyes flashed to the book again. He remembered reading that Rafficer was going to be going to the school soon. Although he hadn't been around Sue for a long while, Raff might be able to sense that he had been there. If Sue said anything, regardless if it were the truth or a lie, he would kill her. "Listen, I don't think you're safe there anymore."

Idona and Minnie starred at Darius in surprise. Sue hesitantly paused. Almost like she was waiting for Darius to add more details.

Darius said nothing. His sky-blue eyes were watching Idona, wondering if she understood what he meant. He knew that she understood what he meant when he saw her eyes widen. Minnie tilted her head to the side in thought until...

"Rafficer? You mean...but he doesn't know about us yet, right? Kathleen got into that accident remember?" Minnie called. Darius shook his head.

"He sensed for me. That was the whole reason for us to leave the school. He knew that I was there. I've been reading, and he's planning on going there to find some clues," Darius informed the girls, and Sue let out a slight grunt.

"What do you mean by read that he's planning on coming here?" Sue asked. Idona looked back to the phone.

"My book of *Project New World* has been rewriting itself with the adventures as they occur. It's like our world has become part or connected to the book world," Idona tried to explain. "You've read before that Rafficer can sense his younglings, right?"

"Yeah...I've read all the books. But this never happened in *Project New World*. Raff...um..." Sue trailed off.

"Rafficer what?" Minnie asked. Darius stiffened when he realized what she meant. He had read that Rafficer intended to kill him during that battle. Maybe, in the book world, before all this, he had succeeded.

"Well..." Sue began.

"He killed me..." Darius finished. Idona gasped and Minnie jumped from her bed.

"But those books are about you!" Minnie cried. Idona shook her head.

"If you remember correctly...they actually follow Rafficer. When the author introduced Darius, she realized that it would be interesting to follow his transformation for a little while. She never had any intention of having him be the main character," Idona whispered. Darius sat back down. He shook his head dejectedly before placing his elbows on his knees and holding his head. Minnie walked around Idona's bed. She put herself closer to Darius and waited. She couldn't find the words to comfort Darius since he had just found out that he was supposed to be dead. In this world, Darius was living on borrowed minutes. "I had hoped that Darius would survive that..."

"Rafficer had me pinned to the wall...I knew even then...that he may kill me," Darius mentioned.

"You had escaped him for a little while. But since he is your sire, he ordered you to come back...you couldn't resist...that was when he killed you. The battle ended seconds later. The rebellion failed," Sue said. Darius shook his head and brought his hands over his ears, it was too much for him to handle. He became overwhelmed. Minnie and Idona watched Darius, worried.

"I can't listen anymore!" he snapped. Knowing that Idona would follow him, Darius decided to deceive the girls. Using vampire speed, he opened the door to the hall and slammed it closed. When Idona and Minnie faced the doorway, Darius snuck out through the glass door to the porch. After hearing the door to the room close, Minnie moaned. She felt deep sympathy for the unfortunate way Darius found out his fate. Idona's gave the porch door a quick glance when Minnie moaned. She saw the curtains still trying to settle in place. Understanding that the vampire wanted privacy, Idona made no move to go see him. Instead she turned back to the phone laying on her bed.

Outside on the porch, Darius sighed in relief when neither girl appeared. He could tell that Idona might have seen evidence of him escaping this way but even she didn't show up. As the rush of the escape and relief of solitude faded, Darius felt empty. Just empty. *Wonder what someone is supposed to feel...when they've found out that they're on a mission that will kill them.* Darius distractedly wondered.

Darius was lost in thought as he watched the cars pass by. During the battle in the book, he'd had a feeling that he might not live longer than a few days. Rafficer had seemed to plan the entire attack carefully. Darius was only at fault for leaving a door unlocked, the others had let themselves in. Darius heard a rumor that they might have opened more doors. Of course, it was pointless to think of that now. Rafficer was going to kill him. It was over. *Unless. Maybe now that I know...I can change things!* Darius thought. He straightened his stance in hope. *Of course...I had an idea. And Sue said that Raff commanded me.'*

Since he had received confirmation of his own death, Darius was very lost. He felt as if there was nothing he'd be able to do to stop it from happening. *I hate the idea of this stupid book. I hate that I'm here!* Darius angrily thought. He looked down before kicking one of the iron bars that made up the rails for the porch. Tears threatened to pour once again. Holding them back, Darius looked at a piece of rust that had broken free and was now drifting down. Sighing once again, the vampire stopped and really thought about what he just thought. *But if I didn't come here...I'd be...and I wouldn't have met...* Darius added before groaning. Squeezing his eyes tight, he shook his head to stop the thought from continuing. No matter how he looked at it, it seemed like this news was only painful.

"Why? Why would I have to die?" Darius asked the still morning air. He dropped his head down and wondered what to do. *Maybe I could leave Idona and Minnie...if I left them; they may not be able to send me back! Then Raff wouldn't be sent back either...* Suddenly a thought occurred. *What happens when they do send me back? Will that fix everything? Maybe Rafficer won't be able to order me around?"*

Darius turned to look at the room. If he were right, it would be a fantastic thing that he was brought here, but if he were wrong...since he was unsure of his feelings, he thought about confiding in Idona to see if she had an answer. Darius turned around and walked back to the room. Darius felt better, so he built up his courage, placed his hand on the door, and went inside.

Minnie paid him no mind when he entered, but Idona faced him. She mouthed an apology to him. Sky-blue eyes looked away from her in response. He couldn't think about it again. Not only that, but he didn't want the girls' pity. Idona felt hurt by Darius's dismissal until she thought about how she'd feel if she was in his shoes. She almost began to cry for him. Pity was something that she couldn't help but feel for him. Idona knew from the books that Darius hated pity but that was the only emotion she could muster. Quickly trying to forget her feelings, Idona focused on the conversation between Minnie and Sue.

"So all we need to do is find a Western Union, right?" Minnie clarified. Idona sighed. Though she was the one to bring up the idea of having Sue leave college, Idona half hoped that the girl would head home rather than join them. –Her presence was not financially feasible. Now they'd have to cover for her flight and hotel room as well. Heck, they'd even have to pay for her meals. Groaning, Idona just nodded. Minnie flashed her a curious glance before noticing that Darius had joined them again. But Darius was focused on something else. He had never heard of a "Western Union" and didn't know what that meant.

"I think that's best," Sue responded. Clearing the negative thoughts, Idona nodded.

"Okay, I'll get to one ASAP, and then I'll call and tell you that it's been sent. As agreed, we'll meet you somewhere in New Orleans," Idona finished. Sue bid them goodbye and hung up. Minnie looked at Idona and Darius before grabbing her computer and turning it on. Idona sighed before looking at her things. She'd need to take out some money to send. Darius meanwhile, sat back down on the couch. He was unsure of how to bring up the topic he had been thinking of. Just as he finally decided to come out with the whole topic, Minnie cried out that she found a Western Union.

"What is this 'Western Union'?"

CHAPTER 13

The Hotel

At the end of the conversation, Idona headed off to a nearby Western Union by herself. Minnie's search led to an outlet in the mall near their hotel. Since it was within walking distance, Idona told Minnie and Darius to wait in the room. Darius could shower if he wanted to, or in reality, Minnie could yet again shower. Minnie did choose to shower first. Darius didn't mind in the least. He had half wanted to go with Idona, but she turned him down. She had sensed that he didn't rest that night.

Not wanting to leave Darius bored, Minnie showed him how to use the remote control for the TV. Like his newfound driving skills, he picked up the remote and pretty much knew how to use it without her quick lesson. The vampire was surprised when his assumption from the night before turned out to be correct. Inside the once blackened screen were moving pictures and sounds that matched. He was so fascinated by the TV that he didn't even notice when Minnie went and took her second shower.

By the time that Idona returned to the room an hour later, Darius was still watching TV and Minnie was showering. Idona entered as

Minnie exited the bathroom. Idona smiled at Minnie, who responded with a friendly nod.

"Did Darius shower?" Idona asked. Minnie shook her head. Idona frowned; she thought it was pointless for Minnie to take a second shower and that Darius needed one.

"He said he didn't want to. He doesn't even smell bad," Minnie explained. Darius lay out cold across Idona's bed. On the TV was a commercial, so the girls couldn't tell what was on. "I guess he wanted to sleep rather than shower…"

"I guess," Idona muttered. She stared at Darius's face and smiled. He looked as peaceful as when she had first seen him in her room. It made her realize that there was no reason to fear Darius. Though he was a vampire, who had bit her, he would never kill her. It was other vampires should she fear. They wouldn't stop. Shaking her head, Idona focused on Minnie. "We should repack our things and take them to the car before we wake him. I don't think he slept all night."

"Maybe we can get some breakfast?" Minnie questioned just as both of their stomachs growled angrily. Idona and Minnie giggled softly at the timing. As the girls calmed, Minnie looked at her things. "I'm gonna grab some different clothes and change."

"But, didn't you just change when you showered?" Idona asked. Minnie gave her a soft smile and shook her head. Knowing that Minnie used to do that at the school, Idona could only laugh at her. Nodding her head in the knowledge of her mistake, Minnie grabbed some clothes from her bag. Once she had headed into the bathroom again, Idona walked over to her bed. Darius was half sleeping on the TV remote. Sighing deeply, Idona looked to see if she could get to the power button. Noting that it was just about within her sight, she slowly reached out for it. Just as her finger touched the button, Darius began to stir.

"Idona?" Darius wearily called. Idona froze before her sea-green eyes focused onto his sky-blue eyes. He still seemed out of it. His state made Idona wonder if he was asleep or simply unconscious. Darius sat up, making every effort of movement seem as though he was in pain even though he only felt slightly stiff. As he sat up, Idona backed away. "When did you get back?"

"A few minutes ago. I was going to shut off the TV," Idona responded. Darius faced the screen, which was still on. Groaning, Darius looked for the remote. Once he found it, he pressed the power button. Idona turned and sat down on the couch. "Did you...sleep?"

"Not really. I felt tired, so I forced myself to rest my body. It's like I said before, I can't sleep," Darius explained. Idona nodded. At the time, Idona had wondered if he lied. In the book, it mentioned them having to sleep. Idona always assumed that the author meant sleep like any normal human. Idona knew it was better to believe Darius since it was...his life. *I wonder if he missed sleeping.* Idona thought.

"Do you have an idea of what it is like to sleep?" Idona whispered. She almost smacked her forehead. Darius was human at one point. Meaning he did have to sleep, maybe even dream. In response, the vampire laughed lightly.

"I used to dream. I dreamt about problems that bothered me. Sometimes I would get the solution of the problem in a dream, other times it just haunted me. Admittedly, I wish I could still dream. Even the bad ones," Darius muttered. He turned away. Idona was focused on the entryway. Her stomach growled again. It felt noisy to her, but Darius made no response that he had heard it. Slowly, he looked back to her. "Speaking about that...I had a thought about if you were to send me back..."

"I'm ready!" Minnie nearly shouted as she exited the bathroom. Darius stiffened as Idona nodded. She looked back at Darius. Minnie quickly walked to her bed and dropped off the set of dirty clothes. Minnie walked back toward the door without worrying about packing.

"We're going to go get some breakfast. I would ask if you want anything, but...anyway, we'll be back soon," Idona told the vampire. Darius could only stare at Idona. Idona gave him a soft smile. "Maybe you should shower while we are gone?"

"Okay," Darius mumbled. Idona nodded and began to leave. Darius sighed deeply and stood up when Idona paused. She looked back at him.

"You were saying something before Minnie came out of the bathroom. What was it?" Darius shook his head. He decided to bring it up later. Idona shrugged and waved goodbye before following Minnie out of the room and down the hall. Darius stood alone in the room. He was uncertain of what to do. After a few minutes, the vampire finally decided to shower. Even if he didn't have a change of clothes.

Downstairs in the lobby, Idona was just finishing filling her plate up. She had three croissants, two plain bagels, an apple, a box of Frosted Flakes, some type of muffin, scrambled eggs, and some white toast. Holding a large glass of orange juice, she looked for Minnie. The older girl had only grabbed a small plate of things before going to choose a seat. She claimed there were too many people around and the table was more important. Besides, it was a breakfast buffet. Meaning, she could always get more plates.

"Idona!" Minnie called, standing up so the shorter girl could see her. She waved her hand back and forth. Idona smiled, to show that she had indeed seen Minnie, before walking toward the table. They were sitting in the far back corner. The furthest table from the buffet line.

Admittedly, Idona loved this type of seat. Normally, this area clears of people before any other, so it's significantly quieter. Idona set her plate down as Minnie began eating something that looked like cinnamon grits.

"Ew," Idona muttered as she watched the other girl eat it. She hated the look of oatmeal or even grits. When wet, or liquefied, she thought it looked like something a baby threw up. It made her sick to the stomach. She looked down at her overflowing plate. As much as she really wanted to put her food to the side, she hadn't eaten anything since Darius had been released from the book. Heck, she didn't even really remember eating dinner the night before he arrived.

"What? Oh, one of those oatmeal haters?" Minnie questioned when she noticed Idona's face. "I'll save that for later than."

"Thanks," Idona mumbled. Minnie nodded her head. She had brought the bowl of oatmeal to the table and a plate with some toast and two sunny-side up eggs. Somewhere along the way, she had also grabbed a small glass of milk. Both girls began eating. "You really don't mind having to do that?"

"Nah. My mom doesn't like it all that much either. When she goes shopping, she never gets it for me. So my dad always makes it up by buying like two to three times the amount I really need. She hates it. So I've learned to eat it in an area she wouldn't go into or wait until she headed out to work. It's no big deal," Minnie explained. Idona nodded. "Besides, I saw you didn't eat much last night. I'd rather you eat something now."

"I plan on it. I also figured we could steal some of the food to bring out to the car." Minnie almost gagged on her milk. She started at Idona in surprise.

"Can we do that?" Idona nodded. Minnie took a bite of her eggs.

"It's a free breakfast. Besides, they leave large napkins out and I think I see something that looks like grocery bags over there. They plan on people taking food. 'Sides, the faster we get down to New Orleans, the faster this will all be over. Heck, we might even get back to school in time for finals!" Minnie gave Idona a skeptical look. Idona shrugged it off and took a sip of some orange juice. The older girl swallowed.

"Speaking of which. Are you sure you want to send Darius off? You two really seem to...you know...connect."

Idona sighed and lowered her head. She hadn't really thought about the fact that Darius would be going as well. And what was worse, now they knew that he was going back to his death. It was getting depressing just thinking about it. "It sucks. What is gonna happen to him, I mean?"

"I'm...we have to fix this. Rafficer is dangerous. Every vampire who was transferred to this world is dangerous. People have been killed, and worse, turned. We can't let this keep happening!" Idona stated, determination holding back the tears. She really wished that what she had just said wasn't happening. Maybe then, she would have been able to enjoy her time with Darius. She had always connected with him. Even when he was just a character in a book.

"I know about Rafficer and Kathleen. But...do we really think that by sending them back that...well, Marc will turn back to normal? Or... will he die because Kathleen wasn't there to turn him during that accident that he had?" Idona froze, mid-bite into one of her croissants. Now that was an idea that she hadn't thought of. *What would happen to all the people the vampires killed or turned? Would they go back to normal, or... would Marc really die?* Idona thought to herself. Minnie calmly finished her plate and looked at the bowl of oatmeal. Idona still had some food left, so Minnie got up. "Be right back."

Idona could only numbly nod her head. Her mind was stuck on the idea of Minnie's suggestion. Not only would Darius die, but Marc could also die. This time, tears did begin to escape out a little. She placed the remainder of the croissant back on her plate. Her appetite was gone. *Maybe when we find someone who can fix this, we'll get answers. I don't think I could do it if I knew I was going to lose both of them.* Idona silently realized. She knew that Marc was a jerk, but he was someone she would miss. She couldn't just forget about him. Or even just read about him in a book. Marc was real. He was part of this world. *He never should have been involved.* Idona declared before picking back up her croissant. She forcefully ripped a large bite off.

"Well?" Minnie asked as she returned. Her plate now held a muffin and a banana. Idona sighed.

"We can only hope that the witch or wizard who can help us will have answers."

"But could you do it?" Idona gave her a quizzical look. "Could you send Darius back even if he'd be the only one who died? Like, say returning him will rewind everything that has happen since he got here?"

"I...I have to."

"That's not what I mean. Can you do it? Emotionally?" Idona looked away from Minnie. She was just too afraid to admit the truth. Minnie nodded. "That's what I thought."

"But I didn't say anything!" Idona cried, shocked. Minnie gave her a smile and took a bite out of her muffin. That was when it hit her. Minnie didn't need a verbal answer. Her body language said it all. Idona moaned and looked down to her plate. She hated that she had very little control over her body language. Minnie giggled for a few seconds before she sobered up.

"Darius will have to drink from me again tonight."

"What? Talk about coming from left field there! Jeez," Minnie stated. Idona nodded. It was an abrupt change of subject. But she couldn't think of a better way to put it. Minnie sighed and sat back in her seat. The plate before her was empty now. As was Idona's. Only the oatmeal remained. "I...I guess I could...you know."

"No. It's best for all of us if he focuses on just me. Emotionally, that is," Idona answered. Minnie nodded and exhaled a sigh of relief. Idona gave her a comforting smile. She looked down at the table and noticed that only the oatmeal was left. Grimacing, Idona turned back. "I'm gonna grab some food to go. Want anything specific?"

"Frosted Flakes, a muffin or two, and a bagel. Oh! And a banana!" Minnie told her. Idona nodded and stood. "A few croissants as well. I didn't get any."

"We're gonna be fighting over them aren't we?" Minnie couldn't help but nod and grin. Idona laughed and walked away. While she grabbed a bag of little goodies, Minnie quickly gulped down the oatmeal before heading over to help. In the end, they took two bags worth of food. Despite Minnie's fears, no one paid them any mind. In fact, another gentleman joined them in packing a bag. Once they were satisfied, they headed to the elevator. There was a large group already waiting so Minnie and Idona said nothing the whole way up. As they entered the room, Idona heard the shower was going. She couldn't help but smile. "Good. He needed that."

"Really? I didn't think he smelled."

"Mental clarity. Not the smell. Showers always help calm down and really think. After everything that happened, we all needed one. I'll take mine tonight though," Idona informed the other girl. Minnie mouthed "oh" and headed deeper into the room. Idona slowly followed.

"Jesus Christ! Did I really leave my stuff out like this?" Minnie called, shocked. Idona couldn't help but laugh. Minnie had always been a bit of a messy roommate. So the fact that she cared about her dirty clothes lying on the unmade bed and the rest of her shower items was new. "Ugh, Idona, can you help me?"

"I helped you last night. Not my fault that you took out a bunch of crap and left it lying all about," Idona told her as she grabbed her phone charger and quickly rolled it up. Minnie moaned and looked at her mess. Laughing lightly, Idona flopped down onto her bed. Very slowly, Minnie began to pack her things. "Don't forget about the laundry bag that they usually leave in the closet."

"Yeah. I know. But don't you need it?" Minnie asked. She headed toward the closet in the front entry. Idona grunted and looked at her bag. Minnie found the bag and grabbed it before walking back over.

"I grabbed some stuff from the dorm that keeps my clothes separated." Minnie nodded as she continued packing her things up into the two bags she had. Just as she finished packing her dirty clothes into the laundry bag, Minnie realized that she had no room in any of her things for the extra bag. She could only hope that Idona wouldn't mind. Not that it really mattered much anyway. They still had lots of room in the HHR. But, Minnie didn't know how much stuff Sue was going to bring. Slowly, Minnie sat down on her bed. Her gaze drifted over to Idona, who was reading.

"Trying to find clues about Marc and Kathleen?" Minnie questioned when she realized Idona was reading *Project New World*. Idona startled at the sudden noise. She looked over to her friend.

"Yeah...but it's basically been following our conversation with Sue for the past couple of pages. I think it might follow us to breakfast or jump to Rafficer. Either way, it's a good heads up," Idona admitted.

Minnie nodded. She turned to the bathroom. Darius still sounded like he was taking his shower. It was taking him a while. Which was a surprise, normally men get ready faster than women did. Shaking off the idea, Minnie faced Idona.

"What do you think happened? I mean, to them?" Minnie whispered. Idona put the book down.

"I...I don't really want to think about it," Idona murmured. Minnie nodded. She knew how Idona felt. It was like if they talked about it, whatever they said would come true. The sound of running water vanished, making both girls face the bathroom. "Darius must be almost done. Which means we really should get ready to get going. Wouldn't want Sue waiting too long for us."

"I guess. Which reminds me, I'll drive today. You've already driven enough," Minnie said. Idona frowned.

"Are you sure?" Idona muttered. Minnie nodded and then smiled.

"Honestly, I'd rather not have Darius drive again. It's creepy when you suddenly remember that he's a character from a book. Never mind that he shouldn't know how to drive. Actually, I have another question. How did Darius suddenly know that? Does the book explain it?" Minnie added. Idona frowned and looked at the book. She had read the scene where Darius bit her repeatedly. Nothing was described. The only mention of anything was that the bite changed Idona's eye color. "How about your eye color change? I don't remember you having hazel eyes."

"The book mentions that my eyes changed color but it didn't describe how or why. I guess it's because Darius drank from me...but that has never happened to anyone before. There is no mention of something like that happening in any of the books I've read before," Idona mentioned. "And I've read almost every book on vampires. Not once had it happened. But, there is mention of some vampires getting a sort of connection to the one they drink from."

"Aren't those normally the romance ones where they two were meant to be together?" Idona couldn't help but nod. Minnie had a point. There was no way that Idona and Darius were connected. Idona knew that there was something strange going on since Darius had bitten her. The bathroom door opened and Darius walked into the room. While in the bathroom, Darius had heard most of the conversation so he knew what was going on.

"Those are the stories...but, I think that's the problem. They're just stories," Idona mumbled. Darius stopped at the entrance to the rest of the room. He looked at Idona.

"I was just a story too."

CHAPTER 14

Dreams

The two girls looked shocked. They hadn't heard him exit the bathroom. Idona took a minute before she realized what Darius meant. He wanted there to be a connection between them. She had insulted him by implying the connection was just fictional. Idona closed her eyes and groaned; she couldn't look at Darius anymore. Even Minnie let out a moan.

"Darius, we don't mean anything by that! It's just a figure of speech," Minnie called. Darius shook his head. "Darius, please!"

"Just forget it. Let's get going," Darius nearly snapped. He turned and stormed out. Minnie frowned and looked at Idona. The shorter girl looked like she was about to start crying. Slowly, Minnie stood up. Idona half looked over.

"Don't...just don't..."

"Idona," Minnie moaned. Idona shook her head. She wiped her eyes and stood up. Shaking her head, Idona bravely met Minnie's chocolate-brown eyes. Minnie waited for a moment while Idona seemed to think about what she was going to say next.

"Let's get our stuff out to the car and head out," Idona muttered. Minnie nodded. As Idona grabbed her things, Minnie watched the other girl. She could tell that Idona was hurting, but she didn't know how to help. Minnie also realized that this was something that Darius and Idona would have to figure out.

Twenty minutes later, Minnie was driving her HHR down the route toward New Orleans. Darius was sitting right behind Idona, who was in the front passenger seat. The vampire looked out the window. He tried not to show his anger or pain. When he first left the girls alone, he wondered if he misunderstood the whole situation. He realized that rationalizing the situation didn't make the pain disappear.

Idona just wished that everything could be over. This was the second time that Darius overheard something she had said to Minnie and took it out of context. *How can I talk to Minnie about things that used to be fake or...some type of dream and not insult Darius? Should I just not even talk about it?* Idona shook her head. She could talk about it. She'd just have to be more careful.

Minnie was not comfortable driving people because she wasn't confident of her skill, but she decided to drive today was because both Idona and Darius needed a break. She wasn't very comfortable with Darius driving because he had never driven before entering this world. As for Idona, Minnie thought that a break from driving was necessary to let her ruminate over her thoughts. Besides, Minnie didn't want a distracted person controlling the wheel.

Time passed by and Darius began to find himself shifting to get comfortable in his seat. He was emotionally drained that it made him tired. It was a feeling that he hadn't experienced in over 600 years, so he didn't know how to react to it. Slowly he found himself, for the first time since he turned, drifting off into a deep sleep.

Once Darius was fast asleep, Idona herself drifting off to sleep. If she knew that Darius was asleep, she would have tried to stay up and give Minnie some company, but in her innocence, Idona slipped into dreamland along with Darius.

Idona opened her eyes again. She thought that she was awake and in the HHR with Minnie and Darius, but she wasn't anymore. In fact, Idona had no clue where she was. Looking around, Idona began to think she was in the countryside.

She knew that she wasn't in the same place because it was darkness here. The shadows made her feel as if she were standing near the edge of a forest or jungle. Off to the right, there was a small, dilapidated cottage from the 18th century. Idona began to wonder if she was in a historic town, like Sturbridge Village. But, there was something else about it that seemed...different—strange almost.

"Idona?" called a familiar voice. Idona turned and noticed Darius was standing behind her. He looked just as confused as she did. Idona stepped closer. He turned to see the surroundings and slowly recognized them.

"Darius? What's going on? Where are we?" Idona asked when she realized that Darius might know. The vampire faced her and shook his head. He couldn't believe what he was seeing. "Darius?"

"I think...I think this is the place where...I was turned," Darius muttered. Idona's jaw dropped in shock. There was no way he was telling the truth. Darius's eyes suddenly focused on something in the background. Before Idona could even turn to look, he grabbed her by the shoulders and pulled her into some nearby bushes.

Through the darkness, Idona and Darius spotted a figure. As it got closer to the light from the cottage, Idona realized that she recognized it. The figure had vibrant green eyes and pitch-black hair. It stood about six feet tall. A thin frame made the figure seem even taller. With each detail, Idona began to recognize it better. By the time the person stepped fully into the light, Idona knew who it was.

"Rafficer!" she cried. Darius nodded helplessly. His assumption was correct. Somehow, Idona and he had travelled into the book. But, Darius didn't remember

anything odd happening before. All he remembered was feeling like he was...I'm sleeping? This is all a dream? But how? Darius thought. His eyes drifted down toward Idona. If he was really sleeping once again, how was Idona here?

Standing before the cottage, Rafficer smiled. He had been watching this young boy for a while. Kathleen even had taken a personal interest in him. The two planned giving this boy to their master for a new vampire. Now that the master was dead, the vampires decided that the boy living in this cottage would be Rafficer's first underling. It would be so easy. Rafficer had seen his master change many humans. So he knew what to do. First, get the attention of the boy.

Slowly the vampire lifted his right hand. Pounding it on the door, Rafficer's smile grew. His vampire hearing noticed the boy inside trying to get up. In the bushes, Darius couldn't help but wince as he also heard the boy inside crashing around. Idona looked at the vampire beside her before looking back at Rafficer. She could hardly tell what was going on. But suddenly she realized that if Darius was right, and this was the night he was turned, but how did she get here? Rafficer knocked again.

"Coming!" screamed a voice from the cottage. Idona gasped. It was Darius's voice. She looked at him. His body had gone stiff.

"Darius, what's happening?" Idona whispered. Darius looked at her.

"I don't really know...," he told her seconds before the door to the cottage opened. Both of them focused onto the new form. It was a teenage boy with sky-blue eyes and dirty blonde hair. He was leaning more on his right leg, which made him seem shorter than his 5'9" frame. Rafficer smiled at the boy. Idona focused on the face. It looked almost exactly like Darius's, but the sky-blue eyes showed the inexperience of youth.

"Is that you?" Idona mumbled. Darius could only nod.

"Who are you?" young Darius asked of the vampire before him. Rafficer's smile changed to a small frown. He suddenly resonated with power. Even from the distance of the tree line, Idona could feel it. Darius felt a chill. His younger self seemed to relax a little.

"I'm your friend. Can we go into the house?" Rafficer questioned in return. Young Darius was uncertain for only a moment. Then his eyes filled with recognition. He opened his arms as though he was going to hug the vampire.

"Yes! Oh my god, how did I not recognize you? It's been so long," young Darius told Rafficer. Idona almost moaned. Though she had read about this scene in the book, it was worse actually watching it happen before her eyes. But, if it was bad for her, how much worse was it for poor Darius?

"It has, hasn't it? Why don't we head inside?" Rafficer prompted again. Young Darius nodded before he backed out of the doorway. Once cleared, Rafficer entered. Idona and Darius stepped out of the bushes just before the door closed. The vampire couldn't help but look away from the cottage. But Idona moved closer.

"I'm gonna go peek in," she told him. Darius focused on her.

"What?" Idona moved even closer.

"I'm gonna go look in." This time, she walked straight up to the cottage. She needed to find the proper window before the whole thing was over. Darius chased after her. He grabbed her hand a moment before she got to the correct window.

"Are you insane?" Idona pulled her hand away and glared at him. "This is Rafficer! And he's about to turn me!"

"I know. I'm sorry, but I have to watch," Idona told him. Darius glared at her. She wanted to watch his moment of weakness. She gave him a sad look before spinning around and looking into the window. There she saw young Darius tending to Rafficer.

"Is there anything else I can get you?" young Darius asked. Rafficer gave the boy a smile. The vampire had the boy light a fire and unnecessarily bring him a blanket, a pillow, and some food. The food was left untouched beside him. A small detail that young Darius didn't notice. Idona frowned as she watched. In the books, the author didn't talk much about Darius's turning. That was why she really wanted to watch. Darius stood by the window, his back to the opening. He already could clearly see the events unfolding in his mind.

"I really could use a drink," Rafficer answered. Young Darius nodded and turned to walk off.

"What kind?" he called. Rafficer's smile grew bigger.

"Come closer, and I'll tell you." Young Darius paused. Something about this was odd. He paused. If this was a friend of his, why couldn't he remember their drink of choice? Or even a name? The teenager turned and looked at Rafficer.

"Hey, I'm sorry, but what's your name again?" Young Darius questioned. Rafficer's smile vanished. Normally, humans only need the small push in the beginning to believe whatever he said. Somehow, Darius was fighting. The vampire almost snarled. He began to use his powers once again.

"Just forget that. Come here, and I'll tell you what I want to drink," Rafficer commanded. Young Darius resisted, but only for a moment. Then he shook the negative thoughts from his mind and walked toward Rafficer only a few steps before halting. Rafficer frowned. He beckoned the boy closer. Again, young Darius hesitated. Rafficer increased the amount of power he was giving off.

"If he keeps on commanding you...you won't turn correctly," Idona whispered. Now Darius was interested. As a human, he couldn't sense the compulsion. Now he could. Idona was right, though. If Rafficer kept on using all this power when he bit young Darius, then Darius shouldn't have been alive for this long.

"Closer," Rafficer stated again. Young Darius smiled this time. The boy was mere steps away from sitting on the vampire's lap.

"Isn't this close enough? I mean, this is just about a drink, right?" Young Darius questioned. Rafficer snarled. His power was almost at full strength. He wouldn't be able to keep this up much longer. Rafficer motioned with his fingers that young Darius still had to move closer. The teen frowned. Sighing deeply, he stepped closer. Now he was within arm's length of the vampire. This time, Rafficer smiled evilly. Young Darius noticed and started backing away, but it was too late. Rafficer jumped from his seat and grabbed young Darius's arms tightly in his hands. "Let me go!"

Rafficer's power surged as the teen struggled. Idona and Darius watched in shock as Rafficer extended his fangs and bit into the boy's neck. Young Darius screamed in pain. Rafficer tightened his grip and bit down harder than before. The poor boy's scream turned into a gurgle. Darius stiffened as he realized that Rafficer still had the compulsion going.

"How?" Idona muttered. "How did you turn correctly?"

Young Darius's sky-blue eyes began to roll back into his head. Rafficer was draining him too quickly. Idona leaned forward. If the vampire didn't stop soon, Darius was going to die before he fully turned. Beside her, the 652-year-old vampire watched on in horror. He couldn't believe that Rafficer turned him while under a compulsion. But even worse, Darius could see that his younger self was being drained too much. And the other vampire didn't seem like he was going to stop or even slow down.

"STOP!" Idona screamed as loud as she could. Darius wasn't sure it was going to change anything. Or if Rafficer would hear. As it was, this was a dream. Somehow, none of that seemed to matter. Rafficer stopped and turned to the window in shock. Idona and Darius barely moved into hiding by the time the vampire fully turned.

"Who's there?" Rafficer ordered. Idona and Darius didn't move. Though Darius felt the command, he didn't have to follow it. It felt different from the normal orders that Rafficer gave him and that was why he was able to resist. Idona looked at the vampire beside her. She was concerned that he would be forced to follow. So when nothing happened, she wondered what was going on. Did some type of magic transport them there or was it a dream? Was all this even real? "Show yourself!"

There was a loud crash. Idona stiffened and squeezed her eyes shut in fear. Darius turned away, not wanting to see what would happen next. Both waited for something to happen, but no one touched them. The crashing sounds continued, and the bitter sounds of battle screams joined in. Idona and Darius both opened their eyes. They noticed that they weren't at the little cottage anymore.

Around them was a huge battle. The surroundings were destroyed; Idona almost didn't realize they were in a warehouse. Darius was shocked to discover that he knew where they were.

"This is the battle just before I vanished! The battle before..." Darius stopped. Idona knew what he meant. She couldn't believe it any more than before. First, she was back in the past and now she was standing before the battle she had been reading in the book.

"Darius! How can this be happening?" Idona asked. Darius was unsure, so he didn't reply. The battle raged on before their eyes. Darius desperately searched for himself and Rafficer. After being at the cottage, the vampire really didn't want Rafficer noticing Idona or him. He was in luck. On the other side of the warehouse, Rafficer was attacking another Darius. Idona noticed the same thing. "Should we move closer?"

"Why?" Darius glanced curiously. She looked at the scene and decided that she didn't care what he thought. Idona felt that she needed to go over there before the situation was over. Looking around, she realized that she would need to skirt around the edge of the battle, which meant that she might not make it in time. Just before she went to move, Darius grabbed her hand. "I'll get us closer."

Idona was shocked. She didn't expect him to bring her closer to Rafficer and his other self, but here he was—dragging her across the battle's edge. At first, Darius was careful to make sure that Idona was following, but as someone's attack landed very close to the two of them, he sped up. Idona was so close to being dragged that he finally had to stop and pick her up. Using vampire speed, he was able to get them within listening distance and hide behind some unbroken crates. Once settled, Idona looked at Darius.

"Thanks," she whispered. He barely nodded. Now that they were closer, Darius noted that Rafficer was holding the other vampire a little differently than he had remembered. The older vampire was holding the second Darius by his shoulders rather than the throat.

"*Did you bring them all here, Daredevil?*" *Rafficer snarled. The second Darius shook his head. He technically didn't bring the others to the warehouse. All he did was open a few doors to allow them in. "Did you plan this?"*

"*No! Rafficer, stop this! You must find your true enemy!*" *the second Darius cried. Idona and Darius frowned. This Darius seemed to be begging his way out of this situation. Rafficer didn't seem to care.*

"*You helped them get in here, did you not?*" *Rafficer demanded. His power increased. The other Darius nodded. Idona gasped.*

"*This is when he'll kill you!*" *she called. Darius nodded. Even he could see that this was where it was heading. Rafficer snarled and looked at the battle.*

"*Are you pleased, Daredevil? Your friends are dying out there! And you are to blame!*" *the older vampire snapped. Shaking his head, the second Darius tried to sneak out of his master's hands. Rafficer gripped the other vampire tighter. He screamed in pain as the older vamp cut through skin with his nails. Idona tensed and looked at Darius. His eyes filled with anger. "Are you happy? I changed you into this amazing creature, and you want to destroy everything! After everything I've done for you!*"

"*Rafficer, stop!*" *the other Darius cried as he winced in pain. Rafficer growled, his fangs releasing. Idona whimpered. She didn't want to watch. Darius looked away from the other two and turned to Idona. When he noticed she had also looked away, he frowned.*

"*Watch,*" *he growled, somehow feeling as though they both should be.. Idona faced him before nodding. Both turned back to watch. Rafficer was red with rage. He turned to look at the battle raging around him. Rafficer noticed that his minions were beginning to fail. Slowly he turned back to Darius.*

"*You will suffer,*" *he snarled. The second Darius gasped as Rafficer dragged him away from the wall and spun him to face the battle. "All of you shall suffer this same fate! Death!*"

All eyes turned to the two vampires as Rafficer's grip shifted. He grabbed both sides of the other Darius's neck and spun it around sharply. With the vampire strength, Rafficer pulled the other's head right off the body. Idona cried out in shock. Darius was stunned to see what his master had planned on doing. The other vampires exchanged glances wondering if the rest of this battle was even worth it. Rafficer turned around. His green eyes narrowed as they landed on Idona and Darius.

"You," Rafficer barked before stepping toward the two. Darius backed away as Idona froze. How can he see us? Wasn't this supposed to be like in the movies? Idona thought. Rafficer closed in on them. He reached out and just barely touched Idona when...

CHAPTER 15

College

Idona woke up screaming. Minnie cried out in shock and jumped; it made the steering wheel spin and Darius tumbled with it. The HHR swerved across the road until the older girl regained control. Once back on track, chocolate-brown eyes looked around. Thankfully, there were no other cars nearby, which meant she hadn't put anyone's life in danger.

"Jeez, Idona, what the hell was that about?" Minnie screamed. Idona shook in fear. Her last memory of the dream was Rafficer reaching for her. She could still feel his fingertips just grazing her skin. Idona had no idea how to begin describing what she had seen. The entire dream was absurd, and didn't feel like a dream. *Was I really the one dreaming that?* Idona wondered. Slowly, Idona turned to look at Darius but Minnie caught her attention first. The girl was looking at her.

"I had a bad dream. That's all," Idona lied. Minnie frowned. *Did she really freak out over such a stupid thing? That was a really loud scream for a "bad" dream.* Minnie thought, and decided to watch the road. Idona sighed, thankful that Minnie wasn't pressing. However, the younger girl knew that Minnie wasn't asking more because she needed to pay attention to the road. Slowly, Idona snuck a peek back at Darius. He was sitting there, looking just as stunned as she felt. Feeling her gaze, Darius looked at her. Idona said nothing, but she did turn back.

"You know you could have gotten us killed?" Minnie suddenly accused. Idona half smiled. Of course, Minnie's freak out would be blamed on Idona. *So much for her not pressing.* Idona thought. Already the fear from the dream was beginning to fade. Idona knew it was going to bother her every now and then, but for now, Minnie's accusations were calming her. "You scared me half to death! And nearly got us run off the road."

"Sorry, Min. Just kind of a natural reaction," Idona explained. Minnie groaned. Idona just turned the guilt back onto her. Even she had woken up in a similar fashion once or twice. But nothing so far as screaming bloody murder. "I thought...I was...going to die."

"So, that made you scream? Who was going to...well, do it?" Minnie questioned slowly. Idona hesitated. In the back of the car, Darius shifted. He remembered Rafficer reached for Idona and then he woke up. Thinking back on it now, the vampire almost wondered if Idona had been in his dream rather than the other way around. Idona cringed; she didn't want to admit what really happened. Idona wanted to talk to Darius about it in private. There was a long pause as everyone waited for Idona to speak. Minnie shifted lanes and used that to sneak a peek at Idona. Seeing that the young girl didn't look ready to talk, Minnie spoke. "I've had some bad dreams in my life, but I've never woken up screaming in the way that you did. Hell, I'll jump, I'll sweat, I'll even shake, but not once like the way you just did."

"Look, I said I'm sorry. I got scared, so I screamed for help. Just so happened that when I went to scream, I woke up," Idona growled in anger. It took her a moment to realize how she sounded and winced. She hadn't meant to sound so harsh. "If I had known that I was going to wake up, I wouldn't have screamed. I did stop once I realized I had woken."

"In your dream, what made you scream?" Darius suddenly asked. Idona opened her mouth to respond but stopped. She did want to talk to Darius, but she didn't want to do it around Minnie. Unsure of how to respond with all that holding her back, Idona stayed quiet. Idona was also too afraid to hear if Darius had a similar dream. She still didn't want to know what was going on. Things were weird enough as it was.

"I...I can't really remember. It's all a little fuzzy. I just...just remember the fear," Idona again lied. Minnie nodded. Most of her dreams were similar in nature. At the end of the dream, she couldn't remember one bit of it. Darius, on the other hand, frowned. He could tell that Idona lied because of her trembling voice, a telltale sign of a lie. Looking into the rear-view mirror to see Idona's face, Darius realized that it was because of Minnie. Unexpectedly, the GPS suddenly called out a new turn.

"Finally, felt like I've been driving down this highway for decades!" Minnie cried in response. Idona laughed, now completely forgetting about the dream. Darius sighed. He had so much he needed to talk to Idona about. But, not even one of the things he wanted to talk about was okay to say in front of Minnie. The girl really was turning into a third wheel. Darius hoped that sometime tonight he could ask Idona everything without Minnie around to hear it. Now that the conversation had ebbed, Idona was stuck with her thoughts, and they all led back to the dream.

It had seemed so real, unlike her usual dreams. Much of what happened was something that she never knew about so she wondered if the dream was her own. How could she have known how Darius was changed? Nor could she have known about Darius's death. Then again, neither could Darius. *Come to think of it. During the dream, Darius seemed to* understand what was happening. It also seemed like he could control it. But, that's *impossible!* Idona thought. Sighing deeply, Idona wondered about the book. *Could it have the answer I need?* She turned to face Darius. He looked at her, confused.

"Can I have the book? I need to see something," Idona told him. Darius frowned deeply. He had just been thinking of glancing at it himself. Not wanting to start another fight, the vampire nodded. Since stopping at the hotel that night, the HHR had been rearranged. Idona's backpack, the one that held the book, was now sitting in the seat beside him. The book was in the front pocket. Yanking it out, Darius began to wonder why she would want it. *Was she looking for information on Rafficer? Or, could it have been about the dream?* Sky-blue eyes curiously gazed at sea-green eyes as the vampire handed the book over to the short girl. Idona took it and acted as if she didn't notice the questioning gaze since she didn't want to talk in front of Minnie. "Thanks."

Why am I keeping Minnie out of all the conversations? Is it because these are personal pieces of information? Am I just not as close as I used to be with Minnie? Idona thought.

"No problem," Darius responded. Idona turned back around and allowed the book to open itself. She had hoped that it would open to the page she needed. Luck was not on her side. When it opened, it actually did it to a brand new page. Idona fought to go back and read the rest. As the book began writing itself, the young girl realized that it was focused on Rafficer. *That was quick.*

"Flying sure does beat the days of travel in our world," called a pretty blonde girl. *Her lithe 5'4" frame bounced through the now private airplane. Shinning aquamarine eyes looked all over the place. The experience of being up in the air was so new and exciting to many of the young vampires under Rafficer's care. But Rafficer and a few of the older vamps that made it through to this new world didn't enjoy the flight.*

The young vamps and even those who were turned from this world were walking around the plane and enjoying their time. Very few humans from the flight were still alive. Rafficer enjoyed that part about this. Hundreds of human passengers locked up together with no escape. Easy meals. None of the older vampires really seemed to mind the flight until they hit some turbulence. The human pilots, who were left alive for the moment, mentioned that if the turbulence hit too hard, the plane could crash. As the pilots noticed that the older vamps began to panic, they told more and more horror stories about plane crashes. So now, Rafficer sat in his seat, gripping the arms rests as hard as he could. Serge stayed by him, almost like a protector.

"Sit down, Crystal," Rafficer ordered sharply. Crystal calmed for a moment before following the order. No one else followed the order, which ticked off Rafficer even more. He was getting sick and tired of their joy in technology. Since he was born in a time without technology, Rafficer didn't like any of these gadgets. None of this. Slowly, mostly the vampires passed Rafficer, and everyone began to take their seats. "How much longer!"

"Only ten more minutes till we prepare for landing, sir," Sam responded from his seat in front. He was in charge of keeping the pilots on track. Sam proved very useful due to his extensive knowledge. Since the takeover, Sam had been counting off every minute Rafficer asked for. However, the 721-year-old vampire did have a moment where he believed Sam's usefulness had run its course. That was when Sam and Serge mentioned that only the pilots could fly the plane. When the pilots went to turn the plane and Sam caught the betrayal, Rafficer let him live.

"Good," Rafficer snapped. He wanted to be off this tin can as soon as possible. Some of the new vampires thought it interesting that he feared flying. None of them had been up front with the pilots when they told their horror stories. Though they had encountered some turbulence, few seemed worried.

"Sir, do you really believe that Darius left a clue?" Serge questioned. The older vamp turned a sharp glare on the youngling. Seeing the glare, Serge almost wondered if it would have been better the stay quiet. Rafficer snarled. He refused to let his younglings know how much power he had. Serge didn't know that Rafficer could tell

all of younglings apart by scent. Nor did he know that his sire could smell this scent for days after the vamp had been at a place. Kathleen and Darius were the only two vampires alive who knew about this power. Too bad for Darius, there was no way around it.

"I will be able to find something. Don't worry about that," Rafficer replied. The plane jolted. Most of the vampires tensed but when nothing more happened, they all began to relax. Rafficer stayed tense. He just wanted the whole hell ride to end. The faster that happened, the better off for everyone.

"Just a few more minutes," Sam whined. Rafficer's eyes narrowed and he glared at the young vamp. As he was about to verbally assault Sam, a call came over the sound speakers. It said that everyone should sit, buckle up, and be prepared to land. Nodding his head, Rafficer leaned back. As a distraction, he decided to try to reach out to the few missing vampires on the east coast. More important, Kathleen.

Idona paused. She almost wondered if Rafficer's side of the book was aligned with their timeline. If it were so, Darius should be feeling Rafficer about now. The teen looked back at the vampire. He was glaring darkly at the back of her seat. Fearfully, she noted that his eyes were solid black. That meant that he felt his sire. Knowing that Rafficer could turn a search into a calling, Idona watched Darius's eyes. If they changed at all, she knew that she'd be forced to protect all three of them. She couldn't even begin to think of how she would do that yet.

Darius didn't notice that Idona was staring at him. He was focused on Rafficer. The vampire learned that if he wasted almost all of his power and energy, he could hide himself from his sire's searching. He didn't want to hide because he didn't want Rafficer to find out that he was capable of hiding. Also, he wanted to conserve energy—the first time he tried to do this, he had turned bloodthirsty.

Just as Darius was about the hit that mark again, Rafficer stopped. Sighing deeply, he looked back out the window. If Rafficer tried again,

Darius knew that he wouldn't be able to pull it off. He was out of energy. He was shocked to learn that he wasn't thirsty for blood despite the lack of energy. Sitting back and resting, Darius finally felt Idona's gaze. Sky-blue eyes turned to her. Sea-green eyes sparkled with concern. He gave her a half smile. It was the book that helped Idona know what happened. Though the book was useful, it was also a pain. It was a pain to be able to read Darius's thoughts and feelings—nothing could be kept from the book.

"Don't worry," Darius told her softly. Idona frowned; she couldn't help but worry. Darius could see that in her gaze and smiled. "He didn't sense me."

"Who didn't...wait, Rafficer? Do you mean Rafficer was sensing for you?" Minnie called, fear tinting her voice. Minnie had finished reading the books yesterday and was processing the information. Idona sat back correctly in her seat. Chocolate-brown eyes looked into the rearview mirror and focused on Darius. He nodded his head. "Oh great! I thought it was bad enough that he knew about our school!"

"Minnie, we talked about this. I already told you that Rafficer would be able to find us quickly. He had a lot of power since he has 721 years of experience, he knows how to use each power to his advantage," Idona cried. Minnie moaned and rolled her eyes. She really didn't want to hear about it.

"And you think I can remember all that? Or even worse that I wanted to?" Minnie snapped. Idona shook her head in dismay. She almost regretted bringing Minnie along. "Remember, Idona. I was the one who said we should abandon Darius and strike out on our own. If we did that in the first place, we wouldn't have had to worry about Rafficer finding us."

"I can protect you better this way. Besides, Rafficer is heading straight to your school. Would you have left if we didn't take you? Or do you think you could have forced yourself to stay away long enough?" Darius questioned back. Minnie stayed silent. Minnie would have stayed, and it would have been her downfall. No one wanted to bring that fact up. "I hid myself. Rafficer couldn't find me. We are in the clear."

"How long can you do that for?" Minnie responded. Darius turned his gaze away. Even Idona couldn't look at Minnie. The girl nodded. It was what she had assumed.

"I won't be able to do it again until I feed a few times. Many would have to be drained and I..."

"You can't!" Minnie nearly shouted. Darius nodded. He did not intend to feed off people. In the back of his mind, Darius knew he'd have to feed soon but he also didn't want to. As he thought about it even more, Darius realized that if he didn't feed off someone tonight, he'd be more a danger to the girls than Rafficer. Just one small nick of blood tonight and one of them could die.

"Minnie, don't worry about it. Remember what I said this morning?" Idona muttered. Minnie frowned. Darius examined their faces to find out what was going on, but their faces revealed nothing. Darius sighed and turned to the window again. He figured that the girls would tell him about their plan later. Idona looked back at the book. It had already flipped a couple of pages. When she looked back at it, the pages were mostly of Rafficer's gang getting off the plane, charting it again, renting a few cars, and then driving from the airport to the college. The rest of the pages where the conversation that they just had. Idona groaned loudly.

"So this is a school?" Serge again asked Sam. The young vamp nodded. Sam was the go-to person because he had studied many things, and until the vampires arrived, not many people cared about his knowledge. Now, since these vampires kept asking questions, Sam figured that he was important to the vampire clan. Almost as important as Rafficer himself. Too bad he hadn't met everyone in the clan. Serge, in the meantime, had been looking around. As they drove around the college in a circle a few times, Rafficer tried a limited sense for Darius and Sam told Serge all about the college. He showed the 70-year-old vampire where the edge of the college's property and talked a little about each building. "All these buildings hold classes? That is outstanding!"

"Actually, some are dormitories. You can tell the difference by the students coming and going," Sam replied. Serge and even Rafficer curiously looked at the youngling. Sam ruffled his dyed blonde hair. How could he explain what dorms were to them? "Dorms are housing for the students who don't have a place to stay nearby. They are like apartments except that they are on school property. Most dorms are cheaper and nicer than apartments offered in the area."

"We'll try one of those first. Darius would have needed to feed at one point, even with his extremely childish views on the subject," Rafficer told the two before Serge could ask about apartments. In their world, apartments didn't really exist. They had small houses, which weren't much cheaper than buying one's own house. Serge looked at Rafficer and noticed his sire was looking at a few of the buildings. Sighing deeply, the young vamp looked around as well.

Meanwhile, Sam looked nervous. Having been to a college once before, he remembered all the security on campus. Sam thought of his now deceased daughter, Vanessa. He remembered the time when he brought her to college; at one point he left the dorm without her to get some food. Going to get the food was easy enough, but returning to his daughter's room was hard. The guard on the lobby floor of the dorm didn't let him leave. He had to call his daughter's cell phone to get her to come down and sign him in. Rather annoying as he was visiting when they were still moving in. It was then that he learned that he could never do a surprise visit. With the school having ID cards for every student and a set of keys for the dorm buildings and for the student's room, it was hard to prove that you belonged if you didn't have keys or an id card.

"Getting into a dorm may be really hard, sir. Dorms have a rather large amount of security," Sam cried, forgetting the abilities that vampires have. Rafficer said nothing. He was getting a little sick and tired of Sam's naiveté. The youngling's knowledge of this new land was the only thing keeping him alive. But, Rafficer also noted that Sam knew that fact. It made the vamp cocky. Soon, Rafficer would prove that all he needed was the knowledge in Sam's head, not the youngling's body. "A guard may ask too many questions!"

"Easy, boy. Don't fret," Serge growled, noticing Rafficer's anger. Though, at this point, even he was getting annoyed with Sam. "We've got that handled."

Sam frowned but nodded. He was a little unsure of how it would happen but he trusted Serge, a fact that he might later learn to regret. For now though, Sam knew he should follow Rafficer. So the three began to look around. As Serge had noted earlier, it was hard to see which building was a dormitory. But Sam was looking for something else. He was looking for students pausing in the doorway to the building, giving them just enough time to unlock it. He spotted two buildings. One was a set of towers, and the other was a shorter but wider building. The towers looked like a good bet, but Sam kept gazing at the other building. Something about it kept drawing him over there. Nodding, he decided that building would be the best.

"Over there. That building is a dorm. I've spotted another one just in case that one's wrong. And there should be a third or even forth somewhere else. Lots of students means lots of dorms," Sam called, as he continued to point to the small dorm off in the distance. Rafficer didn't waste a second. He quickly walked toward it. Serge was by his side in an instant. Rafficer barely noticed. That was how it was supposed to be. Sam gasped in shock. He had no idea how Serge did it. How had the vamp gotten to their sire's side so quickly? It took a minute longer before Sam noticed that he was falling behind. Rafficer and Serge were not waiting for him. At this point though, he'd have to run just to catch up. Thankfully, Sam caught up just in time. There was *a student leaving the dorm as Rafficer and Serge hit the top of the stairs. The young human held the door open for the three vamps before he scampered off to classes.*

Inside, Sam noticed a desk off to the right. More students came around the left corner of the entryway. Rafficer figured that was the way up. Behind the desk, popped up a head. It was a student guard. He was looking for their IDs. The old vamp wasn't paying any attention. His green eyes were focused on the rest of the building. The student stood up even further.

"IDs?" the student asked. Rafficer huffed and focused on the guard. He was pleasantly surprised to see it was a female. That meant that Serge could handle everything. Then he was distracted once again. When he huffed, he caught a familiar scent. Darius had been here at least two days ago. Just about near the end of Rafficer's ability. Rafficer frowned but began to follow the scent. It was coming from the same path the students were walking. The 721-year-old stepped forward and noticed two sets of metal doors. These were elevators, or that was what Sam had told him before. Pleased, Rafficer headed off toward the elevators. The female guard jumped around the desk and got in the vamps' way. "Excuse me! I need to see your IDs, or you need to call the student you are here to visit."

"We've shown you our IDs already," Serge quickly commanded, stepping up beside Rafficer. The girl wasn't convinced. Serge used some more of his power. Her eyes glazed over for a second but she caught herself and glared at Serge. Rafficer frowned. For the past day or so, he began noticing it took more and more power to command the people of this world. Slowly, he added his own power to Serge's. As he added more and more, the girl fell deeper and deeper into their commands. Once it fully hit, she nodded and backed away.

"That's amazing," Sam whispered as Rafficer and Serge rushed past the girl. They reached the elevator just as Sam started moving. Serge hit the up button. Having dealt with these things before, Serge and Rafficer didn't seem too bothered by them. Rafficer stood there staring at both doors. He wondered if Darius had been in both of the elevators. If not, then he'd have to wait around for the other one. Lucky for him and unlucky for Darius and the girls, the 652-year-old had been in both elevators.

They only had to wait less than a minute before the door to the left opened. The three piled on. Rafficer's senses overloaded for a moment. There were so many scents. It took him a moment to pick out Darius's scent. Once he had it, he nodded to Serge. As Sam hit the top floor's button, Serge leaned in and pushed every other one. Rafficer smiled at Sam's shocked look. "Do we really need to stop at every floor?"

"How else can we tell if Darius was on one of them? We need to stop so that we don't waste more time going up all the way and then being forced to go all the way back down," Serge countered. Sam frowned but nodded. The elevator headed up. First floor, nothing. Second floor, same thing. Third floor, nothing. The routine was repeated until the doors opened and Darius's scent continued out there. Rafficer quickly exited. Serge and Sam followed just before the doors closed on them. The scent led Rafficer and his followers straight to the girl's room. Rafficer nodded at the door. Serge smiled and reached forward to try to open the door. For some reason he figured it might have been unlocked. He was wrong.

CHAPTER 16

New Plan

*S*am noticed the photos on the door. There was a white board as well. A long line of black ink separated the board into two distinct parts. One was labeled "Notes for Minnie" and the other was "Notes for Idona." A large "Where are you two? - Sue" was written across the board. Sam frowned and looked up. On the top of the door were two tags that were similar to the ones on the doors down the hall. They read "Idona" and "Minnie." Two girls lived in this room together. Two more girls that Rafficer would kill if they weren't already dead. But what was worse, there could even be a third girl who isn't involved in any of this. Just like his poor little Vanessa. It was now that Sam wished he hadn't met his sire.

"Kick it down," Rafficer ordered. Serge nodded. It had been his intention the whole time. Just barely using his vampire strength, Serge kicked the door in. The lock snapped and part of the doorframe splintered, and the door was now open. All down the hall, more doors began to open and students began to look around. They were curious about the noise. Rafficer and Serge entered the room before a student could clearly see them. Sam stood outside for a moment longer. He noticed all the students and frowned. Slowly, he also entered the room and tried to close the door. It was very damaged and refused to remain shut. Frowning, Sam decided to leave it. Turning his attention to the room, the vampire realized that it was mostly empty. One side had only a bunch of books and sheets on the bed. The other side looked a little lived in.

But there wasn't enough stuff in the room to indicate that both girls were still there. Rafficer could tell that the people who had lived there had packed up and left quickly. Frowning, the 721-year-old focused on the more lived side of the room.

Photos plastered the wall. They caught his attention. But one in particular drew the vampire close. It was a photo of three girls. One girl, to the left, had brunette hair and violet eyes. The middle girl had chocolate-brown eyes and long curly blonde hair. And the last girl had dark chocolate-brown hair but her eyes were closed, so Rafficer couldn't see the color. He snatched the picture off the wall. It was the only one with all three girls. Flipping it around, the old vampire noted the handwriting. Sue, Idona, and me, 2006. Friends forever. *Rafficer turned around. The door was closed. Frowning, he walked over and opened it. There, he noted the tags on the door read the same as one of the names on the paper. Looking down, he noticed the white board. Sue had left a note. That meant the "me" was Minnie. The vamp smirked.*

"You never learn do you, Daredevil?" he muttered. Serge looked at the photo as well. Noticing the two girls, he smiled just as large. Sam frowned as he looked at the wall of photos. Many showed the three girls separately. Not together like the one Rafficer held. But one thing remained the same. The blonde-haired girl was in every photo. It took him a moment more to realize the name Rafficer mentioned. Sam turned to face the two vamps.

"Daredevil?" Sam asked. Serge faced him.

"Darius. The one we've been looking for. He must be with these girls."

"Oh."

"We'll get nothing else from here. They left in a hurry. Probably with no plan. We're at a standstill until I sense for him again. And I'm going to wait. Maybe by then he'll have stopped moving," Rafficer told the two. Nodding his head once again, Rafficer turned to leave. Someone blocked his path. He wore a dark blue uniform, similar to that of a police officer. Serge stepped forward, blocking the "officer" from being able to reach Rafficer. Sam stepped away from all of them. He didn't want to

*be part of a battle. The 721-year-old vampire frowned deeply. All these little dis-
tractions were becoming a pain.*

"Who are you?" *the officer called. Rafficer shook his head. He had no time to
deal with this. The old vampire snapped and forced every ounce of his power into
a mental shove and threw it at the officer. The amount of power tossed the man out
into the hall and harshly slammed him into the opposing wall. They all watched
and waited as the officer fell unconscious and slowly began to slump down. Rafficer
smiled and walked out of the room, heading quickly toward the exit.*

Idona slapped the book closed. *At least Raff has no idea where we
are headed. Thank god, there was no clue left behind at the school. Now...*Idona
thought. *Now he knows what we look like.* All the advantage that they once
had was slowly drifting away. Rafficer will soon find out where they
were headed. All he had to do was call out to Kathleen. Once they
meet up, she'd tell him where they were headed, and it'd all be over.
With that large plane they chartered, Rafficer could catch up to them
no matter how large of a head start they had. Idona almost wondered
if they would be better off not going to New Orleans. They could just
make it seem like they are still on the path there. Then she remembered
Sue. They had just sent her to New Orleans. It would be horribly wrong
to leave her there by herself. Sue had no clue what was going on. *But if
we change course now...never head into New Orleans...would that protect her? Or
would Rafficer want to find her as well?*

"Idona? What is Rafficer doing?" Darius suddenly asked. He sat
further up in his seat. Closing her sea-green eyes, Idona sighed and
looked over her left shoulder at Darius. Her eyes focused on Darius's
face and what she saw frightened her. It looked like Rafficer had tried
sensing for him again. This time, he would have been successful. Idona
frowned and thought back. Rafficer had been working on leaving the
school, not sensing for anyone.

"Last I read he was in my dorm room. He uh...just found a photo of Minnie, Sue, and me. It was on Minnie's wall of photos. From that photo and names tags outside our door, he's learned our names," Idona told him. Now it was Darius's turn to sigh deeply, though it sounded more like a groan. Minnie frowned. She really didn't like the sound of what Idona described. Taking a quick glance at Idona's face, Minnie noticed that she also didn't like that idea.

"That's not good. I was hoping to use his lack of knowledge. It would have been easy to play you two off as a food source," Darius muttered. Idona had been planning the exact same thing. With that option out of the bag, Idona didn't know what to do. Not only was she trying to protect herself from Rafficer, she needed to protect Minnie, Sue and even Darius. "It won't take him long to realize where we are headed."

"We can't turn around now! I've been driving all day! We're only a few hours away!" Minnie cried. Idona nodded. She agreed with both Minnie and Darius. She was thinking about the same idea.

"We have to stop in New Orleans. I suggest we just stay one night. We can gather our wits and make a new plan," Idona stated, forgetting to mention picking up Sue. Minnie sighed and looked at the GPS. It still read about two hours away from the city. Chocolate-brown eyes then turned to the speedometer. She had been going the exact speed limit the whole trip, but if she went five miles per hour faster than that, she would be able to cut down the time. Heck, if she wasn't afraid of cops catching her, she could go even faster.

"How long does it take to get to New Orleans by other means of travel?" Darius questioned. He remembered the phone conversation with Sue. Though he hadn't been there for most of it, he thought he heard that she'd arrive before them even if she hung around the college for a while. Idona and Minnie tensed when they realized that Rafficer would be there in the same amount of time it would take them. But

Idona knew that Rafficer had a private jet, so he wouldn't have to wait for plane times.

"Around two to three hours. Maybe less. Rafficer has a private jet. All he had to do is board and state his destination. But, he still has a little while to get from the school to the airport," Idona responded. They hoped that traffic would stall him. Darius frowned. Even though Idona didn't state the rest of that, he could tell that that was what was going to save them.

"If that's true, Rafficer could be in New Orleans within an hour or two of our own arrival. It's not a good idea to go there. We should just pull over now and come up with a plan. The more time we waste going to New Orleans, the easier it will be for Rafficer to get a clue of where we are going to next," Darius growled. Idona almost screamed in frustration. Everyone had their own points. Points that good either sealed their doom or saved them. Each plan was good and depended on many things going their way. If even one thing went wrong in any of the plans, it would ruin everything. But there was one major downfall in Darius's plan.

"Sue's waiting for us in New Orleans. We at least have to go and pick her up," Minnie suddenly mentioned. Darius growled angrily. He really didn't want to go to New Orleans. That was the last place he wanted to visit now. But he also didn't want to leave Sue there. She had no idea that Rafficer was on his way there. Nor did she know that he recognized her. Darius didn't want anyone else getting hurt because of him. The vampire knew he'd have to give into Rafficer soon.

"Fine. There doesn't seem to be any other option but going to that city. Just know that we can't stay long. The faster we leave, the better off we'll be," Darius finally told all of them. Idona and Minnie nodded. They agreed with him. It would be better off. Too bad that his plan wouldn't work.

"Darius, I know you don't sleep but...we're going to need to rest for the night. Sue's gonna be tired, and Idona and I are going to need to rest in an actual bed. Never mind we need to stock up on some real food. Most of what we took from the other hotel is already gone," Minnie stated. Darius frowned. He had forgotten that he was the one who argued about them resting the night before. He had also forgotten that they needed to eat actual food. Idona moaned. She did agree with Darius more than she agreed with Minnie now. Though the girls needed rest and food, they didn't need to spend the night in New Orleans.

"We'll talk to Sue. If she's too tired, then we'll stop for the night. But if she can drive or even stay awake, and then we'll head off. Where? I don't know. Maybe we'll stop and get some dinner or something and make plans then. But for now, the new plan is to go pick up Sue," Idona told Minnie and Darius. They both nodded. Each one could tell that Idona was trying to find common ground. They hoped that their agreement would work to their favor. Darius sat back in his seat. Though they had a plan, Rafficer was on the move now. Suddenly the vampire realized that he should be watching Rafficer.

"In the meantime, you're gonna call Sue and find out where she is, okay? I can fix the GPS to the new location," Minnie mentioned. Idona hung her head. She hated talking on the phone. It was just one of her pet peeves. The main reason was that most people couldn't understand her on it. At times, Idona felt that once someone picked up the line on the other end they lost all normal brain function. But knowing that the call had to be made, Idona sighed and looked around. As she reached for her phone, Darius leaned forward again. The book was just about within his reach. He snaked his arm around Idona's seat and snatched the book. Idona looked at him, surprise all over her face.

"I'll follow Rafficer as best as I can," he informed her. Giving him a relieved smile, Idona yanked her cell phone out of her pocket. She hadn't really thought about the book. He was right though. Someone did need to watch Rafficer. If only to make sure he didn't get on a plane faster than Minnie and Idona first estimated. Sighing, Idona turned back and began to dial Sue. The other girl picked it up on the second ring.

Darius stopped paying attention to Idona once she said "hello." He knew that Minnie and Idona could handle planning the meeting with Sue. With that in mind, Darius flipped open the book. Quickly scanning the words, he noticed that it was focusing on Rafficer. But he was speaking to someone. Flipping back a few pages, Darius found where it switched from the girls and him to Rafficer. It started with him leaving the school grounds.

Rafficer got into his private car. The driver was beginning to look a little nervous. Maybe he heard over the radio that there was an attack. Rafficer didn't even care. But it could have caused an issue later on. Serge stepped into the car after him and Sam sat in the front passenger seat. Once all the doors were closed, the driver looked at Sam.

"Well?" the man asked. Sam frowned.

"Back to the airport," Sam replied. The driver nodded and quickly started the vehicle. Sam turned to look at Serge. "That is where we're going, right?"

"Yes. We may stop once or twice. But that is the final destination," Serge muttered. Sam sighed deeply. He was surprised that he had actually guessed right. It was the first time he had done so since meeting Rafficer. With that done, Sam turned around. Relief flooded him. Knowing that Rafficer might not need him for a while, Sam shifted, trying to get comfortable. In the back, Serge looked at his sire. He knew the old vampire enough to know what he wanted. But there were times that Serge was wrong. Since Rafficer didn't interject Serge's response, the younger vamp assumed he was right.

Beside the young vamp, Rafficer grumpily looked out the car window. Something *was off.* Yes, Darius would know that he'd have to leave the school. But why would he bring the girls? *Rafficer thought. Darius was smart, but Rafficer didn't give the younger one enough credit to actually know what he was going to do. Frowning, Rafficer wondered what was going on. He needed to figure out what was going on in Darius's head. Since he couldn't read Darius's thoughts, Rafficer had to think of another way. That was when he realized one.*

Closing his eyes tightly, Rafficer forced himself to focus. Finding this particular vampire was harder on the old vampire as compared to finding others. He wanted to send a call out to Kathleen, but she also had an ability to hide herself from him. Rafficer sent out a powerful call to her asking her to come to him quickly.

"Sir? Did you just send out a call?" *Serge suddenly questioned. Rafficer opened his eyes and faced his underling. It amazed the old vamp that, at times, some of the younglings could feel him send out a call to others. He almost wondered if he had turned them differently than the others or if they were somehow different when they were humans. The latter of the ideas made Rafficer half wonder if humans themselves were different from each other. And if that were true, that would explain a little bit about each vampire having a unique ability.*

"Yes. I'm going to call Kathleen to me," *Rafficer responded. Serge frowned. He had a feeling that Rafficer actually didn't need Kathleen. It had the potential to prove useful, but since they were on the move it didn't matter.*

"Are you going to waste all your energy by calling her every few minutes?" *Serge wondered aloud. Rafficer groaned. He hadn't really thought about it. Yes, they were traveling and Rafficer was calling as though he was in a fixed position. He got the idea to try to call Kathleen but give a destination that was different from his current location. Rafficer had done that before with lesser vampires. But since Kathleen was as strong as him, Rafficer wondered if he'd be able to do it. With nothing more to lose, Rafficer sent out the new call, telling Kathleen to meet him at the airport where his private jet was waiting. Now all Rafficer could do was hope that it worked and continue down the path he was on.*

Rafficer leaned against his window and began to drift off. It wasn't that he was sleeping—he just kept losing consciousness. He wasn't the only one who did. Everyone, outside of the driver, also did the same. As all three vampires drifted in and out, the car rattled down the road, getting closer and closer to the airport. Hours passed, until finally the driver pulled into the airport and parked the car. The still and now silent engine stirred the vamps.

"We've made it," the driver told them. Sam reached into his back pocket as though he was going to pay the man. Rafficer took a deep breath before opening his door and exiting the car. Serge leaned forward in his seat. His mouth sitting right in the open space between the driver and Sam. Surprised, Sam looked at the older vamp.

"Sam, get out," Serge ordered. Sam paled. Knowing that he'd regret it if he stayed, Sam slowly nodded and opened his door.

"It'd be easier to just simply pay him, you know that right?" Sam asked. Serge smiled slyly. Knowing now that he'd never be able to change the other vampires with him, Sam just shook his head and got out of the car. Just before he pushed the door, the young vampire heard the snarl from Serge as he turned and attacked the driver. Sam walked away, knowing the once clear windows were becoming drenched in red blood. When he caught up to Rafficer, he said nothing. Rafficer's look said it all. The old one was getting sick of dealing with his naiveté. Sam was beginning to feel like he may not last much longer.

"Driver being dealt with?" Rafficer inquired. Sam nodded. Sighing, Rafficer walked closer to Sam. "You understand why he must die, correct?"

"I'm not fully positive," Sam admitted. Rafficer nodded.

"He's seen us. That's all," Rafficer answered, a smile spreading across his face. Sam frowned. He didn't like that answer at all. If Rafficer continued to either kill or change every human they come across, being with them was going to get very dangerous.

"RAFFIE!" cried a loud female voice. Rafficer winced and looked across the parking lot. Coming out from a black Camaro, Kathleen raced forward. Behind her was a muscular boy who looked a lot younger than he actually was. One good look at him though, Rafficer was shocked. This boy with forest-green eyes and dirty blonde hair was a vampire. A day old vampire. Kathleen had turned him. That made Rafficer angry. He forbid Kathleen from turning humans without letting him know. Yet, here was a boy whom she had turned.

"Kathleen! Who the hell is that?" Rafficer screamed. Kathleen froze. She had forgotten about Marc. Slowly, she turned and noticed that he was walking toward her. His forest-green eyes angrily focusing on Rafficer. Kathleen slowly began to curl up into a defensive position. She didn't want to be in between the two vampires when they started their territorial battle. "KATHLEEN!"

"Kathleen!" Marc called at the exact same time. Kathleen curled up even more. "Who is that? Kathleen!"

CHAPTER 17

Rafficer vs. Marc

*S*narling, Rafficer rushed forward. Using vampire speed, he slipped right by Kathleen and caught Marc's left cheek with a punch. Marc took two steps backward, recovering his balance. He glared at Rafficer. Rafficer showed his teeth. Marc didn't back down. He also streaked his teeth and gave a growl to boot. Marc then began to turn, as though he was going to leave, but instead lifted his right leg and roundhouse kicked Rafficer. One thing about vampires was that they didn't dodge. Rafficer took the blow directly into his left ear.

"Stop!" Kathleen cried out. Rafficer gave a dark laugh. Marc's kick didn't even make him move one step. The kid was too weak. Ignoring Kathleen, Rafficer sent his right fist directly into Marc's gut. Marc coughed as the punch knocked out all the air from his lungs. Growling, he went to do a roundhouse kick in the opposite direction. "MARC!"

Rafficer smiled and caught Marc's leg with one hand. Kathleen screamed as Rafficer gripped the leg between his hands. There was a loud crack and Marc cried out in pain. Rafficer had snapped his leg in two. As the old vamp dropped Marc's leg to the ground, Marc lost his balance and fell. The day-old vamp glared at Rafficer. He knew he'd heal. But more than likely, once he did, it would too late.

"Rafficer, stop! We need him!" Kathleen called out, hoping that it would stop him. Rafficer paused for a second. Shaking his head, Rafficer looked at her.

"I already know. Darius is with two girls. They are down south," Rafficer told her. Kathleen paled. She had thought that Marc's information about the girls would save him. But if Rafficer already had the information, then there was nothing that could save the human now.

"Darius? You mean that guy with Idona?" Marc snarled. Rafficer looked at the boy. The name he had mentioned was one of the names of the girls from the room at the college. That meant he did know them. But Rafficer didn't know how well. Could he risk destroying the boy if he actually knew the girls well enough to know where they were going. Growling, Rafficer backed away.

"What do you know of this...Idona?" Rafficer questioned. Marc struggled to sit up. Surprise on his face. Why does this old coot want to know about Idona? Marc wondered briefly. It almost made him not want to answer. As his eyes gazed over at Kathleen, he noticed the fear in her eyes. Marc began to think it might be better if he simply answered. But something still held him silent. "Well? What do you know of this girl?"

"Marc told me before that she and Darius plan on going to a city called New Orleans. I don't know what they plan on doing there...but from what I understand, there is a good reason for them choosing that city," Kathleen answered for her youngling. Rafficer snarled and looked down at Marc. He hated when people made others answer questions for them. But then again, he never minded when someone did it for him.

"New Orleans...I already knew that. Anything else?" Rafficer snarled. Kathleen grimaced. She knew he had lied. He hadn't known about New Orleans. But Rafficer survived by lying. Rafficer used his age and power as an intimidation technique. "If you don't, I might as well kill you now."

"Idona and Minnie know about all of you. Minnie claimed it was from a book. Idona is a big reader...she must have owned the book from long before," Marc quickly called. Rafficer focused on Kathleen. If the kid is telling the truth, then these humans know what we are. But how much do they really know about us? *Rafficer thought to himself. Seeing in her eyes that Marc might actually be telling the truth, the old vamp looked back.*

"What do you know about this book?"

"I don't pay attention to what she read! Wait...I may know. I remember a book...from when we first met. She said she was re-reading it...Project...Something or other...I can't really remember," *Marc informed Rafficer. Rafficer sighed. He was getting somewhere now. But was it going to be enough? Rafficer stepped forward and grabbed the front of Marc's shirt. Lifting him off the ground, green eyes glared into forest-green eyes. Awakening his power, Rafficer stared.*

"What was the name of the book Idona was re-reading?" *Rafficer commanded. Marc's forest-green eyes went a little hazy as his body slumped into Rafficer's hand. The youngling easily fell under the compulsion. Kathleen twitched. This was getting hard to watch. She always hated watching Rafficer try to command information from someone.*

"Project Old Life. It's part of a series," *Marc responded. Rafficer frowned. He had never heard of anything like that. Dropping Marc onto the ground, Rafficer turned away. Kathleen now stood by Sam. Behind them, Serge, still cleaning himself off, was walking up to them. Rafficer gave them all a rather large smile.*

"We are heading to New Orleans," *Rafficer told them all. Serge nodded, and before fully walking toward Kathleen and Sam's side, he turned back around. Sam faced Serge and slowly began to follow. Meanwhile, Kathleen walked toward Marc and Rafficer. Rafficer glared at her, prepared to fight if she wanted to pick one.*

"I didn't get into the series. But the book was about a vampire named Rafficer," *Marc continued. Rafficer turned to the youngling.*

"Shut up," *he snapped. As Kathleen passed by Rafficer's side, he looked at her.* "We'll speak of your betrayal, later."

With that, Rafficer walked away. Kathleen stopped by Marc's side. The new vampire's leg had almost already healed. It was good news. She hadn't wanted him to travel with a damaged leg. Rafficer didn't like any signs of weakness. Marc looked up at her, confusion and sadness hidden deep in his eyes. Kathleen snarled. She did take after Rafficer's disapproval of weakness. But she knew that Marc was valuable. It was the main reason she broke her word with Rafficer.

"Come on. We have to go," Kathleen snarled at Marc. He looked shocked. She had been so sweet to him before. Now suddenly he was seeing her dark side. Thinking back to the accident that would have killed him, Marc realized he didn't really have any option but to follow her. Groaning not at his limited options but really at the pain, Marc slowly began to get up.

"Why does that guy want to know about Idona?" Marc suddenly inquired. Kathleen paused. Sighing, she looked away.

"He actually wants the man with her. Darius. He ran away from us. And Rafficer doesn't like that. The girls are just in the way," Kathleen answered. Marc nodded. He knew from the first moment that he met Darius that he was dangerous. Now he just needed to convince Idona before she got hurt. "Come on. Let's just go. Rafficer is waiting for us, and he doesn't like being kept waiting."

Darius suddenly became aware of the world outside the book when he couldn't hear the HHR's engine. Shocked, he looked up. Both girls were looking back at him. Minnie had a slight smile on her face. Almost as though she knew something that he didn't. Frowning, Darius focused on Idona. She looked worried. It was strange that she looked so worried. She almost looks as worried as I feel. But, how can she? Is there something that I'm missing? Darius shook the thoughts from his head.

"We're gonna go and get some dinner. Do you want to come in with us?" Minnie questioned. Darius looked back and forth between the girls. He looked to see if either of them left a clue as to whether they wanted him to come or not. Neither one really seemed to show any sign. Darius sighed. He had no idea what to say. "Sue should be meeting us sometime soon. She's gonna try and get here before we finish eating."

"Okay...then I'll go in with you," Darius told her. Minnie nodded and started to get out of the car. Idona stayed still, getting Darius to focus on her. She looked like she wanted to say something important, but she was holding back. Just as Darius went to ask Idona about it, Minnie leaned back into the car.

"Come on. I'm starving!" she informed them. Idona looked at her, the worry on her face relaxing into humor.

"You're always hungry," Idona joked. Minnie laughed and backed out of the car. As she closed the door, Idona also began to get out. Darius stayed seated for a moment longer. He still wondered what she was thinking about. Darius was determined to ask her about it. Slowly, he got out of the car.

With everyone out of the car, Minnie locked it and headed for the restaurant. Idona followed close behind. Darius again paused. He looked down at the side mirror on the HHR. His eyes were still sky-blue but he could feel the need for blood. Frowning, the vampire wondered if his eyes were ever going to change back like last time. Shaking the idea from his head, Darius wandered off after the girls.

Inside, Darius stopped. He hadn't been in a restaurant like this before. The main entrance was set up similar to a store of some sort. It was filled with all types of different things. Forgetting the store area, Darius wondered where the dining room was. Looking around he finally spotted Idona waving to him. Minnie was not by her side. Rushing over, Darius spotted a secondary room filled with tables, chairs, and other guests. That was the actual dining room. Darius smiled.

"Ready?" Idona asked. Darius nodded. Together the two headed into the dining room. Way in the back corner, all by herself, sat Minnie. When she noticed the two coming her way, she waved. Idona waved back and rushed forward. As Darius drew closer, he noticed that Minnie was sitting on one side of the table and Idona was heading for the other. The only two other available seats were right next to either girl. He'd have to choose whom to sit next to. The choice was made easy when Idona looked back at him. She patted the seat beside her, a clear indication that he was to sit there. Nodding, he joined the girls.

"So, can you actually eat real food?" Minnie questioned as she looked down at the menu before her. Darius sighed. Technically, he could, but he really didn't like to. Food in his lifetime in the book world had changed since he was last human, so now most of the food actually made him sick. Darius simply shook his head. Minnie frowned. *So much for making this seem normal.* Minnie thought. As she tried to forget what was going on, she lifted her menu. She was really hungry and there was a lot on the menu that she liked eating. Idona also frowned.

"Speaking of eating, we need to figure out what we are going to do," Idona muttered. Darius looked at her. She slowly lifted the menu before her. Minnie groaned, dropping her menu back onto the table.

"Please, not while I'm here!" she cried. Darius looked between the two girls.

"Figure out what?" he inquired. Idona ignored Minnie and focused on the vampire beside her. She knew this wasn't going to be an easy topic to talk about. Letting out a deep breath, Idona began to speak. Just before a sound came out of her mouth, Idona noticed movement at the edge of her vision. She turned to look and noticed a waiter coming over. Closing her mouth, Idona faced forward again. Minnie looked over the top of her menu to see why Idona didn't speak. Darius took a deep breath and turned to face the table.

"Hello, my name is Jeremy. I'll be your waiter for tonight. Can I interest you in a drink?" the waiter asked. Minnie put her menu down and faced Jeremy.

"I'm all set to order. How 'bout you Idona?" Minnie mentioned. Idona nodded. Jeremy smiled and took out a notepad and pen. Darius drifted off into his own thoughts. He was worried about Rafficer catching up to them, he was worried about the need to consume blood soon and he was worried about whatever had been bothering Idona. The vampire was caught up in his own thoughts that he missed both girls ordering and Jeremy asking what he wanted a few times. Idona finally nudged his side. Jerking into awareness, Darius looked at Idona before finally focusing on Jeremy.

"Water," was all Darius said. Jeremy frowned but nodded and jotted it down on the pad before walking away. There was a long pause as everyone waited to be certain that no one would return to the table. Once certain, Idona shifted in her chair to face Darius. Minnie quickly stood.

"I'll be in the restroom," she informed them. Darius raised an eyebrow at the comment but nodded nonetheless. Idona also nodded, barely even paying attention to her. As the taller girl began to walk away, Idona placed her hand on Darius's right arm as a way to call attention to herself. Shocked, sky-blue eyes focused on sea-green ones.

"You need blood. And even though your eyes aren't showing it, I can tell you need it soon, if not now," Idona told him. Darius growled very lightly as a way to show his displeasure. Idona brushed it off. She had known this wasn't going to be easy. "You should continue to feed from me."

"No." The vamp said and Idona glared.

"Darius..." Darius shook his head. When he was done, he looked away from her.

"No."

Idona could tell now that he was getting mad. She really didn't care. The longer Darius went without feeding, the worse it would be. Darius, meanwhile, was focusing on anything other than Idona. He didn't want to hear this.

"You have——" Idona began.

"No. We should focus on something else. Like how about Rafficer coming to New Orleans?" Darius interrupted. Idona filed that information away silently. She was worried, but Darius needing blood now was more important. Since Idona wasn't going to change topics, Darius growled lightly. He wasn't going to listen to this stupid idea anymore. Slowly, he began to stand. Idona grabbed his arm. She caught it and held him still.

"How else are you going to get it?" she questioned. Darius glared at her weak hand. He knew that if he simply jerked his arm away, he could leave. But he stayed.

"Any other way," he said and lightly pulled his arm free. Idona stood as Darius began to walk away.

"And if you attack Minnie?" she asked and Darius froze. He had thought of that before. But he didn't want to drink from Idona. "What about Sue? Or someone else?"

Darius sighed. Idona was winning this battle. She had great points. Points that Darius himself had tried to argue against before. Even knowing that Idona was going to win, Darius still tried fighting her ideas. He didn't want to drink from her again, but it was too dangerous for him to drink from anyone.

"I can't do that," Darius finally admitted. Idona frowned.

"Can't do what? Attack Minnie or Sue?"

"Drink any more from you," Darius answered. Idona paused. She wished she didn't hear the lust in the vampire's voice, but it was there.

As much as Darius said he didn't want to drink from her, Idona could tell that he actually did. Slowly she turned and sat back down. Darius hesitated. He wondered what she was going to say now. There was no way that he won the fight.

Idona sighed. Her eyes shifted slightly to see if Darius was watching her. He was indeed. That was good for her. In the blink of an eye, Idona grabbed for her knife and sliced a bit of her hand. Blood began to pour freely from the wound. Darius stiffened at the scent. He couldn't believe she had just done that. Especially in such a public place. Her sea-green eyes were focused on him. But Darius was watching her hand. He was short of breath. Idona raised her hand closer to him, making the vampire snarl. Darius moved closer, dropping into the seat beside her. He couldn't fight his hunger any longer. Then a cell phone began to ring.

Pulling her bleeding hand from a hungry vampire, Idona reached for her cell phone. Sue was calling her. Idona moaned in displeasure. And when her sea-green eyes focused on Darius, she could see that he was in pain as well. Having the blood so close to him, yet not being able to even taste it was almost like being dipped in acid and then set on fire.

"It's Sue," Idona explained. Darius didn't care. All he wanted was the blood. As Idona answered the phone, Darius realized he wasn't going to be able to hold himself back anymore. He quickly stood up once again and walked off. Darius headed straight for the store attached to the restaurant. Halfway there, Minnie stopped him.

"Darius?" she called. He paused and looked at her. She could see the hunger in his eyes but there were still sky-blue. "Did she talk to you?"

"She cut herself, and then Sue called," Darius responded. Minnie frowned. That was not the plan, and then realization struck her.

"Your eyes are still blue," Minnie accused. Darius crossed his eyebrows. He knew they had been blue before but...there was no way possible that they would look normal during such hunger. Darius was so deep into his bloodlust that his eyes should have turned red. If not red, then black. Surprised by her admittance, Darius stormed off and headed into the store area. Looking around quickly, he found the signs for the restroom. Darius noticed Minnie watching him. He could see the fear in her eyes. She was terrified of him.

Without another glance, Darius escaped into the restroom for the men. Locking the door, Darius paused. Quickly using all his vampire senses, he made sure the place was empty. Sighing gratefully, Darius turned to look at the mirror and was shocked. Minnie was right. His eyes had not changed color in the slightest. Something was going on and it wasn't good.

Back at the table, Idona was just hanging up the phone when Minnie and the waiter arrived. Minnie sat down in her seat while the man handed out their drinks. He noted the empty seat where Darius had been but said nothing. Before he walked away, Idona looked sharply at him.

"Can we get the check? We may have to bounce once the food gets here," Idona told him. The waiter frowned and Idona could tell that he was thinking that they might not pay. She could have almost decked him for that. But she didn't. Finally, he nodded and walked off. Once he was gone, Minnie looked closely at her roommate.

"Darius said Sue called?" she asked. Idona nodded and showed the phone off as though it explained everything. Minnie noted that Idona seemed a little distant. Idona did feel slightly distant because of the conversation with Darius. She knew that Rafficer was coming to New Orleans. The information didn't faze her because she had prepared for him to. Shaking her head, Idona decided to focus on Minnie and Sue.

"I told her where we are at the moment. She's gonna get a taxi and meet us outside. That's gonna be like five maybe ten minutes at most. Then we have to come up with a new plan. So, basically it means that when our food gets here, Sue will be waiting for us," Idona informed her. Minnie sighed and looked at her glass of Coke. Idona then reached for her napkin and began cleaning her hand. Her thoughts were scrambled. The other girl watched her for a moment. Feeling her gaze, Idona looked up.

"Darius?"

"No...well, yes, I guess. I cut myself to show him he needed blood. Got close to him drinking from me when Sue called." Minnie shook her head in sadness. Idona couldn't say anything more. Both girls went silent. Neither were really thinking of anything. And they stayed that way until the food arrived at the table. As Minnie began to delve into the food, Idona noticed that Darius hadn't returned. "Where's Darius?"

"Don't know...think he might have gone to the restroom. Mentioned that his eyes never changed, and he got spooked," Minnie muttered between mouthfuls of food. Idona was stunned. She had no idea what to say. "Which, what's with that? The book mentions that their eyes change to red when hungry and black when absolutely desperate for food or really pissed off."

"My eyes, as well. We can't forget that. Something's going on," Idona answered. Minnie shrugged it off. But Idona couldn't help but think about it. Darius was changing, and Idona was as well. *Could there be something else going on?* Idona wondered. Focusing again on her friend, Idona stood up. Minnie looked at her. "Pack my food up when the waiter comes back. I'm gonna go find Darius."

Minnie simply nodded. Idona sighed, turned, and walked away from the table. Minnie focused on her food while Idona paused to pay the bill. As she watched two men enter the restroom, she assumed that Darius wasn't there. So headed outside.

Once there, she spotted the vampire leaning against the side of the HHR. He looked confused, upsct, and definitely hungry. With her hand still cut, Idona knew that Darius would sense her long before she even got close. But that didn't matter to her. She needed to speak to him before Sue got there. Walking closer, Idona found she could only reach a car length away before Darius's attention snapped onto her. She felt frightened when he looked at her as if she was food. Then she remembered that she had offered herself to him just minutes before.

"Darius?" she called. The vampire simply nodded as a form of acknowledging that she wanted to get closer. Idona began to walk toward him. In an instant, Darius was on top of her. His hands were on either side of her head, pushing her against a silver Sedan. She didn't even have time to scream. Her sea-green eyes stared at Darius in shock. The vampire looked so hungry that he seemed ready to tear into her throat. But he didn't move.

"Don't," he commanded her before backing off. Idona knew it was a command but didn't feel compelled. Either he was too weak or the commands just didn't affect her. Idona wasn't too sure, nor did she really care. Darius had almost ripped out her throat, proof enough that he needed to feed. And he was still refusing to do anything about it.

"You just almost attacked me, and you still won't feed? Don't you see what is going on? God forbid Sue has even the tiniest of scratches on her. You'll drain her dry before you realize whom you're attacking! Darius please, just a little to tide you over!" Idona cried. Darius walked away, shaking his head. He knew that Idona was right. Knew that he couldn't fight it anymore.

Slowly, he turned and faced Idona. He watched as her sea-green eyes shifted to knowing what he was about to do. And all she could do was give him a relieved smile, letting him know that she was pleased with his decision. Darius walked closer to her. He grabbed her shoulders and she twisted her head to open her neck to him. Taking a breath, Darius got ready, but he was interrupted when a taxi pulled into the lot.

The two separated quickly and looked at the vehicle as it slowed. Both were breathing heavily, almost as though they had been ready to do something other than feeding the vampire inside Darius. All that mattered now was making sure the person inside the taxi hadn't seen much of anything. Thankfully, they were in luck. The door to the taxi opened, and a young girl stepped out. Idona's eyes widened as she realized the girl was Sue. She had finally arrived.

As the taxi pulled away, Sue turned around. From the car, she had seen two people standing between the parked vehicles. Though she could barely see, one of the people had looked remarkably similar to Idona. As Sue turned and focused them, Idona stepped out from between the cars and smiled. For a brief second, Sue was relieved but then she wondered who was accompanying the girl, but Idona's smile comforted Sue.

CHAPTER 18

Reunited

"Sue," Idona muttered. The older girl laughed and walked over. They hugged as Darius slowly began appeared from between the cars. Sue didn't have a chance to see Darius. Idona twisted to block the girl's view. As the two broke away from their embrace, Minnie walked out of the restaurant holding boxes. When she saw the older girl, Minnie squealed in delight. Dropping the food onto the ground, Minnie began to run toward the awkward group.

"SUE!" she cried. Idona backed off, moving to stand beside Darius. The vampire focused his attention on the dropped food. Minnie's hug was as brief as Idona's, because Sue caught sight of Darius. Her eyes widened at the sight of him. Darius couldn't help but flinch, he felt objectified by the girl's gaze.

Sue was startled and frozen. Idona switched her vision from Sue to Darius. The vampire was fidgeting. He tried hard not to run from Sue. Wanting to think of something else, Darius focused on Idona and instantly smelled her blood. She still had an open wound. Letting loose a distressed breath, Darius began to try to find a reason to stop Sue's gaze. Idona turned back to Sue with a regretful sigh.

"Is that..." Sue began. All Minnie could do was nod. She wasn't sure what to say. Minnie knew that Sue had read all the same books as Idona. After staying with Darius for so long, she had forgotten what it was like to be reminded that he was just a book character. Sue watched Darius like a hawk. Every twitch of his muscles made her eyes twinkle in glee. Every breath he took made her nearly faint. No matter what he did, it affected Sue. She was focused on only him, so she missed when Idona moved to grab Darius's hand in an attempt to calm him. Sue's eyes scanned his body, looking for signs for something. Anything that either proved he wasn't real or that he was actually there.

Idona watched as Darius shifted uncomfortably underneath Sue's gaze. Idona noticed his sky-blue eyes desperately searching for an escape. Her hand had done little to placate him. It was almost like they weren't even touching. Darius was fighting a multitude of emotions. He had already gone through the idea of draining Sue dry, ripping out her eyes, slitting her throat, grabbing Idona and running, stealing the keys to the HHR, and driving off and finally telling Sue to get over it.As Idona watched the events transpire, she began feeling strangely uneasy by Sue's watchful gaze. It was plain to see that Darius was indeed uncomfortable, but that didn't stop Sue. Idona watched as Minnie walked to the food. But Darius could only think about the girl watching his every move. He hated that Sue was staring at him like this. It made him feel nonexistent. For the first time, Darius realized how lucky he was to have met Idona and Minnie first.

"Hello?" Darius questioned Sue. That snapped her out of her examination of the vampire. She looked as if an animal had spoken words. Darius felt uncomfortable by her reaction but braced himself for her gaze to be on him for a long time. Utterly shocked, Sue began to stare at Darius like he was an alien. While her reaction made sense, no one could help but judge the girl. Minnie returned to see the change in atmosphere and audibly groaned.

"Sue, this is Darius," Idona introduced the girl. She reacted by screaming like a teenage girl seeing her famous idol for the first time. Darius, Idona, and Minnie winced at the sound. Idona had hoped the older girl could keep a level head, but she had been proven horribly wrong. Sue couldn't believe that this was really happening. Here was Darius, a character from a book series. He was standing right in front of her. How could someone not freak out?

As Sue began to jump up and down in excitement, Minnie looked around. Darius was too busy making sure that Sue kept her distance from him and Idona was waiting for the hungry vampire to snap and suddenly attack the crazed girl. Minnie noticed the group of people suddenly watching them. There was a crowd of people staring at the scene. Minnie frowned and quickly directed Idona's attention to the crowd.

Agreeing that this was becoming a volatile situation, Idona placed herself between Darius and Sue, who focused on Idona. The younger girl nodded at the crowd, who quickly dispersed. Fearing that they'd be back, Idona spoke. "Sue, there is a lot that needs explaining right now. Judging by the way these people here have perceived us, I suggest we move this conversation elsewhere."

"Like where?" Darius muttered sharply. His discomfort with Sue and Idona's small cut was really getting to him. The biggest issue was Sue wasn't focused on Idona anymore. Instead, she was trying to sneak another peek at Darius. Noticing that Sue and Darius were going to be no help, Minnie came up with an idea.

"I'd vote for hotel. We're gonna be talking about many strange things that other people aren't gonna want to hear. And I've been cooped up in that car for far too long. Never mind needing another shower," Minnie suggested. Idona nodded to Minnie and faced Darius. The vampire had heard but he hesitated to see if there would be any other suggestions. Seeing that there wasn't going to be any, Darius was the first one to turn away from Sue and walk toward the car. Minnie and Idona quickly followed after.

Sue hesitated, watching Darius walk away, before she took hurried steps after them. Being taller than the two younger girls, she was able to pull right up beside them before they got directly in front of the car. When they reached the HHR, Minnie stopped at the driver's seat, Idona stopped at the front passenger seat and Darius stopped by her side. Sue headed for the back seat behind Minnie. Her eyes were focused on Darius as though he might run for it or simply vanish like he had never even been there.

"Please, don't make me sit with her," the vampire whispered into Idona's ear, almost begging. Idona looked at Sue. Idona noticed the desire in the other girl's eyes. Looking back at Darius, she nodded and walked toward the back seat. Darius relaxed, but he couldn't help but notice the disappointment flooding Sue's body. Thankfully, though, she didn't fight. Everyone got into the car and buckled up just before Minnie started the engine.

"So, where is a hotel?" Minnie asked. Idona shrugged and looked at Sue. Sue frowned but said nothing. Minnie hadn't expected an answer, but she was a little disappointed when no one responded. "Okay, driving around aimlessly it is."

With that decided, Minnie pulled the car out of its spot and headed on toward the road. A minute or so later, Sue seemed relax enough to begin staring at Darius from her seat. Darius could feel the gaze. He tried to ignore it but it almost right away began to give him chills. Feeling some shifting from the seat beside her, Idona turned to look.

Seeing Sue staring at Darius, she tried not to react. But as she faced Darius, she watched as a chill raced up his spine.

Sue's eyes displayed with a mix of surprise, confusion, happiness, and fear. Idona wasn't sure how to respond to Sue's various emotions. It almost made Idona sick that Sue was acting like Darius was something other than an everyday person. Darius was obviously trying to ignore the gaze. Considering how Idona felt, she could only assume that he was succeeding. Minnie was focused on driving and finding a hotel so she didn't even really register what else was going on.

Becoming disgusted with Sue's idolized view of Darius, Idona suddenly remembered the danger they were all in. Her mind flashed back to Darius's offhand comment of Rafficer coming to New Orleans. Then suddenly she realized, Minnie and Idona didn't idolize Darius because they knew that he wasn't the only one around. But this was the whole reason they were heading to the hotel. As Idona thought about it more, she realized that talking about it now might save money.

"Darius isn't the only one here from the books," Idona mentioned as if this was an everyday occurrence. Sue stopped staring at Darius and faced Idona. The bluntness of the statement made it hard to believe. But Sue's eyes looked ready for more "happy" news. Idona frowned. It was then that she remembered Darius was Sue's second favorite character. Idona couldn't recall whom Sue liked best.

"What? Who else is here?" Sue asked excitedly. Darius winced but didn't look away from the window. It bothered him more than ever that Sue seemed to think he either couldn't understand her or didn't care. Minnie shook her head as she turned her attention back to the conversation.

"We know of at least Rafficer, Serge, and Kathleen," Minnie answered as if Sue should know that. Sue looked at Minnie with eyes full of skepticism. She found it difficult to believe that a larger number of villains from the book had escaped into her world. Since Sue didn't know about the book, she had to trust what the others told her.

"Really?" she asked, the disbelief in her voice was apparent. Darius snapped back to Sue and gave her a nasty look. Minnie shook her head.

"Minnie has read the books," Idona muttered as if that added value to the conversation. Sue frowned; she didn't care if Minnie had read the books—she thought they were insane. She looked at Idona, wondering what the truth was. She knew there was something else. "Rafficer has already turned a few people from our world. And Kathleen..."

"We don't know if Marc is indeed changed. He might have said no," Sue said because she didn't know about the updates in the book. Idona sighed, wishing Sue's statement were true. Though Darius hadn't mentioned that he read of Marc's plot in the book, Idona knew the obvious truth. Marc was now a vampire, and there was nothing to do about it.

"He's been turned, and he's with Rafficer right now. They're on a plane heading down here as we speak," Darius suddenly informed everyone. Minnie closed her eyes, holding back a tear. Idona looked down at the floor, upset by Darius's confirmation of Marc's state. Sue stared at Darius. Although they were going into detail, Sue was looking for anything that would prove that they were lying. "How do you know that?"

"The last book. It's been updating itself," Darius tried to explain. Sue scoffed; there was no way they could prove that. Idona picked up the book that was lying beside her feet and handed it over to Sue. She pushed away the book, without looking at what it was because she was too busy staring at Darius. Idona frowned and lightly held the object.

The book slowly opened to a blank page. Before it could even begin to write anything down, Idona looked away.

"What do you mean by updating itself?" Sue asked. Darius turned in his seat to look at her. His sky-blue eyes focused on Sue before he noticed the book in Idona's hand. She was holding it open and it had already finished writing Sue's comment and was beginning to describe other things.

"Look at it," Darius told her while signaling to the book beside her. Sue took a quick look just as it paused its narration. Darius frowned when Sue turned her gaze back to him.

"I read it already," Sue muttered. Darius sighed deeply at her response. Idona pushed the book closer to Sue. Sue grabbed it and dropped it by her feet. "If you guys aren't gonna tell me the truth, I might as well return to school. Hell, I might even report you guys for ditching."

"You can't!" Minnie cried in surprise. Sue leaned her head back against the seat, mulling over the idea. She wasn't serious at first, but what other choice did she have? There was no way she could believe them.

"Let her go back. Since Rafficer's coming to New Orleans, she should be safe in school," Darius snapped. All Idona wanted was for them all to be safe. That was the original idea in asking Sue to leave the school. Now that she had permission to leave, Sue realized that she didn't want to go. It was in that moment that Sue looked down to her feet and screamed. Idona leaned forward and caught sight of the book turning pages at Sue's feet. Unbuckling her seatbelt, Idona quickly began climbing into the back. No one was sure of what had happened.

It was complete chaos. Minnie was screaming while trying to keep control of the car. Sue was freaking out over the book moving on its own. Idona was pushing Sue back toward her seat. Darius was avoiding Sue's scrapping nails. Through that entire ruckus, Minnie was somehow able to spot a hotel and pull into the parking lot safely. Once the car had fully stopped, everyone glared at Sue.

"Sue! Go get us a room before I kill you!" Minnie snapped. Sue didn't even try to argue as she rushed out of the car. The girl slammed the door shut like a little kid throwing a tantrum. As Sue entered the large building, Minnie turned to look at Idona and Darius. The vampire was sitting there, terrified. Idona was simply upset. "You sure we should have gotten her involved?"

"I was up until two minutes ago," Idona said, nervously laughing. Minnie nodded in agreement. Darius sat back, wondering briefly if this "nightmare" was ever going to end.

"So what should we do now?"

"Get the room, rest for the night, and let everyone decide what they want to do after. If we all want to go our separate ways, then we can," Minnie seriously responded. Idona nodded hearing the underlying message that Minnie was fed up with the situation. But she really couldn't believe that Minnie would just leave. Idona was not going to convince her to stay, but Idona thought Minnie had invested too much in this to stop.

"Would you leave?" Darius asked, unsure of Minnie's actual feelings. Minnie turned to look at him with a puzzled look. Even Idona focused a questioning gaze on the vampire. "If given the chance, would you leave?"

Minnie took a moment to consider the idea. As much as her previous statement sounded like she had thought about it, she actually hadn't. Her response was directed at Sue. Minnie thought about it and gave a soft smile to the waiting vamp.

"If you wouldn't care and Rafficer would leave me alone. Oh, and if I knew that Idona was going to be safe, I probably would. But knowing that isn't possible, I won't," Minnie answered. Darius then looked at Idona for the answer to his question. Idona's smile spread far faster and wider than Minnie's did.

"Never," she said. Darius softly sighed and smiled at the friendships he had cultivated.

CHAPTER 19

The Hotel: Night Two

Sue ended up getting two rooms. She did not want to stay with Darius but she also didn't want any one else to room with Darius.. After a long discussion, they reluctantly decided that Sue and Minnie would share a room while Idona and Darius shared the other. Sue did not appreciate this decision, but she couldn't say much when Idona handed her the book to be caught up on the situation. They decided that after Sue was caught up and Minnie was done with her shower, they would meet to discuss a new plan.

That left Idona and Darius alone in their room with an hour to kill. Sue was a noteworthy and fast reader. Darius quickly placed himself on the bed at the far end of the room. Idona stood in the conjoined doorway between the rooms. She looked at Darius, who was watching her and knew where this situation was going to lead.

"No."

"No, what? No, you aren't going to drink? No, you aren't hungry?" Idona countered.

"Idona, I can't!" Darius pitifully called. Idona let out a heavy breath before walking toward the vamp. He tensed up. Her wound had not healed fully. In the car, he had been able to ignore it because of Sue. But here, alone, with nothing to stop him, the smell was overwhelming.

"Darius, you need to feed," Idona moaned. Darius shook his head before turning his back to her. She groaned lightly before playing with her wounded hand. As she messed around with the cut, she reopened it. Darius was on her before the blood could even bubble up. Pinned against the wall and Darius's chest, Idona could barely gasp. When she looked up, all Idona saw was a hungry vampire with sky-blue eyes leaning forward to bite her neck.

The pain lasted as long as it had taken Darius to cross the room. Once it passed, Idona could see into Darius's mind. He loved the taste of her blood. It was like an aphrodisiac; so strong, yet sweet and innocent. Drinking it, Darius could feel Idona's desire to help. But it was more than that, both of them could feel a locked away emotion. Unreachable...untouchable.

Then it was over. Darius pulled back, and Idona sagged into him. Surprised, Darius almost didn't catch her in time. She melted into his arms and he carried her. Darius placed her on one of the beds. As she settled into the bed, Idona became aware that someone was watching her. Slowly she opened her eyes and Darius gasped. Idona's eyes were no longer sea-green. They were turquoise.

"Idona," Darius softly began. Idona immediately knew something was different. Darius also looked different. As she looked him over, he watched her eyes. "Your eyes...they've changed..."

Idona grimaced at his comment. She knew that they had changed to sea-green, but if they were different again then something really was going on. But even with her sudden need to go check her eyes, Idona was still trying to work out why Darius seemed different. After a few more seconds, Idona turned to go find a mirror and that was when it hit her. Her attention snapped back onto Darius.

"Darius, your skin isn't pale anymore," Idona stammered. Indeed, Darius's skin wasn't the vampiric pale white any longer. It had turned back to the lightly tanned color he had been before he met Rafficer. Within seconds, both of them had gotten up and rushed to the nearest mirror. There they confirmed each other's statements. "What is going on? Why does this keep happening?"

"I...I don't know...I've never heard of anything like this before. Have you?" Darius questioned as he backed away from the mirror in shock. Idona fell back against the opposing wall and watched as the vamp began pacing the room.

"I've heard about something similar to this but...it was in a TV show or maybe in a book...but it never happened in real life," Idona explained. Darius snarled so softly that Idona couldn't hear it. *Just like a character coming out of a book*, he thought to himself with a dark sneer at the ground. "Darius, what could this mean?"

"I can't see why these changes would mean anything. I don't understand what the result will be. If I knew that, then I'd be able to answer," Darius mumbled. Idona didn't respond. Darius's comment was so obvious that there wasn't much to argue with. Their silence was interrupted by a knock. When Darius had bitten Idona, they lost track of time.

"So, Sue finished nearly all the book," Minnie stated. Idona nodded as Minnie and Sue went to sit on the bed closest to the conjoined door. With a deep sigh, Darius sat on the other bed. All attention drew onto Idona. She hadn't moved toward either bed. Focusing on Sue, Idona tried to take the gazes off her.

"So, what do you think?" Idona asked. Sue didn't answer. Both she and Minnie were fixated on the new eye color.

"Your eyes!" Sue cried out in surprise when she finally realized her own eyes weren't deceiving her. Idona frowned but nodded in confirmation that she knew they were different. Minnie then took a quick glance at Darius. His attention was suddenly riveted on a slight rip in the carpet before him. "How long have they..."

"Been turquoise? Only a few minutes. But they began changing colors after...well..." Idona began but suddenly didn't want to finish the reply.

"It was mentioned in the book," Minnie scoffed as though it had been an important part of the story. Sue cast a suspicious glance her way before returning to gaze at Idona. Beginning to feel uncomfortable, Idona stormed over to the bed Darius sat on and dramatically flopped down. "Speaking of the book, Sue, what do you think?"

"About?" Sue inquired. Minnie rolled her eyes. "Oh, the book? Right. Well, it's interesting. Doesn't explain much about what happened. Actually, it rather seems to just be going with the flow of things."

"So, you're cool with the idea of it," Minnie muttered when it seemed no one would respond. Sue nodded. This was going to happen with or without her.

"I noticed that you guys plan on sending them all back," Sue mentioned. Idona shook her head yes while she turned away from Darius. She really didn't want him to leave anymore, but there didn't seem to be any other choice. "And you planned on doing what down here?"

"Uh..."Minnie intelligently responded. Sue nodded with a hum of contentment. She had assumed as much when the book never mentioned a good reason for going to New Orleans.

"You were just hoping to drive around and have some voodoo person stop you and help, right?" Sue questioned. When neither girl answered, Sue said "hmm" angrily. "And what if there were no actual voodoo people in New Orleans after Katrina?"

"Katrina?" Darius echoed softly.

"We were a little freaked out," Minnie said in vain to defend Idona and herself. Sue shook her head. Sighing, she picked up the book. As she began flipping through the pages a thought crossed her mind.

"What about the author?"

"What?" everyone called.

"The author? This Amanda chick. She lives in Florida. Hell, she might have a better clue of what is going on than some crackpot," Sue explained. Darius whined. Idona snatched the book out of Sue's hand and flipped open to the author information page. Amanda did live in Florida. A retirement community called "The Villages." She stayed with her mother and took care of her and her pets. Minnie then gave a short snort of amusement.

"I mentioned Florida before, but Idona thought New Orleans was a better choice," she happily cried. Idona scoffed as she looked up. But Darius beat her to the punch.

"You mentioned a place called Disney...not going to see the author," he snapped. Minnie's happiness quickly diminished. Darius's comment was laced with so much anger that everyone knew he wasn't done. "I'm not going to see this...'author.' It's ridiculous."

"Do you have a better plan?" Sue growled back. Darius didn't. But he also couldn't see this author plan helping them. Sue smirked. "Thought as much."

"Okay, so we rest here tonight and then head to Florida in the morning. Sound good?" Minnie declared, showing her support for the older girl. Idona stared at the ground in disapproval. Like Darius, she could care less for the idea of talking to the author. Speaking to this woman was only going to make matters more difficult. But, she knew better than to fight with Minnie and Sue. Especially since the group was using Minnie's car to get around.

"If we are all agreed, I suggest we rest. Good night," Sue announced before turning and walking out of the room. Minnie waited an extra moment to see if Idona was okay. Darius was seething in rage. This new girl came along, put herself in danger, and now suddenly believed she knew the right thing to do? That ticked Darius off more than he had ever felt before. "Minnie!"

"Go," Idona whispered when Minnie hesitated a bit and then left. Once alone again, Idona shifted over to her bed and focused on Darius. He was still glaring at the last place Sue had been standing. Idona said nothing to the vampire. She could see that he wasn't going to let Sue get away with her plan. Sadly, for now, there was no stopping it.

"I want to strangle her! I want to tear her throat out!" Darius said so softly that Idona began to wonder if she imagined it. As she focused on his features, she knew that Darius had said those words. And he meant every single one. She knew it should frighten her. It should also make her want to stop him. But she agreed with him.

"I understand the feeling. And I wish I could allow you, but we just don't have another plan right now," Idona stated. Darius turned to her. He could see her own rage coursing through her and he knew that she really did understand. With a deep sigh, he let go of nearly all his rage. Feeling that Darius let go of his, Idona released her anger.

"So what? We just go with it?" Darius growled. Idona could only nod.

"Rest now. Maybe in the night we can come up with a better plan," Idona answered. Darius snarled but let it go. Slowly he nodded and laid back in the bed. Idona did the same. Both of them wanted to lay in silence with their thoughts. Too bad, it wasn't meant to be.

Idona opened her eyes, after having believed that she only closed them for a second, and was stunned to find herself in a log cabin. It was dark, save the areas around the roaring fire or small candles. The couch, placed in the middle of the room, looked like it was made of stained wood and had a tattered white sheet on top. Beside that was a small square end table that had a three-pronged candlestick, all three filled with an extra tall candle. The fireplace wasn't really decorated with any particular flair. It just seemed to be there only for necessary heat and light. Focusing her attention behind the couch, Idona noticed an opening leading to another part of the cabin. Since she didn't know if anyone was home, she made no move to head over there.

Spying about the room, Idona tried looking for a way to identify where she was. All she could figure out was that she was tucked away in the corner of the room with a perfect view of everything. Too frightened to make a move toward the front door, Idona felt safe. There was a loud crash, followed by the sound of a door smash and that of a body dropping to the floor. Frightened, Idona froze and waited to see what would happen. There was no movement for about a minute, which gave her enough time to build up her courage. Slowly, Idona moved closer to the body and saw that it was a man.

He seemed injured, tired, and in desperate need of help. Looking closer, she could see his torn clothing, open wounds, sores, and even some healing scars. His body was ragged and bloody, almost looking like he had been living outdoors for a long period. When he finally looked up, Idona was shocked to see it was Darius. Eyes as red as rubies and filled with a starving need like a person who hadn't eaten in weeks. Idona was stunned by his condition, and frightened that he might suddenly attack her. But his eyes seemed to be focused on the wall behind her. He let out a loud groan before rolling over onto his side.

"Hello?" called a soft female voice, responding more to the groan than the crashing of the door. Darius and Idona stiffened. Suddenly Darius didn't look hungry, but

he was now filled with terror. Trying to curb her shock, Idona watched as the woman entered through the opening behind the couch.

The second her eyes caught sight of the woman, Idona was stunned. This woman could have been her twin. There were only some slight differences. Her hair was a bit darker, the skin slightly more tanned, and the woman seemed possibly an inch or two taller. After seeing that, Idona knew who this was. This was no mistake. Her description in the book had been thorough.

"Robyn," Idona whispered so softly that even she almost missed it. But Darius's hungry eyes snapped toward Idona before facing Robyn. Idona wondered if he could see her, and something was holding him back. She ignored the idea and watched the two instead. Robyn's eyes were wide as she looked the vampire over but there was no fear in them. She looked curious and sympathetic. Just as the woman began to move toward the downed body, Darius jumped to his feet and used his vampire speed to trap himself in the back corner, across from Idona. Robyn didn't react.

"Oh, did I frighten you?" Robyn softly asked. Darius's breath was coming in short quick gasps as he focused on her neck. He almost seemed to be panicking or fighting a war with himself. Robyn held up her hands as though she meant no harm. The movement made Darius tenser. Idona silently watched it all as she tried to remember this scene in the book. "I swear that I didn't mean to frighten you. I was only coming over to check on you. Trust me, I won't hurt you."

"But I was frightened that I'd hurt you," Darius's voice declared, but the injured vampire hadn't said a thing. Idona twisted and was shocked to see a completely unin-jured Darius. His sky-blue eyes were focused on the scene before them. Idona looked between the two vamps. The one beside her seemed older, wiser, and more alert than the other version of Darius. Both seemed more focused on the other woman. "Robyn nearly spent over two hours trying to calm me down. She asked about my injuries, my life, and when that didn't faze me, she talked about herself. She said anything in an effort to get me out of that corner. It barely worked. I was too hungry to listen, but I was too defiant to feed."

"Oh, you broke my door," Robyn said with a slight note of despair. Idona frowned.

"What happened?" Idona muttered, this portion of the book wasn't written in much detail. Darius sighed before the scene changed. Idona could tell that time had passed because of the size of the candles and the fire in the fireplace. The injured Darius was curled up in the corner with his now black eyes focused on Robyn. She had now moved to the far side of the couch and was comfortably sitting there.

"I see that most of your injuries seem to be healing themselves," Robyn voiced. There was no response from the frightened vamp. Idona looked at Darius. It took a second for him to notice her gaze, but once he did, he looked at her. The two said nothing. "So, are you ever going to talk to me?"

"No," the other Darius muttered as he curled tighter into a ball. Robyn raised an eyebrow as Idona and Darius focused back on the situation. This was the first word she had got out of her newest guest since he arrived. A hint of a smile formed on her face before she shifted in her seat. Darius tensed.

"You barged into my house. You know that, right?" Robyn questioned.

"It is a mistake," Darius sharply replied. Robyn frowned. "It looks abandoned."

"What?" Robyn cried in shock. She made her way toward the door, but when Darius shifted, she paused. She then focused on the vamp. "Were you joking?"

Darius smiled showing his fangs, before he began laughing lightly. It wasn't an evil laugh, and didn't sound like he was fully at ease. He laughed because her comment was humorous. After calming, he shook his head. Robyn now had a smile on her own face.

"Yeah, guess you're right. I haven't really been taking care of this place," Robyn muttered. Darius frowned and shifted toward the two different women in the room.

"And this is where I make the biggest mistake of my life," Darius mentioned beside Idona.

"I could help with that," the other Darius offered. Robyn focused on him and the vampire relaxed. She could now clearly see that in their conversation, nearly all his *wounds had healed. Idona nodded. The rest of this was in the book. Knowing what happens next, Idona lightly grabbed Darius's hand and the two walked off. She led them to the opening behind the couch, and as they passed through it, the scene changed.*

"Darius, you have to go!" Robyn cried out in horror. The two now stood in the kitchen. Robyn was pushing Darius toward the door, but he was fighting to stay. "Rafficer is on his way here!"

"All the more reason for me to stay!" Darius countered. Robyn shook her head.

"Please, just go!"

"I can't! Robyn," Darius nearly whined. Outside there was a loud crash. "No. Robyn."

"Go!" Robyn ordered one last time before shoving Darius out the kitchen door. As she closed the door, the vampire spun around. She mouthed, "get out of here" before she turned her back on him and headed back into the cabin.

"This is where Robyn got changed?" Idona softly asked. Darius shook his head.

"No, I ran. It wasn't until three days after that I came back and found her missing. There was a note, telling me to go to Raff. I went and there I saw him...but she had changed," Darius responded as he watched his younger self turn and run from the cabin. "I still regret this decision. Because I left, she died."

"It wasn't your fault. Rafficer was the one who killed her," Idona challenged. Darius gave her a forgiving smile.

"But it was my fault that he found her. My fault that she was tortured. My fault that she was changed. And my fault that she was destroyed," Darius explained. Idona frowned and tried to disagree with him, but the scene changed and Darius was gone. Idona realized she was back home.

CHAPTER 20

Chaos at the Airport

"Darius. Come back to me. Come see me," Rafficer's voice whispered in Darius's mind, waking up the younger vamp. Darius snapped to attention. The call was overpowering. He needed to go. There was only a small portion of his mind that said "no, don't go," but Darius couldn't help himself. Twisting off the bed, Darius stood up and began to leave the hotel room. He quickly glanced at Idona, who was still sound asleep in her bed. A frown formed on his face before he slipped past the door and into the hall. "Darius. Come to me."

"Darius?" softly came a familiar voice. Darius turned around and noticed Minnie leaning out of her room. She was watching him with a curious gaze. Knowing he couldn't explain, the vampire continued walking. Minnie knew something was amiss when he turned toward the elevator, even though there was a sign showing where the stairs were. She rushed out of the room and down the hall after him. "Darius? Where are you going?"

When he didn't respond a second time, Minnie figured that Idona might have a clue as to why the vampire was leaving. She sadly watched as Darius stepped into an elevator and disappeared behind closed doors. Biting her lip, she rushed to Idona's room and began pounding on the door. She was lucky that Idona was a light sleeper. The other girl opened the door in less than a minute.

"What?" Idona groggily asked. Just as Minnie was about to speak, the door to her room opened and Sue leaned out. She looked groggy, but a little more pissed off than Idona did. Minnie ignored the older girl.

"Darius just left," she explained. Idona frowned.

"Since when is that a big deal?" Sue questioned. Idona and Minnie both ignored her. Neither one of them wanted to deal with her skepticism right now.

"Do you know why?" Idona muttered. Minnie shook her head no. Letting worry get the best of her, Idona turned away from the taller girls and looked inside the room. She wondered if there was some sort of sign in there.

"He didn't say anything to me. Just kind of looked at me sadly before getting into the elevator," Minnie mentioned. Idona then rushed back into the room. Trading a glance, Sue and Minnie followed her inside. They both turned from the entry only to see Idona digging around for something.

"What are you looking for?" Sue inquired as she watched the girl rummage through her things. Idona didn't respond. The other two girls continued watching her search before finally it hit Minnie. She suddenly knew what Idona was looking for.

"The book!" Minnie cried before joining Idona in the search. Sue rolled her eyes and watched the two. Idona victoriously cried when she found the book under her bed. Sue sighed deeply as Minnie jumped to her feet and rushed to Idona's side. They silently read the book and realized what had happened. "We have to go after him."

Meanwhile, Darius had already made it downstairs and was walking across the parking lot. He didn't want to use his vampire speed until he saw the girls. But with the way Minnie looked at him, Darius was unsure if she'd even alert the others. Just as he reached the edge of the parking lot, he looked back. No one followed him. Darius felt anxious and concentrated to find the place Rafficer was calling him to "Darius, you need to be faster. We need to speak. Come to me," Rafficer softly called again. Darius shivered, he felt compelled to go. All he wanted was for Idona to come out and try to stop him. Just like Robyn had done in the past. But the longer it took her to come down, the more time Darius had to be called to Rafficer's side. Another call sliced into Darius's mind. Very slowly, Darius took a step forward, followed by another and then another until the vampire was out of the hotel. That was when his inhibitions snapped. Using his vampiric speed, Darius raced off to find Rafficer.

Darius arrived at an empty looking airport within five minutes. There wasn't a single car in the lot, not a single light turned on in the buildings. But when Darius went out back, he found a small jet sitting on the tarmac. Darius paused as he looked the contraption. For the first time since he appeared in this world, Darius wasn't afraid or confused by the technology. Of course that held little concern to him at the time.

Standing next to the large jet, almost looking rather dwarfed considering his size, was Serge. A large "I know more than you" smile was plastered over his face. Darius shuddered as he stared at his once best friend. As he continued waiting, Darius began to wonder how long he could hold off before going inside the jet. Slowly, he began pacing the large vehicle. Serge followed him with his eyes and the tilt of the head every now and then. Darius circled the area three times before Serge spoke.

"Did 'Daddy's' calls make you come running?" he sarcastically asked. Darius snarled. Rafficer's calls didn't ever just go to the intended target. It went to everyone under his command. No one would miss it.

Just like no one would be able to resist the call if it was sent to them. "That girl couldn't stop you this time I see."

"Leave her out of this," Darius growled deeply. Serge laughed. It was a deep throaty laugh that made the older vampire just want to clock him. Not wanting to get closer to Rafficer's den, Darius stood a good distance away and so wasn't able to do anything to Serge.

"Believe this new one is called Idona? Or is it Minnie that you like?" Serge questioned. Darius balled his hands up in anger. He so badly wanted to destroy Serge. Instead, he decided to taunt back.

"Those girls? Oh, I drained them dry a while back. They tasted wonderful. So sweet, innocent, and oh-so-pretty," Darius taunted knowing about Serge's disability. See each vampire has a certain taste that they looked for in their victims. Some go for virgins. Others are gender-specific. Serge went for the young ones. They tended to be "nice girls." A little better than average. But always virgins. That was until he turned 50.

Serge got careless. He was not discreet while drinking from a young daughter of a very rich family. When the family found out about him, they set out a reward for his life. A vampire hunter found the young vamp hiding in a cave outside of town. At the time, this hunter believed that fire would kill a vampire. Sadly that was a mistake. It did hurt Serge and forced him to hide in the cave for two months longer than he had intended. But once he left the cave and went on a hunt, he found that his sense of taste was gone.

"Oh, no. You can't bother me today," Serge answered back. Darius stopped pacing making Serge smile. "Rafficer is going to—"

"SERGE!" screamed a female voice. Darius and Serge snapped to attention and focused on the door to the jet. There stood Kathleen. Her eyes had returned to their normal color, and she seemed freshly fed. Darius slightly reached out for her power and quickly noted that he was slightly weaker than she was. His use of power and lack of feeding was getting to him. "Darius needs to come inside now. Stop distracting him."

"Yes ma'am," Serge dutifully responded. But when the other two vamps turned to Darius, he didn't move. Rafficer had stopped calling once Darius made it onto the airport territory and so he didn't really have to stay. But he knew that if he turned to leave, Rafficer would order him inside. All this stalling was hopefully giving the girls a chance to get away.

"Darius! Inside! Now!" Kathleen ordered. Snarling once again, Darius very slowly made his way toward the jet. Kathleen glared at him the entire way. When he was close enough to the jet, Kathleen turned and headed inside. Darius paused after she disappeared, but Serge pushed him forward and the two entered. It took a second for Darius to get his bearings straight but that second would cost him. Suddenly he was attacked from both sides. Fighting back, he dropped to the floor with his would-be attackers falling on top of him. With them now having most of the control, they were able to manhandle him into their arms.

Slowly the three then worked themselves into a standing position. Now having adjusted, Darius could see Serge to his left. The larger vamp gripped Darius's arm so tightly that if he tried to get away he would end up dislocating his shoulder or breaking it entirely. On his right was a new vampire. One that Darius didn't recognize, but judging by his appearance the older vamp could only guess that it was Sam. Sam was holding Darius in a similar fashion but much looser than Serge. Knowing this, Darius decided to bide his time and wait for the right moment to try to escape.

Darius quickly looked about the jet. He noticed that nearly all of Rafficer's younglings were in the jet. Many seemed drained or tired, but they were all there. Crystal, an ex-girlfriend that Rafficer never approved of, waved to him lightly. Her worried smile made Darius wonder about the purpose of this event.

"Hello, Daredevil," Rafficer said mockingly. Darius looked at him. The old vamp was sitting in the middle of the jet surrounded by his younglings. Kathleen was leaning against the chair to his right and another vamp was on his left. It took Darius a few seconds before he realized who it was.

"Yes, I'm who you think I am," the vamp mocked. Rafficer smiled and gave a deep chuckle. The young vamp had an evil-looking smile on his face.

"Marc?" Darius questioned. Marc nodded. His forest-green eyes glinted with glee. Darius was disgusted. Marc had only been turned a few hours ago, but he was acting as though it had been a lifetime. Seeing the younger vampire's feelings about Marc, Kathleen reached across Rafficer's lap and began to stroke Marc's cheek. The teenage vamp closed his eyes and leaned into her cold hand. Darius looked away.

"What? Don't you like what I've done to him?" Kathleen asked. Darius knew better than respond. It seemed like Rafficer and Kathleen tortured him the entire time. They didn't beat him; they forced him to do things he didn't want to do or hurt others because of his betrayal.

"No," Darius admitted. Kathleen smiled and looked up at Rafficer.

"We are not here to bother him about the new one. Nor are we going to ask about his travel companions," Rafficer declared. Darius raised an eyebrow. He had figured it was about Marc or the girls.

"Yes. But are we going to get to that subject?" Marc inquired. Darius shifted his attention over for a second. In that second he missed

Rafficer's dark glare toward the young vamp. Deciding it was instead best to ignore the ignorant newbie, Rafficer focused on Darius.

"I want to offer you something. The offer I wish to make has never been done by any vampire before me," Rafficer informed everyone. Darius simply stared at his sire. Not only was he unsure of what to say, but last time something very similar to this happened and that was when he saw Robyn again. Darius sure as hell didn't want that happening again. But one glace over to Marc made him realize it already did happen, just not to someone as important as him. "I want to offer you your freedom."

"What?" everyone in the jet had cried out. The interruption bothered Rafficer. Already not liking most of the younglings he had around him, they then had to do this.

"You're all dismissed!" Rafficer commanded as he sent out power to mostly everyone there. Only Serge, Sam, Marc, Kathleen, Darius, and Crystal stayed. Why Rafficer allowed Crystal to stay, no one really knew. Darius almost figured that she might be there because Rafficer wants her to suffer for having loved him at one point. It took a few minutes for everyone to clear out of the jet. Once empty of everyone but the remaining few, Rafficer cleared his throat. "I said I want to offer you your freedom from me."

"I'm sorry, but can you do that?" Sam questioned. Rafficer growled and leveled a gaze on the now terrified vamp. Sam thought that Rafficer would get used to his little quirks, but he hadn't.

"Technically, we all know you will never be free from me. But, what I really mean is that I will never call you. Will never command you do anything. And I will never bother you again even if it's to say hello," Rafficer clarified. Darius nodded but was still skeptical. Something was up.

"What's the catch?" Darius muttered. Rafficer laughed.

"Catch? No, no catch. Just a little condition."

"Okay. What's the condition?"

"I get the girls you've been with."

"What?" Darius cried as Marc also called out.

"I knew the girls were gonna be involved!" Rafficer responded to that with a prompt backhand to Marc's face. The vamp used his strength to make it more painful and in the end actually broke Marc's nose. But Marc quickly healed because he was a vampire.

"In trade for your freedom, I get the three girls you are with. I believe their names are Idona, Minnie, and Sam," Rafficer mentioned.

"Sue," Marc grunted. Rafficer raised his head and the young vamp winced.

"Why are you so interested in them?" Darius countered. Rafficer smiled.

"I'm not. Why are you?"

"They were a ride and a quick bite," Darius explained as truthfully as possible. It was indeed true. They were giving him a ride and he did have a quick bite. But his tone gave away the lie. He did his best to make it sound like he didn't care about them.

"That is not what I've been told," Rafficer cooed as he began absently stroking Kathleen's face. She tried hard to avoid away from his touch but everyone there could see that it was a losing battle. "So, are you rejecting my offer?"

"What happens if I do?" Darius muttered. Knowing Rafficer too well, there always had to be a horrible consequence. It was just a matter of what was he going to say.

"Are you rejecting my offer?"

"What happens if I refuse?"

"Answer the question!" Rafficer ordered.

"I will not hand over the girls," Darius answered. He was shocked to see Rafficer smile after that comment. Darius realized all of this had been a trap. The book was right.

"I was hoping you'd say that. Kill him."

Everything after those two words happened so fast. Serge and Sam spun Darius around breaking both his shoulders in an instant. Marc lunged forward and drove a fist to his gut so hard that it felt like something burst. Kathleen pulled out a knife and took a swipe for his neck but Serge pulled back on his broken shoulder and then grabbed his arm with two hands and snapped it over his knee right at the elbow. A loud crack echoed through the jet. Darius barely had time to shout out. Then things got strange.

Suddenly Kathleen and Rafficer were tossed to the front of the jet. Marc was thrown into a wall and Serge and Sam were pummeled. Surprised, Darius sat back and watched. He had no idea what was happening, but every time a vamp would get close enough to attack him, something would drive them away. After a minute of a battle, which seemed more like three or four hours, the attacker stopped and faced Darius.

"GET OUT OF HERE!" Crystal shouted as loud as she could. Unsure of how to react, Darius stayed put. Growling in anger, she rushed over and lifted him by his shirt collar. It felt like the time Rafficer held Darius by the neck. "I said get!"

Once Crystal dropped him outside of the jet, Darius took off running. He just about made it to the other side of the tarmac when he turned around to look. Crystal had been tossed out of the jet and was lying on the ground. Her back was to the plane and she didn't notice

Serge coming out with a machete. He watched in dead silence as Serge walked up to Crystal and coolly sliced her head off. She was still staring at Darius as her head separated from her body. The second the head touched the ground, Darius was off again. He really didn't want to go back.

CHAPTER 21

Aftermath

"**D**arius!" Idona screamed out the window of the HHR. The book had revealed that Darius was heading to the airport so all the girls piled into the car and took off after him. Sue was in the driver's seat. Minnie in the front and Idona right behind her. The girls reached the airport just as the other vamps unloaded from the jet, so they had to circle around the place a few times. As they were circling, they noticed Darius. Sue quickly sped to catch up to him, but the vampire speed was just slightly faster. His hearing had also improved.

"Idona?" Darius questioned before slowing. They remained about ten feet behind him. When both car and vamp halted, Idona rushed out of the vehicle and ran into Darius's chest, pulling him into a tight hug. He had already pretty much fully healed from his attack earlier.

"Oh my god! I was so worried about you!" Idona gushed as she held the vampire close. Darius frowned. He had wanted them to run. Hell, he even intentionally thought of them running to safety so that it would show up in the book.

"What are you doing?" Darius asked in a slightly dark tone. Idona quickly released the vamp and looked into his now pitch-black eyes. Shocked, she backed up even more. "We were coming to help you,"

Idona meekly answered. Darius sighed deeply and turned to face her. When he noticed that she was completely serious, he had to fight not to laugh.

"Three girls, human girls, against that many vampires?" Darius nearly snarled out. Idona was clearly hurt. Now seeing that he was hurting her, Darius bit his lip. His eyes began to change back to sky-blue and his demeanor even seemed to relax a bit. Unsure what was happening, Idona just hoped she didn't cry in front of Darius again. "Sorry."

"Hey, love birds! We should get going?" Sue cried from the driver's seat before honking. Darius glared at her darkly. Thankfully, Idona saved her from any attack.

"She's right. Raff is still going to hunt you down. We're going to go to Florida. Once we're there, I'll try to change their minds about seeing the author. I promise," Idona muttered. Darius nodded and took her hand. As they made their way over to the car, Darius suddenly felt like his head was going to explode. He screamed out in pain. It was so much that he completely missed Idona calling him, Minnie and Sue jumping out of the car, and the three girls dragging him into the back seat of the HHR.

When he returned to his senses, they were already driving on the highway. Idona was stroking his head lightly and whispering soothing words. Darius couldn't fully hear the words, so he just sat back and listened to the sound of her voice. The car was rather silent. It made Darius wonder if that was his fault. "I will get you Darius. There is nowhere you can run too. I will always find you," came Rafficer's voice in his head. Darius moaned, and Idona looked down at him. She immediately understood what was going on.

"Darius, you're too weak to fight this right now. Please, suck my blood," Idona whispered. Darius shook his head. Sighing deeply, Idona continued to rub his head. "Darius, just stay with me. That's all I want."

Darius felt better after that comment. Then the pain began again. He cried out again. And just as he closed his eyes, tears began to form in Idona's. As she watched the vampire writhe in pain, all she wished was that Rafficer would just stop. *Why can't he just leave things alone? He lost, end of story! Right?* Idona thought as she cried for Darius's sake.

"What is happening to him?" Minnie whined.

"Rafficer," Sue mumbled. All three girls looked at the poor vampire. None of them could wait until it stopped. They all felt slightly bad for him. They didn't know what to do for him. All they could do was continue to drive to Florida and hope that it all stopped soon.

"Oh, Darius. Fight back! Don't let him control you like this. You can be stronger than he can. Please," Idona said softly. Looking quickly about the car, she wondered if she could find something to open a wound. Sadly, her search turned up in vain. "Darius. Don't do this to yourself. All you need is some blood."

"Yeah, Daredevil. Just drink some blood. Go ahead, drain her dry."

"You're better than this. You've beaten him once before. Just keep it up! I swear it will all be over soon."

"All be over as soon as you hand me those girls. Or I find you. Either way, you'll be rid of me. So why not come back with the girls? Tell them to go back to the airport. You forgot to get Marc," Rafficer mentioned. Darius groaned and shook his head no. Idona frowned.

"Robyn helped you through this. She said you were stronger than he'll ever be. You are the better vampire, not him. Being your sire doesn't automatically make him the leader. Please, remember that,"

Idona replied, thinking that he was telling her no. "Darius, is this even helping?"

"Tell her that she's a hindrance. She should just shut up. TELL HER!" Rafficer ordered, but Darius kept on screaming in pain. The mental attack was very painful, but Idona's soothing voice was helpful. It kept him focused on keeping her safe. Then the worst thing that could happen happened. The HHR hit a hole in the road and Idona fell onto Darius. Her neck only centimeters away from his fangs. Her soft gasp was all the others heard when Darius fell silent.

Darius's pain invaded Idona's mind so quickly that she couldn't scream. She let out a gasp. The vampire's normal endorphins were on overload trying to handle the pain, and it was just too much. Idona couldn't believe that Darius could stand this type of pain. It felt like her head exploded, imploded, and then was boiled in the sun. The worst part was that she only had about half of the pain. Darius was undergoing the other half. Mentally, she was screaming louder than humanly possible, but no one other than Darius heard her.

Together they shared the pain. But while sharing that, their minds also filtered through the other's life. Darius saw Idona grow up. He watched as her father abused her verbally and mentally. Her mother was distant and never there for her. Even though she was a single child, Idona never got the attention like many single children do.

Meanwhile, Idona watched as Darius's life as the fifth child in a family of sixteen. But of the sixteen children, only seven survived past age eight. Darius was the second child to make it. His older brother was killed three years before the change during a territory brawl. Then for the second time she watched him change. And the next scene really made her wish she could stop watching. She was forced to see his first kill.

It was a little girl. No more than six years old. Darius went up to her and talked for a few minutes. Then as she got comfortable, he asked her into a darkened alley. She willingly followed. Once in the shadows, he spun on her so fast that she couldn't even drop her stuffed teddy before being drained dry. Despite her disgust, Idona couldn't help but see the artistry in it. He barely left a mark on her and not a single drop was left on her skin, clothes or ground. Not even a stray droplet was left on his lips.

Darius viewed Idona's first day of school through her eyes. And he saw every single other day as well. It was just a never-ending show of her life. Barely a second was skipped over. Until college. Darius was watching her the night he showed up. He saw her stand and go to the window. He couldn't hear what she said. Then he noticed her going to bed before the same light showed up and he appeared at the door.

Death after death. Moment after moment. Idona saw it all. She could hardly believe it all. The entire time she read the books; there was barely any mention of Darius feeding. But he did feed. He wasn't as truly innocent as she had always made him out to be. Stunned, Idona could only see the images go by in a blur. Her mind processed all the information to look over later but right now, she was just there.

Finally, it ended. The two were there, together. All they cared about was that they were together and not in pain. But that was a surprise. Neither could remember when the pain stopped. Did Rafficer quit attacking? No, they could both feel a slight bit of pressure but nothing serious. That was when it hit Darius.

Darius let go of Idona so fast that they jumped apart as if electrocuted. Thankfully, they didn't make enough noise to attract attention. Once in his right mind again, Darius quickly looked Idona over. He needed to make sure he didn't take too much blood. But as he checked her out, he noted that she looked perfectly fine. Idona only had a mild headache and dizziness that was quickly passing.

"What was that?" Idona muttered as she reached for her head. Darius shook his head. He knew just as much as she did. That was when he noticed that her eyes had changed color for a third time. Now they were aqua. Not wanting to say anything, Darius focused on the pressure point in the back of his head. There he felt Rafficer. He was calling but the voice was weak. Darius completely blocked it. And he could tell it was blocked because there was no more pressure. "Darius, has anything like that ever happened before?"

"Not that I am aware of," Darius responded. His voice prompted Minnie to turn around. She gave him a large smile.

"No more screaming then?" she asked. Darius frowned but nodded. "Good. Sue's bringing us to The Villages. We'll find a hotel there tonight and then tomorrow, we'll figure out the path we want to take. But we've ten more hours of driving or so ahead of us."

"So that gives us ten hours to talk about it here rather than later," Idona countered, easily switching to the new, less confusing topic. Minnie groaned but didn't argue back. Neither did Sue. Darius just sat back. Unless asked a specific question, he intended to stay out of it. "There has to be something better than going to the author."

"It worked for *Inkheart*," Minnie pointed out. Idona rolled her eyes.

"*Inkheart* is a book. That stuff doesn't happen in real life," Sue mentioned, almost sounding like she was thinking she was smarter than the two other girls were. Minnie and Idona didn't say anything. Darius seethed. Oh, how he wanted to beat her. She just wasn't getting it. "But either way. I think visiting the author is best."

"Is that actually what you think, or are you being self-centered?" Minnie suddenly asked. Sue gave her a quick surprised glance before focusing on the road again. Even Idona was a bit stumped by Minnie's sudden attitude.

"What the hell...where the hell did that come from?" Sue inquired.

"Ever since you joined us, you've been sarcastic, rude, hard to convince, and I for one am sick and tired of it. If you didn't believe us in the first place, why did you come all the way down here? Was it the free plane ticket?" Minnie cried out loudly. Sue winced. Minnie's words were very harsh. Even Idona cringed in the back. Now Darius had turned his attention to the conversation. "No, it wasn't the ticket. And I did believe you!" Sue defended. Minnie shook her head. "That was the whole reason I came down! I wanted to help!"

"No, you wanted to order everyone around," Darius mumbled in the back.

"What? No! Why would you say that?" Sue cried.

"Cause you like being in charge. That's why you're the R.A.! You like having power," Minnie added.

"That's ridiculous," Sue called. "I come here to help and suddenly I'm getting attacked! This is so not cool!"

"Guys, just stop," Idona softly muttered. Everyone looked at her. "We're all tired. We're exhausted and we have a long way to go. I think Minnie and I should get some sleep now so that we can take over when Sue gets too tired. During that time, we can all think up different plans of action. I can't defend Disney and I can't fully argue the author because I have no other idea. If I can think of something, then we'll try it. But for now, we should all just leave each other alone."

And that's exactly what they all did. Darius focused outside his window for the whole trip. Sue, surprisingly, drove the remaining nine and a half hours to The Villages. Minnie rested in the front seat. Sometimes she'd make polite conversations with Sue about school. Idona fell asleep with her head against Darius's side. The whole thing went by rather slowly. By about four more hours in, everyone was in need of something to happen.

"Ugh, I forgot how boring a long drive could be!" Sue moaned as she twisted her neck around to stretch it out. Minnie nodded in agreement. Idona was still fast asleep against Darius, and he quickly looked at the other two girls before focusing on Idona.

"So, seriously, why do you want to go to the author?" Minnie asked. Sue groaned and rolled her eyes. "No, I mean it. I want to know."

"Well. I know that when I work on any type of writing I make sure to have a few different versions of the idea. And with the book being called *Project: New World*, it doesn't make sense that nothing like that really seemed to happen. Yeah you could use it figuratively, as in Rafficer created a completely new world by using the vampires under his control. Or you could use it like them coming to this world. Either way it can technically mean the same thing. But, I felt like she had been planning it as actually going to a new world but then changed it around the area in the book where she kills Darius," Sue explained. Minnie nodded as Darius suddenly gained interest in what they were talking about.

"So you mean we could have a similar thing to *Inkheart?*"

"No. That had a guy reading people out of the books. This would mean the book is written about us. Like we are fated to do this. But if that's the case then the author would kind-of be like a prophet or something."

"Oh, okay. I guess that makes sense."

"But prophets don't always see everything correctly," Darius called, his hopes of life being restored slightly. Sue nodded.

"That's true. It could be why she messed up in the first place. She might have the ability to control the characters in the book but when it came to the rest of us, we have freedom of choice. So, rather than praying that the second idea would work, she went with one she knew could," Sue said.

"She doesn't control me," Darius growled.

"I didn't mean it like that. I think of it as her writing persuades you to do things. Like you have two options in front of you. One feels more like what you want to do than the other. She could be doing something like that," Sue told him. Darius grunted and turned his attention to the window once again. Sue sighed. "Look, I know you don't like this plan, but what other option do we have?"

"You could let us all stay," he whispered. Sue shook her head.

"And have how many more die? Or be turned?" Darius had nothing to say against that. So instead, he fumed in silence. Minnie turned her attention to the road along with Sue. But Sue felt like something more had to be said. "If you want, Minnie and I can go to her. You won't have to see her. We can act like would-be writers and get the information that way."

"Fine. I don't want to see her at all," Darius ordered. Sue nodded. She could easily agree to that idea.

The rest of the ride was silent. Sue spent the whole time wondering what she was going to say to the author. Minnie sat there wondering how to pull off the meeting with the author without looking insane. Darius was thinking of unique was to kill Sue if she broke her promise. At around almost the same time they left New Orleans the day before, they arrived at The Villages. They were starving and luckily found a McDonald's nearby, so they passed through the drive-thru before they found a hotel and set up for the night.

Because Idona was still sleeping, Minnie had ordered something for her and Darius had carried her into the room that Sue got for them. Minnie and Sue told Darius good night before heading across the hall to their own room. They were asleep in less than thirty minutes. But Darius was still wide awake in his room. He wasn't sure what to do now. Of course, he didn't have to wait long. With Idona having slept nearly the whole ten-hour drive, she was waking up.

"Where are we?" Idona questioned when she realized that she wasn't in the car anymore. Darius looked at her.

"At a hotel. A Hampton? In The Villages. Sue drove us all the way here," Darius answered. Idona sat up.

"I slept the whole drive?"

"Yes."

"Oh god. Was Sue mad?"

"No. Minnie offered to take over a few times. She declined," Darius informed her. Idona nodded. She was just thankful that everyone was getting along better now. "Minnie got you some food. I believe it was called McDonald's?"

"Oh. Okay," Idona called before getting up. She noticed the bag was sitting on the coffee table in front of Darius, so she headed over that way. Taking the food out, she began to dine. About halfway through, she saw that Darius was watching her. Halfway through a bite she asked, "What about you?"

"Hmm? Oh, no. I'm good."

When Idona finished eating, she sat back on the couch. "Tomorrow, Sue and Minnie are going to see the author. If you want, you can go with them."

"I thought we were going to decide that in the morning?" Idona called, sitting up. Darius shook his head.

"We all talked while you were sleeping. Sue made some very good points. But I made her agree that I wouldn't have to meet the person."

Idona nodded. Now she could only hope that Sue would keep to that promise. Sue tended to keep to her own devices. If she thought it was needed, she'd force people to do what she wanted. "So, now we just wait till morning."

"Yup."

CHAPTER 22

Final Show

The next morning came faster than anyone really wanted it too. Minnie and Sue barely felt rested and left without speaking to Idona or Darius. Darius knew they left because he heard them whispering in the hall as they began to leave. He didn't say anything to Idona though. Most of the night the two had watched TV. They avoided thinking of the book, the author, and the next morning. It seemed calm.

"The girls should be up by now," Idona suddenly remarked. Darius looked at her. They had left over a half hour ago. Darius simply nodded. "Maybe I should go check on them."

"They'll be fine. They were exhausted when we first got here. I wouldn't be surprised if they were still asleep," Darius informed her. Idona sighed.

"I just still can't believe that you guys made a decision without me."

"Would it have changed things? Do you have another idea?" Idona turned away. "I'm sorry. But that was the only thing that could have changed their minds. And even then, by the way Sue was speaking it would only delay her."

"I think Sue just wants this all over so she can bring Minnie and me back to the school."

"Sounds like her," Darius snorted. Idona smiled. She was glad that Darius could joke about her friend. All she hoped was that it could continue. "So, continue watching TV?"

"Actually...I was thinking about the changes we've been going through during the feedings," Idona stated. Darius looked away, embarrassed that he had to feed off her. Idona gave a light smile and placed a hand on his leg. "I don't blame you for needing to feed. Besides, I offered myself to you."

"I don't feel comfortable with the idea. I mean, I've been able to hold off for a long time before."

"Yeah, well...no offense, but the author said that you were close to going feral. Robyn was distracting you," Idona mentioned. Darius frowned. "Look, I'm sorry. I don't want that to happen to you. I'd rather die than let that happen!"

"Can we talk about something else? Why don't we check out the book?" Darius offered. Idona sighed but nodded. Checking out the book was a good idea. She almost wondered if she could see what Sue and Minnie were doing. But when Darius grabbed the book and came back over, Idona noticed it wasn't about the others.

Rafficer was pissed. He kept trying to send out calls to Darius but something was stopping him. This had never happened to him before. He had been mentally attacking Darius when suddenly he felt like the power wasn't reaching the youngling. Shocked, he tried again with a higher amount of power. But it still didn't work. Frustrated, Rafficer stopped and looked up. Serge was standing directly front of him.

"I want everyone out searching for him," Rafficer ordered. Serge nodded and turned to leave. With his second in command following his order, Rafficer turned to his wife. Kathleen was holding Marc by his arm. "Find out if he knows anything."

"Yes, sir," Kathleen responded. She began to drag him out.

"But, I told you everything I know," Marc declared. Rafficer smirked.

"If he has nothing left, we're done with him," Rafficer mentioned. Kathleen nodded and continued to drag the ex-human out. In the meanwhile, Rafficer turned his attention back to Darius. He may not be able to attack or call, but he could try other things.

Kathleen brought Marc out into the fields behind the tarmac. Once a good distance away, Kathleen tossed the new vamp down to the ground. Marc looked up at her like she had betrayed him. But he knew she was going to do this even if it bothered her in any way.

"Better come up with something good, boy," Kathleen snapped. Marc could say nothing. He had no idea what they wanted. "We need to know how those girls found him. What do they know?"

"Idona is the one who knows the most about it! She like studies vampires for a living!" Marc called. Kathleen shook her head and kicked out, catching him in the gut. Marc grunted in pain.

"Knowledge of vampires is rather widespread. How did they knew where we are?"

"I don't know!" he screamed as Kathleen kicked him again while also sending her own mental attack against him. Marc screamed in pain. When she stopped attacking, she waited for only a few seconds for him to speak again. Rather than speak, Marc tried to sit up. That just pissed Kathleen off more.

"I don't want to do anything to you, but I will to get answers!" Kathleen said. "Now tell me, how does she know?"

"I don't know! Maybe in one of her books!" Marc cried. Kathleen went to kick him but stopped. She remembered at the Cracker Barrel parking lot that Minnie had also mentioned a book. But she never caught the name.

"What's the name of the book?" Kathleen questioned. Marc paused. In that pause, Kathleen snapped and backhanded him.

"I don't know! My god! What don't you people get about that?" Marc screamed. Kathleen frowned.

"If you don't come up with something, then I'll have to kill you. And we both know you don't want that," Kathleen mentioned. Marc shuddered before thinking back to the day that he had been allowed in Idona's and Minnie's room. He had been on both sides of the room, but his memory wasn't very great.

"I don't really know! It could be Dracula, Vampire Academy, Twilight, any vampire book! I have no idea!" Marc called. Kathleen frowned. "But I can look it up online! I swear. Once I see it again, I'll know it!"

Kathleen growled and debated what to do. She really had no idea. If she brought Marc back with barely an answer, Rafficer would be upset and might kill him before getting the answer. But if she asked Sam to look up the information before she returned, the info might not be right. Looking back to the jet, Kathleen figured that Rafficer would want to be right more than having a full answer.

"Follow me," she ordered. Marc nodded and the two headed for the jet. As they got inside, Rafficer focused a narrow gaze on them.

"What are you two doing here?" he growled.

"Marc has an idea of finding out what the girls know," Kathleen answered. Rafficer snarled as Marc watched. "He needs Sam."

Rafficer looked at Marc briefly before nodding his head behind him. Kathleen nodded and grabbed Marc's arm and dragged him behind her husband. Once there, Marc headed over to Sam, who was sitting at a makeshift table with a small laptop. Sam looked up.

"What?" he asked.

"I need that," Marc snapped, thinking he was considered more important than Sam was. Sam growled and looked at Kathleen. She placed a hand on Marc's shoulder.

"Sam is the one who uses computers," Kathleen said. Marc shrugged her hand off.

"I can use computers too. Besides, I work faster if I'm the one typing," Marc replied. Nodding, Kathleen looked at Sam. He frowned but got out of the way. With the laptop clear, Marc sat down. He was lucky that the Internet was ready loaded. Clicking on the search bar, he typed Amazon.com and hit enter. Once that loaded, Marc began typing away different search functions throughout the site.

"What is taking so long?" Rafficer questioned. Marc didn't respond. He just kept typing away.

"The kid is an idiot," Sam growled before pushing Marc over and sitting down himself. Marc snapped. He jumped to his feet and punched Sam.

"Don't touch me!" he cried. That got the two of them trading blows.

"STOP IT!" Rafficer screamed. The two froze mid punch. "Get back to work, one of you. I don't care who, just as long as I get my answers."

Sam smiled. He was still sitting in the seat, so he was closest to the computer. Getting out of Marc's search, Sam went to Wikipedia.org and typed in Rafficer. The search came up with a character profile of a Rafficer St. John who was born nearly 700 years ago. Scanning through the page, he found out information about a book series called Project.

"Looks like it's a series. Only three books are out right now," Sam read. Rafficer stood and walked toward the computer. He stood directly behind Sam and read the page. He couldn't understand most of it. But the few bits he did understand made him realize that those books were about Darius and him.

"What are those?" Rafficer snarled. Sam looked up to him. "How could people know so much about us?"

"In this world we have such workers called 'writers.' Do you not have such a thing?" Marc sarcastically questioned. Rafficer glared at him, but Marc just ignored it. "They write fiction. So here, you guys are all fake."

"What?" Kathleen cried. Her fear was getting the better of her now. She, like Rafficer, couldn't understand how this person knew enough about them to write stories. And if someone was, how did they know about them? "But, I'm standing right here!"

"Kathleen, shut up," Rafficer snapped. Right away, she stopped making any noise. It wasn't that he commanded her or anything. His attitude showed that if she pissed him off, she'd regret it.

"At least you weren't that pissed off," Idona muttered as she sat back. Darius laughed, and Idona got confused. "What? What did I say?"

"Raff is only pissed because he can't understand it. He shows anger more than he'll ever show fear. Being the leader, he always tries to act like nothing can bother him. Only anger is his way of showing that he feels something. But, vampires being naturally angry, many don't even notice," Darius explained. Idona nodded while mouthing, "Oh." Slowly she got up and began to do a little stretching. "Going somewhere?"

"No. Just stretching. But now, how can you notice the things about him if no one else can?" Idona questioned. Darius shrugged his shoulders. He had never really thought about it before. It wasn't like anyone had taught him. Just, from the day he first met Rafficer, Darius had been able to read the older vamp's emotions.

"I always have done it," Darius answered. Idona frowned. All these different little non-connecting traits were making her wonder. If Darius was special, then maybe this could be one of those stories where she could change him. She could now only hope that she was right.

"So, do you think we should keep reading? Or will they spend a good while freaking out?" Idona muttered. Darius looked down to the book.

"Apparently keep reading," Darius said. Idona rushed back over and sat down.

"Author?" Rafficer inquired. Sam nodded.

"Another name for writer. The author, Amanda, she lives only half a day away. We can always go to her," Sam responded. Rafficer walked away. He kept on wondering if maybe this "writer" could be some sort of prophet. If that was true, then maybe she could tell him what Darius would be doing long before.

"We could ask it a lot of questions," Rafficer agreed. "We should go."

"Well, there is an issue with that. If Marc is correct about them being able to find out what we are doing, they may be able to get there first," Kathleen pointed out, speaking for the first time since Rafficer told her to shut up. Rafficer turned to face her. As much as he didn't want to admit it, she did have a point.

"Never mind that. The closest airport to where the author lives is at least an hour away. Maybe even more. We'd never be able to beat them," Sam added, forgetting that Darius and the girls had at least a ten-hour drive before them as they only ran away over an hour ago or so. And every minute that they spend looking for Darius or even arguing the ideas of what to do next, the others got closer and closer to the author.

"We will go to this author now," Rafficer declared.

"But Rafficer, what about the others whom you sent after Darius?" Kathleen asked. Rafficer snarled. It was going to take to gather them. Some of them were a good distance away. And even more had given up the search to feed. Aggravated, Rafficer screamed before punching his chair, snapping the weak material in half.

"Get them here!" Rafficer shouted at Kathleen before walking off the jet to go stomping around the grounds. He wasted so much energy attacking Darius that he needed to feed. No one had noticed before. Of course, no one had really been around him that distracted.

In the end, he found a young man coming into work for the airport. He had been running late and so missed the announcement to get out as fast as one could. Rafficer found the man walking across the tarmac to the jet. He intended to ask the jet to move off the runway and go to the docking area. Too bad, it was going to be the last thing he ever did. Rafficer was vicious in his takedown, like normal, and didn't really get as much blood as he truly needed. So, the hungry vamp took to the streets of New Orleans.

"Could they have beaten us already?" Idona muttered. Darius frowned. The book was still busy writing away on the next few pages. But it didn't focus on Rafficer anymore. It was still trying to write out the car ride to Florida.

"I don't know. We can only hope that we have. Raff is low on power. And if he keeps on attacking his victims so viciously, then it's going to take a lot of people to completely fill him," Darius answered. Idona sighed and got up. She began to walk around. Darius watched her as her walking slowly turned into pacing.

"Why did the book suddenly get so slow at updating?" Idona moaned. Darius looked down. He did have to say a lot had been happening. It was trying to follow two different stories at the same time and both were affecting the others. So of course it was running slow. "It used to be so fast. Updating both sides so well."

"Maybe we're getting to the end?" Darius suggested. Idona stopped pacing and turned to him. They both then looked down toward the book. It did seem to be running out of pages. They never thought that something like this would happen.

"But what does that mean? Are we sending you back to your death? Did we rewrite every book? Is this world going to change?" Idona asked in a flurry of questions. All Darius could do was gaze at her, dejectedly.

"I don't know."

CHAPTER 23

Amanda

It took less than thirty minutes for Sue to find the address in the back of the books. Surprised that she would have her actual address published on the back cover, Sue and Minnie actually debated whether to go in or not. But Minnie built up the courage.

"We have to go. She may have the answers we need," Minnie told Sue. Sue nodded.

"I know. But what if this is the wrong address?" Sue asked. Minnie shrugged her shoulders.

"Then we look like total nerds. Who cares?" Minnie mentioned. Sue shrugged. Slowly the two got out of the car and headed to the front door. As they reached it, they heard multiple dogs barking, followed by a voice.

"Quiet down! Shush! Tira, Pippy, Chloe!" called the voice. It was no use; the dogs kept on barking. Sue and Minnie traded glances. There had been a mention that Amanda's mother owned dogs. "Tira, no! Chloe, go out?"

The barking continued. Sue and Minnie backed away from the door and waited. It took only a few minutes for the door to open. As

it opened, a chubby, little black, brown, and white dog jumped outside. The animal looked like a Yorkie. Following the dog was a woman around the age of twenty-four. She had dark-brown hair and brownish-green eyes. She was chubby and her hair fell down to her shoulders.

"Oh, hello?" the woman said to them when she noticed the two girls.

"Hello, are you Amanda?" Sue questioned in a rather hyperactive voice. The woman could only smile and nod with a hint of laughter.

"Yes, I am she. Who are you?" Amanda replied. Sue laughed and placed a hand on the back of her head in embarrassment.

"Sorry. My name is Minnie Matsu and this is Sue Koto," Minnie answered. "We were here to ask you about your book series, the *Project* books."

"Oh," Amanda called before Chloe pulled on her leash. Amanda jerked forward between the girls and began to be slowly dragged down toward the street. "Sorry, she really has to go."

"No problem, we can follow," Minnie laughed. The three then followed the chubby dog.

"So, what do you want to know?" Amanda muttered as she watched Chloe sniffing around for a good place to go to the restroom. Sue and Minnie traded a glance. "Well…"

"Well, we were wondering. For the newest book, is…I mean was there another version of it?" Sue inquired. Amanda looked at her.

"Do you know what it takes to write a story?" Amanda questioned. Sue shook her head. Minnie also shook her head. "I rewrote that story at least thirty times. I edited the crap out of it so much that it doesn't even follow the first idea I ever had for it."

"But, don't most authors follow a type of story script?" Minnie mumbled. Amanda nodded.

"Most do. I let the story flow out of me. Sometimes I make a rough guideline of how I would like the events to play out. But there are times that the story just flows right through my hands and takes a new path. I normally never have any idea how my story will turn out until it is complete," Amanda explained and smiled. "I know I'm not much help on learning how to write or anything. But that's just how it works for me."

"Well, actually. I had always wondered by the title of the third book. *New World*, did you actually mean for it to be like going to a new world or having the story world change?" Sue asked. Amanda sighed and focused on the dog again. Chloe was laying on the grass panting after finishing her business. A quick tug on the leash and the pup was up and walking back toward the house. Amanda nodded her head in that direction and slowly they all headed over there.

"To be honest, I had no idea. At one point, I was following the idea that the book world crossed over to this world but it seemed a little bit too strange so I stopped it. I went back and rewrote the whole idea. Now I'm beginning to think it was a big mistake. I hated that second storyline that I followed," Amanda admitted.

"So, if you went with the first version, what would have happened?" Minnie called. Amanda shook her head and tried to think back. It had been a couple of years since she last saw those pages. Minnie and Sue just stood there waiting.

"Wait, what did you say your names were again?"

"Sue and Minnie," Sue replied. They had reached the house. Amanda quickly leaned down and took Chloe off the leash before turning and heading to the right and down a small hall. Turning another corner, she entered her office. Sue and Minnie followed her. They turn the corner just in time to see Amanda digging through some boxes before pulling out some papers. Scanning them, Amanda gave a cry of triumph.

"Sue, age 20. A junior in college. Minnie, age 20. A sophomore in college. Both friends with Idona, age 19, also a sophomore in college," Amanda read. Then she looked up to face the two girls before her. They slowly watched as her eyes began to widen in surprise. Neither girl spoke as Amanda looked back and forth between the girls and the papers in front of her. "Oh my god, the descriptions are perfect! Every detail an exact match!"

"What do you mean by that?" Sue cried before grabbing the papers. She quickly scanned them herself and noticed that it was indeed true. Amanda's papers had everything about her, even down to the scars on her back that no one but her parents and a few doctors knew about. "How can you know this stuff?"

"It all just came to me, like how I told you. I sit down in front of a computer or a notebook and write. The words flow through me. I just get the briefest ideas. This whole series started with Rafficer. Then I introduced Darius and it began to follow him. After that, I got an idea to create a love interest for Darius. But I couldn't think of a good character profile in Darius's world so he had to leave his world. That was when I thought of Idona...I didn't know she'd be real," Amanda explained.

"So, what happens to us?" Minnie whispered. Amanda shrugged. She pointed to the sheets.

"That's about all I had written. I have no idea what happened next," Amanda replied. Minnie frowned and quickly looked the sheets over. It only went about as far as them leaving the school. "But, if you guys are real and here, then that means Darius must be around!"

"Well, yeah. But...we can't. Darius has requested not to see you," Sue explained. Amanda frowned. She was beginning to look a little pissed. Sue sighed. "Look, how would you feel? Suddenly finding out that your whole life was a lie? And someone was controlling your choices?"

"I guess you're right, but I don't care. I want to see him," Amanda pretty much ordered. Minnie looked at Sue. They still needed her help. Now they were beginning to wonder if she could even offer them any help. Amanda walked toward a bookshelf in the room and picked up a book. It was *Project: New World*. Confused, Sue and Minnie watched her. Amanda opened the book toward the back. She scanned it and smiled. "You're going to bring me."

"What?" Sue asked as she took the book, and at the bottom of the page it read that Sue finally gave in and allowed Amanda to follow them to the hotel that Idona and Darius were staying at. Sue looked up toward Amanda. "I thought you said you didn't write this?"

"We're almost at the end of the story. It could be that all the books changed to the first storyline because that was what happened. If that is the case, don't you think we should follow it?" Amanda questioned with a large smile on her face. Sue and Minnie again traded a look before they both faced the ground.

"Fine," Sue muttered, giving in to Amanda and the book. As they all turned to leave, Amanda was skipping on her way out.

Meanwhile, back in the hotel, the book had finally caught up to the girls. Many little details had been skipped over, but Darius and Idona were able to read the final lines just as they were happening in real life. Idona could barely wince in surprise before Darius bellowed in rage. He was more than furious with Sue.

"WHAT THE HELL! SHE PROMISED ME!" Darius screamed. Idona curled up on the couch. Unsure of what to say, she just let the vampire vent. "I don't want to see that woman! She is so arrogant!"

"Darius, please," Idona softly called. Darius began stomping around the room in his anger.

"She thinks she knows what is best! I bet that author knew this was going to happen and planted that book a long time ago! I can't believe this! I'm gonna kill her! I'm gonna kill both of them! I can't stand them!" Darius continued to rage. Idona couldn't do anything but watch him. "They aren't going to live past today! I hope they understand that!"

"Darius calm down," Idona begged. Darius faced her, his eyes red with rage. He looked like he was going to attack her. Idona jumped. He began to calm down after gazing at her face for a few minutes.

"I'm sorry. I just...don't want this to end," Darius muttered before sitting down on the bed closest to the couch. Idona furrowed her eyebrows.

"What do you mean?"

Darius looked up at her confused. He had no idea what she meant. "What don't you want to end?"

Darius sighed and looked at the floor. Now he was embarrassed. He hadn't meant to say that. Idona patiently waited for an answer. She knew that he was going to give in soon. It took a few minutes before suddenly it hit Idona. Darius was afraid of going back. He had mentioned it a few times before but she never really considered it. Well, from what they did know, he was being sent back to his death.

"Oh, Darius. This doesn't mean it's the end. There could be more to do! There is always some type of quest where we have to get certain things that all add up to the final solution," Idona mentioned. Darius frowned but nodded, praying that she was right. He still had the feeling that if he saw the author of his book, then it would all be over.

"Idona, please. I don't want to see her," Darius whined. Idona sighed.

"I don't know what to do. If we want to figure out how to send Rafficer back, then we need her help." Darius jerked up at that. Idona looked away.

"You don't want to send me back?"

"Well...honestly, not if I can help it," Idona admitted. Her cheeks were now beginning to flush. Darius was surprised. He had hoped that she would care for him but he lost all hopes after he fed from her. "I...I don't want you to go. But you know we have to get the others back at least. And that..."

"Means sending me back too...I know...the one thing I'll regret is that you can't come too," Darius mentioned. Idona smiled.

"Same here...I...mean...It's so weird...we've only known each other for a few days," Idona called. Darius nodded. "But it feels like we've been together forever."

"I get it...I just wish...Well...I wish that we could stay together," Darius responded. Idona sighed. How she so wished that could really happen. But to fix what had already happened in this world and to stop more from happening, they needed to figure out how to send Darius back. There was a soft knock on the door. Darius and Idona looked at it. The ding of a key card unlocking the door made Darius turn to Idona. "I'll miss you."

The door opened and Amanda stepped in. Darius turned to look at the woman just before there was a bright flash. It was so similar to what happened to him before Darius figured out what was happening. A tear began to drop from his eye before the light made him shut them. When he opened them again, Rafficer was standing before him, hand closed tightly on his throat.